Midge Sumpter Mystery Number Two

THE INDIAN MOUND MURDER

Emerson Littlefield

The Indian Mound Murder
© Emerson Littlefield

ISBN 979-8-35097-163-7 (Print)
ISBN 979-8-35097-164-4 (eBook)

DEDICATION

ONCE AGAIN, TO MY WIFE, NANCY, FOR HER LONG SUPPORT and encouragement, and to my son, Josh, ever an inspiration to me with his dedication to the arts. And, again, to my daughter, Laura, my first reader and best critic, who has made several notable suggestions that improved this novel.

TABLE OF CONTENTS

THE SOFT AND NOISY DARKNESS

SHE COULD HEAR THE SOUNDS IN THE DARKNESS. IT MIGHT be big: a bear? A deer? Someone moving about the camp? Of course, even small critters—possums, raccoons, rats—could make more noise than you'd think.

But noise or no noise, she had to pee, so she took the flashlight with her, scanned the ground carefully so she wasn't squatting over poison oak or a cottonmouth. She wished there was a portolet, but there wasn't one.

The dark was nearly complete out here. Once lights went out at the camp and everyone was asleep, the darkness closed in, absolute and stifling. It was almost a physical sensation, like weight or constriction. When the moon shone, there was some light, but the moon tonight was only the thinnest crescent, and she couldn't have said whether it was waxing or waning. Wasn't her thing. There were stars visible, but cloud cover and the thick humidity obscured most of them.

There was a noticeable rustle over by the Indian mound, and she shone her flashlight in that direction. An armadillo, caught by the light, froze for an instant and then scampered away far faster than she would have thought. That was slightly scary, she thought; but armadillos were harmless, though digging in the mound they were likely to disturb ancient remains. Nothing she could do about it in the middle of the night.

When she was far enough from her tent to make it sanitary, but not so far that she'd get lost in the woods or risk stepping on a cottonmouth in the middle of the night—who wants to get bitten in the bum by a snake in the middle of the night?—she scanned the ground carefully, squatted, and turned off the flashlight for privacy.

She could hear breathing. It was heavy and regular and slow. For an instant, she couldn't tell whether it was hers or someone else's. She was breathing hard herself because squatting to do your business was a little taxing, especially when, even at night, the temperatures were in the eighties and the September humidity was at least as high as the temperature. She wasn't sure of her conversions, but wasn't the low eighties Fahrenheit somewhere around thirty Celsius? She occupied her mind with such trivia as a matter of habit.

But thinking of temperatures didn't obscure the breathing.

And it definitely wasn't hers.

And it sounded human for certain.

"Hey, you, whoever you are. Mind if I do my business in peace?" She wiped and stood up and quickly pulled up her shorts. She was out here in the woods with a number of people, including at least two young men who might well be interested in her, Tuco and Stan. She hadn't pegged either of them as the pervy sort, but, then, one never knew.

She swiveled around fast and aimed the flashlight at the sound of the breathing. Nobody, nothing. The flashlight just shone into darkness, illuminating only the trunks of tall old pines, fan-leafed palmettos as high as her head, and shadows in every shape imaginable, dancing in the flashlight beam against the green screen of palmetto fronds. She directed the light back and forth, but nobody was there. Okay, she thought, I was imagining it. There was no breathing.

Except, she couldn't shake the feeling that indeed there *had* been breathing. And it wasn't that silent, and it wasn't hers.

One last careful three-sixty with the flashlight. She could see palmettos and pine trunks, the leaf litter on the ground, their big Toyota Land Cruiser with its wagon still attached. Then, the cluster of tents for herself and the other researchers and volunteer workers. One for Stan and Tuco, one for her and Becky, one for Professor Morgana. There'd be another for Professor Lavida when he arrived tomorrow. Then, the light shone on the mound where they'd be digging. On the side of that mound, obscured by night and intervening trees and palmettos, was a trench started months ago by Professor Lavida. She and Becky and the boys had visited it just yesterday; they'd be working to expand it today. Slow and painstaking work. Paleontological work.

It was exciting work, even if it was physically very hard and draining in this heat. Here in the remote pine woods of North Florida, an ancient group of PaleoIndians had set up camp. The team knew it was paleo because Lavida had discovered a mastodon tooth months ago, and fossilized bone fragments with clear cut marks on them. Early American Indians had penetrated this far east and south when the great, lumbering beasts still flourished in Florida, then a drier and cooler and grassier place. They all prayed for human remains, except none of them actually believed in prayer. This was a scientific outfit, and they approached the dig as scientists.

She walked toward her tent and switched off the light just before she got in, so as not to wake Becky. When she was in the tent, she could swear the breathing returned. And Becky wasn't in the tent.

Within minutes, as she waited almost in a panic, she was about to go rouse the boys so they could search the camp. But just as she was about to go out again, here came a flashlight swinging back and forth, and Becky squatted before the tent flap and crawled in. There was barely room for the two of them.

"Hey, Beck, you have to go, too?"

"Nature's just got this way of turning beer into urine, know what I mean?"

"Yeah, I know. Say, what direction did you just go?"

"Out behind the truck. Why? Don't matter where you pee out here. Bears and deer do it on the ground all the time. I ain't goin' to that tiny shit-shed, not just to take a leak." The "shit-shed" was their primitive toilet, where they had all agreed they'd do their poops. It was just a pit with a bench over it, and a big hole in the middle of the bench for the obvious purpose. Primitive, but without a portolet out here, it was the best they could rig up.

"Well, I could have sworn I heard breathing out there." It wouldn't have been Becky, though. She'd gone behind the truck, in exactly the opposite direction from her.

"Wooo! Creepy. Seriously?"

"Yeah, seriously. And I'm ninety percent sure it wasn't me."

"You don't think one of the boys was spying on you? Creeper!"

"I don't know. I shone my flashlight around, but I couldn't see anything."

"Well, you're safe now. You've got me to protect you!" Then Becky giggled. She was all of five and a half feet tall with an athletic build—still, Regina thought, not a physically imposing presence. She was tough, though, and in fantastic shape. Regina had noticed this when they were digging.

"Yep. Appreciate that. Think I should broach the subject with the boys in the morning?"

"Sure, I guess so. You sure about this?"

"Ninety percent, yes."

"I mean, nights out here are so damn dark, it makes you feel kind of closed in. You could have been hearing your own breathing, but, I don't know, like projected back from the trees—no, reflected, that's what I meant to say."

"Maybe, Beck, but I don't think so. Oh, well, g'night."

"Yeah. Nighty-night. I'm not crawling down in my bag; it's too damn hot."

"Me neither. Let me check the zipper on the tent—keep out wandering armadillos and rattlesnakes."

"Oh, God, please."

In minute, she could hear Becky's quiet, shallow breathing, with just a hint of a snore. The quintessential cute volunteer, all smiles freckles and pigtails. Learn a little about digging a mound, get out of the school environment for a bit, out of the musty hallways where specimens were kept, the labs where reconstructive work was done to restore fragments to their original shapes: pottery shards, scapulas, long bones, hip joints, skulls.

Except that Becky seemed to know more about anything they'd turned up on their preliminary, quick overview, than anybody else at the mound, even Doctor Morgana. And Becky, beneath her cuteness, seemed strangely wired for action. Regina felt that Becky must be hiding something, but what? She listened to Becky for a moment, but hers did not seem the breathing Regina had heard.

It took her a while to fall asleep, but she did. She fell asleep thinking: There was definitely breathing, and it was definitely human. Why the flashlight hadn't shone anything she couldn't make out. The dark was so thick, though, like the palmettos and the trees, maybe he—whoever it was—was there, but she just couldn't see. It would be easy to hide, in the dark of night, amongst the broad-leaved palmettos. She couldn't imagine anyone wanting to do that: snakes, spiders—God knew what would slither and crawl in the heavy bushes.

The next morning brought light and a camp breakfast: bacon, no eggs, and potatoes fried in the bacon grease. Coffee. No juice or milk. Somebody would have to take the truck into Seminole Pines, the little town nearby, in a day or two, for groceries. But they'd have to draw straws. Even if the work was sweaty and hot and they were all filthy, the excitement of digging further and further into the mound and uncovering yet more and more evidence of PaleoIndian activity was just too great. Nobody wanted to be the gofer. Professor Morgana was in charge, at least until professor Lavida arrived; she'd probably choose somebody to send. Maybe they could convince her to pool their money and have an uber driver come out here with groceries.

A few quick questions at breakfast occasioned mostly jokes and a few comments about hearing things at night. Stan was the worst. "Probably hearing your own breathing. The night out here does crazy things to your senses. You can't see squat, the darkness is so thick. Makes your other senses extra sharp, so you hear your own breathing, but you mentally project it away from yourself. There wasn't anybody spying on you while you were tinkling on the tussock grass, Regina."

"Did I say there was?"

"You were sure implying it."

"No, I wasn't."

"Yes, actually, you were. Did you shine your flashlight around?"

She was quiet for a moment. Then, she answered: "Yes, I looked around, very carefully."

"Did you notice the breathing sound while the light was on?"

She hadn't thought of this, but in fact, she didn't know the answer. "I don't know," she said.

Stan laughed. He was a bit of a prick, she thought. An undergraduate volunteer, a few years older than most undergrads. Earn a few field credits for his methods class. He clearly liked to feel superior to the girls, even though Regina herself was a third year grad student, only months away from acquiring enough material on Florida's paleoIndians to begin organizing her doctoral dissertation. In the scheme of things as paleontology at the university went, he was junior to her by several years, though he was actually about her age.

"Well," Stan added, "If you hear the boogyman again tonight, come and wake me up. I'll protect you while you pee, but only for a price."

"Oh, for God's sake, Stan. You are too much. Keep on with that shit and I'll ask Professor Morgana to send you home."

He glanced at Tuco, who was silent. Another undergrad volunteer, but not much like Stan except for being a little older than most undergrads. Tuco was quiet and intense. He loved paleontology; it seemed almost a kind of release for him, but from what, Regina couldn't say.

"All right, Stan. Let's just drop it, okay? I thought I heard some heavy breathing last night. I admit I didn't see anybody. It was very dark. Could have been somebody, but lots of places to hide in these woods. Maybe it was just my fevered girlie imagination." She said this ironically.

But there *had* been breathing. She was certain. And it had been human. And she was going to listen for it again tonight with her phone concealed and on voice record. Then, let's see who's the silly one.

By that time, Professor Morgana was up, already organizing materials at her table under her little makeshift tarp. The day's digging would begin very soon.

A PROFESSOR APPEARS WHERE HE SHOULDN'T

I INTRODUCED MYSELF IN ANOTHER BOOK BEFORE, BUT IN case you didn't read it, it's called *The Motel Murder*. Read it; it's good!

My name's Denise Sumpter, deputy sheriff, Wassahatchka County, Florida. My sheriff's name is Beaumont Marion, but I call him Pee-Wee. He's six foot seven and weighs in at about 330 pounds, my guess, but he's putting on weight with all the desk work he does, so he may be up to 340, for all I know. He needs to get out more. He's getting to be an office manager as much as a sheriff, though he still helps us out on tough cases. Like the one I'm gonna tell you about now.

Oh. How come I call him Pee-Wee, even though he's about grizzly bear size and getting bigger around the middle all the time? Well, he calls me Midge. That's short for Midget. Ain't my name, but compared to him, it fits. I'm all of five foot three if I stretch, and 130 pounds after I eat dinner. He started raggin' on me for my size the day he hired me, so the same day, about the millionth time he said, "Hey, Midget," and told me what he wanted me to do, I looked right at him and said, "What you want, Pee-Wee?" That startled him, but he didn't fire me. He just smiled that tough-guy smile of his, and we've been at this game ever since—over four years now.

Sometimes when I tell stories, I throw in random stuff happens to be on my mind. Story's comin', so keep your britches buckled, we'll be there in a minute.

Speaking of my "diminutive" size—I like that word: "diminutive." Cool. So, my favorite dinner in the world? Right now, it's sausage and chicken gumbo at Willie's Restaurant, served over white rice, side of fried okra. You don't like my taste? You ain't never had it. Willie's gumbo is spicy and got lots of flavor; don't know what kind of sausage she uses. Oh, "She." "Willie's" is short for Willamena's. Willie also makes up the best fried okra this side of anywhere you want to name. Damn good! Dip it in some spicy tomato sauce, you can't stop eatin' 'em. Why I eat at Willie's every once in a while and can't put on a pound to save my life, I don't know. Pee-Wee looks slantwise at a donut, he gains ten pounds.

Gotta get that man out more.

So I'm on my way in to the station about 7:15, same as every other mornin' of my life, hoping I don't have court duty or speed trap. Them's the dregs of working as a deputy in this or any other county. You think it's fun sitting on your butt in your cruiser, waiting for some poor sucker to speed by so's you can give chase and ticket 'em? Good source of revenue for Wassahatchka County, but about as boring as watching paint dry. *More* boring. I live for solving crimes. That's my specialty. I'm about five blocks away when Pee-Wee comes on my radio: "Midge?"

"Yessir, sheriff, I'm almost there. Know you can't wait to see my cute little face poke in through the front door. Hold on, keep your heart still. I'll be there in just a minute." I ain't actually due in 'til seven-thirty.

"No joking around this morning, Midge. Have a mysterious deceased out in the woods by the old Indian Mound. There's a crew out there from the university doing archaeological work. They seem pretty shook up."

I don't tell Pee-Wee it ain't archaeological work; it paleontology work. They ain't digging up an old Roman town; they're digging up something been buried way, way back before Columbus' time—back when there were them old animals don't exist no more. I heard about this excavation. An article about it in the Seminole Pines Gazette.

"Okay, Pee-Wee," I say. The Indian Mound's a local legend. Indians camped or built towns in lots of places in Florida way back before Columbus' time, going back thousands of years. I know a little about this. They threw out their garbage—broken pots, animal bones, shells where they were near the sea, in mounds, and over time they built up into what they call "middens." Trash heaps from a long time ago. But the article I read in the paper about it said the folks from the university working on this mound believed it may well be over ten thousand years old. Think about that! Maybe even thirteen or fourteen thousand years, nobody knows for sure. One of 'em found a mastodon tooth last year in the mound, and that brought the team out to dig this year. Mound was beside what probably was a lake way back then, but now the lake is long gone and the whole place is just pine woods, scrub oak and palmettos. A palmetto and a pine tree are the logo of Wassahatchka County—on our sheriff's uniforms.

Only problem: the mound couldn't be more off the beaten track. On National Forest land at least four miles from any paved road. They got a camp set up out there so the crew can dig and do their research without having to drive into town every damn day. Wouldn't want to be out there myself; don't like campin'. But the paleontology itself is really interesting to me. Think of it: people ten thousand years ago was living in this state, way before people from Europe or Africa came, and they left a little evidence behind of who they were and how they lived. That's fascinating, you ask me.

So I pull in, park and get out of my ancient cruiser—a hand-me-down from the Florida Highway Patrol. I'm no sooner in the door than Pee-Wee's on his way out with my partner, Jake Leon. So me, Pee-wee and Jake climb in Pee-Wee's Chevy Suburban, and we're off to investigate.

Takes us near a half hour to get there. Once you get off the main paved roads and onto national forest roads, you ain't got no idea how easy it is to lose yourself in these woods. The word "roads" is a joke—ain't but trails with ruts, puddles, slick clay and soft sand. And sometimes you're on a trail and think you're goin' somewhere, and the road just stops, and you've got to back up. But we're finally there, and we pull up as close as we can get next to the crew's big SUV—a Toyota Land Cruiser—and trailer. I know when we get out, Pee-Wee's gonna let me ask most of the questions because if it turns out to be a murder inquiry, he'll put me in charge. Guarantee.

We get out and a whole group of 'em is standin' together near a campfire middle of their circle of tents. I can see the mound about, maybe, twenty yards away through the trees. Bigger than I thought it would be. Never seen it before. Indians—PaleoIndians, proper—must have lived in this spot for years.

Pee-Wee, me and Jake go up to 'em, and I can see their faces are pretty sunk, most of 'em. There are two younger women, one older woman, older but not old, and really pretty, and two young men. "Hey, folks," Pee-Wee says, "I'm Beaumont Marion, Sheriff of Wassahatchka County, this is Deputy Denise Sumpter, and this is Deputy Jake Leon. They'll be helping me with this inquiry—or investigation, if it turns out we need one." They introduce themselves: Professor Felicia Morgana, grad students Regina Gentiles, Becky Rubin, Stan Assice and Tuco Fairweather.

"You'll need an investigation," the older woman says. "Go on up to the mound and take a look. I'll come with you."

So, I'm expecting to see a skeleton, something that might have been a paleoIndian, but no such thing. Partially revealed in a trench they were digging is a man in shorts, with lug-soled boots on, his lower half clearly visible, the upper half covered by a little soil and muddy sand. His face is completely obscured by dirt and debris.

"You know who this is?" Pee-Wee asks the professor.

"I'm not sure, sheriff. We didn't uncover the face, even though the boys were anxious to do so. I told them to stop. But I recognize the boots and the shorts, or I think I do." She covers her mouth quick with one off those gestures that says she's worried and afraid. Seems a might exaggerated to me, but I understand her emotion.

"So?" Pee-Wee persists.

"I'm not sure. It looks like it might be Professor Lavida. He is, or was, supposed to be leading this dig, but he wasn't supposed to be here until tomorrow or the next day. He was supposed to be at another dig on the coast south of Sarasota—a newer one, more likely Calusa or Tocobaga. I was afraid to uncover his face."

"Midge," Pee-Wee says, "Could you take some pictures please? I don't want to miss anything, but I want to uncover his face." I say okay. He wants me to take pictures because in case he uncovers anything suspicious—a bullet casing, a knife, could be anything—he wants a picture of what the site looked like exactly before he disturbed it. We could have the Highway Patrol's CSI team in before we actually touch anything, but, first, they could be days, and second, Pee-Wee likes to do things his own way. He's a pretty careful crime scene guy himself. Ain't no fault of the Highway Patrol— they're stretched thin, and a scene like this? Way out in the boonies? More likely animals would dig it up and disturb the remains before they could get out here, so better we do it ourselves.

So I shoot a dozen pictures from different angles, slidin' around some on the slick clay mud, then Pee-Wee puts on gloves and starts to brush away the dirt.

The professor—Morgana—screams like crazy. You've never seen nothin' like it. Dead white man, one long wooden stake through each eye, one through his mouth, pounded down into the skull. Don't know whether they go all the way through into the dirt or not. Professor Morgana runs off, I guess to throw up in the bushes. Can't say I blame her.

Feel a little the same way myself. This is murder, and really bad stuff.

When we get Morgana calmed down, Pee-Wee gets her to identify the man. It's that professor she mentioned, Toulouse Lavida. The guy who was supposed to be leading this project.

"Hey, Midge," Pee-Wee says. "Could I get you and Jake to go talk to the folks back in camp. I want to stay and take a look around."

"Okay," I say. So me and Jake hike down through the little trail to the camp. Along the way, I'm goin' slow looking at the ground and the bushes.

That man got in there somehow, or was put in there somehow. May have been killed there; may not have. Don't know yet. Who knows what we may see on the ground. One problem I see right away: Any signs of how he got there have been obliterated by the team themselves when they walked the path to start their digging this morning, and then we all walked over the same trail ourselves. Footprints ain't likely to help us none.

"So, folks," I say when Jake and I get back, "It looks like your lead professor, Mr. Lavida, is dead, and it looks a little grisly. Pretty certain it's murder."

"How do you know that, officer?" That's the one named Stan, I think.

"It's Deputy. And we know it's murder because the man has wooden stakes pounded through his eyes and his mouth. Might be all the way through his skull and into the ground, but I ain't sure of that. Sometimes them sharp wooden stakes come flyin' out of nowhere and just happen to stab somebody in the eyes, but I'm bettin' against it this time."

I see the professor, Morgana, off by herself a little. She looks shook up, though there seems a steely underside to her emotion. What's that all about? The rest of them, all younger, just look stunned, best I can tell.

"I got to ask you some questions," I say.

They all nod their heads.

"Let's start with, do all of y'all know the victim? Professor Morgana here says it's Mr. Lavida, who I hear was supposed to be leadin' this dig."

"It's Professor Lavida, officer, not Mr. And yes, we all know, or knew, Professor Lavida." This is Stan. He seems to be the only one to talk amongst this group.

"You're Stan, right?"

"Stan Assice. Yes, *deputy*," he says. He emphasizes the "deputy" in a weird, unnatural way. I'll tuck this in the back of my mind for later.

"So, you-all discovered the body this morning?"

"Yes," Stan says.

"How?"

"We walked up to start working on the trench through the center of the mound that Professor Lavida started several months ago, found the body almost right away. We were all up at the mound yesterday late afternoon, but there wasn't a body there then."

"Everybody else, that sound right to you?" They all nod. "Okay, then. Question: how'd the body get there? Professor Morgana says he wasn't supposed to show up 'till tomorrow or the next day. So how's he here?"

"We don't know," says Stan again.

"Anybody here talk except for Stan?" I say.

One of the girls speaks up: "I don't think anybody expected him to be here until tomorrow, like Dr. Morgana said. We're all surprised as heck to find him here. More surprised he's dead."

"What's your name, honey?"

"Regina," she says.

"Okay, so, everybody, an obvious question. Don't tell me it's obvious. Just answer the question. You all sure he didn't come in with you?"

They all nod their heads, and a jumble of voices say "We're absolutely sure," "No way he came in with us," and so on.

"But he's here," I say. "Any idea how he got here?"

"Only thing I can think of is, he must've come in some time last night, deputy." That's Stan, again.

"But no car? No motorcycle? No truck? How'd he get here?"

Nobody has an answer, so I go on with the questions. "You said you started digging on the mound yesterday?" I say.

"No," Stan says. "We visited the mound just to check things out. Late afternoon, early evening. Maybe five o'clock? Sure there was no body there then." They all nod in chorus.

"So there's no chance he came in before you-all got here?" I add.

Stan just shrugs, as if to say, "Obviously not."

"Okay, group. If he came in separately from the rest of you and later, he must have come in by a vehicle. Any other cars you've seen or heard in here: vans, motorbikes, whatever, other than your SUV?"

They all shake their heads, and the same jumble of voices say "Nope," "No, deputy," "No other vehicles that I've seen." "We didn't hear anything." Someone adds, "Stan and Felicia went to town yesterday evening for some beer, but they were back easily by maybe seven or seven thirty."

"They went to town for beer?"

"Yes," say a chorus of heads.

"But no body, obviously."

"Obviously not," says Stan. Dr. Morgana just laughs. Seems she finds Stan funny, even in a terrible situation.

"Just beer," she says.

"You all helped unload the beer?"

A chorus of nods and "Yesses."

"Obviously, no body in the back of the SUV?"

A chorus of "Nos" and shakes of the head.

"But Lavida is here. He must've come in here some way. So, Stan and, ahh, Felicia—that's professor Morgana?—you're both *sure* you didn't see no other vehicles going out last night when you were coming in with your beer?"

"Absolutely sure," Stan says. Morgana nods assent.

"So, while Stan and Professor Morgana were on their beer run into town, you're all sure nobody else showed up at this camp?"

"Yes, ma'am." The same chorus. I'm looking carefully at the group, and a few of them seem more curious than afraid. Somebody just killed their lead professor, and a couple of them don't seem fazed by it. That seems odd. I'm thinking right now, the perp could be right here amongst this group.

"Last time, then: you-all didn't hear *any* vehicles driving up the trail after you arrived? Nor last night?"

A chorus of no's and head-shaking.

"Okay," I say, "So, let's talk about how all y'all know Professor . . . shoot, I just forgot his name."

"Lavida," a chorus of voices says, but kind of jumbled up and not in synch.

"Professor Lavida. So, how y'all know him?"

Stan seems to be their designated speaker, so he answers again: "He's a professor of paleontology at the university. He specializes in pre-historical and ancient Indian sites. What we're doing here is trying to find out as much as we can about paleo-Indian culture in Florida. How far does it go back? What were they living on? Where were they active? That sort of thing. We've all taken courses from him, or from Professor Morgana here, though she's not at the university." He nods in the professor's direction.

"I see," I say. "Where d'you know her from, then?"

"Took a course from her at JC," says the other, silent young man.

"You teach there?" I ask the professor.

"I do," says Dr. Morgana.

Okay. So, Professor Lavida was gonna lead this dig, but he wasn't supposed to show up 'till tomorrow or the next day. That right?"

"That's right," they all say. Same discordant voices. I see they're all answering together except the one young man who isn't Stan.

"Say, young man," I address the more silent student. "You don't seem to be answering with the rest of your gang here. What's up?"

"Nothing," he says. "Just really spooky. I don't like digging into the sacred sites of my ancestors. Reason I got into this is, it's a trash midden. We can find out about them by studying what they threw away. Not supposed to be any human remains in these middens. All of a sudden, our own professor shows up. It's kind of like a desecration. Not supposed to be this way."

"What's your name, sir?"

"Tuco Fairweather."

"You said your ancestors. You a Seminole?"

"No, ma'am. The Seminoles are late comers to Florida. I'm Micossukee. We were originally part of the Creek Nation, long ago, and came to Florida in pre-historic times. But some of us believe we're partly descended from far more ancient groups, mostly the Calusa, who date back to times as ancient as this mound. There are other ancient groups, too: the Tocobaga, the Apalachee—others. This is kind of a duty for me, a ritual recognition of my ancestors and therefore of my own history."

"I see," I said. Truth is, I knew about the Seminoles. They're the most famous group of Indians in Florida, but until that minute I'd never heard of the Micossukee or the Calusa, or the others. So, I thought, we have an Indian student digging into an Indian mound. I write all this stuff down; can't put all the threads together until you have all the threads. Don't know now how it will all weave together, but I'll figure it out. Eventually.

"So," I said, "Anything unusual going on around here recently?"

The girl named Regina raises her hand.

"Okay, shoot."

"Well, deputy, last night I had to get up to go . . . do my business, you know. I took a flashlight with me. I could have sworn I heard human breathing. In fact, I'm *going* to swear I heard human breathing. And it wasn't mine." She looks right at Stan when she says this.

"Heavy breathing. Okay. When was this?"

"I'm not sure exactly. Maybe two, two-thirty in the morning."

"You said you had a flashlight. Did you see anything?"

"I didn't. Just an armadillo scampering over the mound." When she says this, I look carefully around. The palmettos and scrub oaks are thick in here. I can easily see that someone could hide and not be seen, even with a flashlight aimed straight at where they were hiding.

"What direction did the breathing seem to come from?"

"I'm sorry, deputy, I just don't know. It seemed to be coming from everywhere. All around me. It gets so dark out here. The darkness hides everything, and I think the palmettos' wide leaves reflect sound. I'm being serious."

"I believe you," I say. "We're going to need to get statements from each of you about last night, this morning, your preparations for coming out here, your knowledge of Professor Lavida. We'll take all those statements individually. One last thing, Professor Lavida was supposed to be some-where else. Where was that, exactly?"

"I can answer that, deputy," says Professor Morgana. She speaks in a sort of husky contralto that suits her good looks: very glossy black hair pulled back into a pony tail, a perfect oval face that could belong to a cover-girl model, large dark eyes, and full lips that part when she speaks to show a row of perfectly straight white teeth. "He was supposed to be down at a Tocobaga site south of Sarasota. It's a historical site rather than a pre-historical one. Probably pre-Columbian, but not really ancient—maybe six, seven hundred years old."

"And who'd be running that dig, ma'am?"

"A woman named Estella Rodriguez. She works at the University, too. Her specialty is pre-Columbian Indian culture and early European contact. She's done digs around the state, and sometimes beyond: Alabama, Mississippi, Louisiana, Texas Gulf Coast." I'm writing all this down.

I turn to Jake, talking just between the two of us. "Jake, we'll need to call this Professor Rodriguez first thing after we leave; this guy clearly couldn't have been clear down in Sarasota last night and shown up here this morning—I don't think. We also need to get individual statements from everybody. You take who you want; I'll do the rest."

"Okay," says Jake. "I'll take the statements of the two guys; you do the two girls and the professor."

"You got any questions for the group?"

"Just a couple," he says. "So everybody," he starts out, "Anything odd happen last night before you all went to bed?"

"No," everybody replies. The same cacophony of mixed voices.

"What were you all doing last night? Before you all turned in, I mean?" Jake goes on.

"A little partying," Stan replies. "Today was going to start the heavy work, so we thought we'd kick off the hard week with a little relaxation. We had a few beers, watched the fire, tried to sing a few songs. Except Becky here kept giggling. I guess she thinks we're not such good musicians."

"So, blunt question, anybody get falling down drunk? Drunk enough to miss something obvious happening?"

"Probably all of us—except Becky here," says Stan. "She sipped one beer all night. Reggie wasn't much better. She couldn't have had more than two."

"So, I'm guessing you drank the most?"

Stan shrugs his shoulders. "Likely."

"So, nothing untoward, nothing unusual, over by the mound?"

"Not a thing." Still Stan, evidently the group leader, or someone who thinks he's the group leader.

"One last thing," Jake says. "You're pretty isolated out here. Has anybody else been out here that you know of? I mean, since you got here?"

"No," says Stan, "but there was somebody out here before we came."

"Oh?"

"There were discarded cigarette butts on the mound, and a crushed Bud Lite can or two. Somebody'd been out here, but don't know why. Doesn't seem to have disturbed anything."

"Okay," Jake muses. I'm thinkin': Good question, Jake! We'll have to find out who that was and what they were doing out here. That won't be easy, most likely, but could mean somebody has a tie to this place and could, somehow, be connected to the killing.

"Last thing," Jake says. "Miss . . ." He's looking at the one named Becky.

"Rubin," she says, "Becky Rubin."

"You're the only one who hasn't said anything. We'll take your statement later, but anything preliminary? Anything to add to what we have now?"

"Nossir," she says. She smiles pretty broadly, acting shy. I don't know whether she really is shy or not. I think it's a bit of a flirt. Jake is a good looking guy. My friend Phoenix says he looks like Errol Flynn—a movie actor from back in . . . long time ago. Jake's got that swanky mustache and a curl of dark hair falls over his forehead. His dad, Dr. Alphonse Leon, is from Cuba, and Jake has a little of that sexy hispanic look to him—kind of exotic and romantic. Becky wouldn't know that he's gay.

"Not a thing?"

"Well, officer, I got up to pee about the same time Reggie did. That's Regina here. I went behind the truck. I didn't hear the whispering Reggie mentioned. Didn't hear nothing; didn't see nothing."

Pee-Wee comes walking up just then and motions us over. I see he has several evidence bags, one with a couple of discarded blue cans. One with a handful of cigarette butts. One has a piece of something: a rock? A pottery shard?

We talk amongst the three of us. "Been somebody here before this crowd," says Pee-Wee. These cans are a bit faded, and I haven't seen anybody here smoking. Also, weird, a half dozen of the cigarettes were planted butt-first into the mound, not with the butt-end sticking up like they were crushed out. Weird as hell. You guys are going to have to explain that one to me. Hey," he says out loud. "Anybody here smoke cigarettes?"

They all shake their heads, and the same mixed up chorus of "no's."

"Thought so," Pee-Wee says, and he turns to us. "Okay. You-all get their statements individually. See if we can get anything helpful out of them."

"Okay, Pee-Wee," I say, "But I don't think we're gonna get a lick of nothin'. Nobody saw nothing nor heard nothing, except the one named Reggie, that girl there, who says she swears she heard breathing last night." Jake chimes in to agree with me.

"Any other visitors, other vehicles, whatever?"

"Not a thing, not since they got here."

"Jesus," groans Pee-Wee. "So we have a dead man, obviously murdered. Was supposed to be somewhere else, but wasn't. This whole crew here didn't see anything coming in, didn't see or hear anything but some breathing. How the hell'd this guy get here? Where was he killed? Who killed him? Why? Right now, all these guys are suspects. Shit," he swears emphatically. "Jake, tape this mound off. Tell these folks they're gonna have to break camp, but they've got to stay in the area. See if they can camp out in Lake Seminole Park, or maybe stay in Midge's grandma's motel for a few days."

Then he turns to me. "You figure it out," he says. "What I hired you for." Then, he walks past the group to the suburban.

THE TOCOBAGA TIMES

AS USUAL I DON'T HAVE A CLUE WHERE EXACTLY TO START, SO I sit down to figure it all out. Got to remove the body and take it to the morgue for a pathology examination. Our pathologist is Alphonse Leon, Jake's daddy. Then I've got to find out why our deceased wasn't at the dig he was supposed to be at, the Tocobaga site south of Sarasota. Then I've got to find out who left the cigarette butts and beer cans on the Indian mound. Eventually I'll have to figure out why he was killed and who done it.

One thing at a time.

Jake and I take individual statements, but not a thing comes up that wasn't in the group interview. Not a single particle of information.

Pee-Wee, Jake and me have to exhume the body—well, not exhume, exactly, but uncover. It wasn't really buried; it was just covered over partially with loose soil and sand. Pee-Wee does the hard part, moving the man's head. But he doesn't remove the stakes from the eyes and the mouth. Before he touches a thing, he carefully takes about a dozen pictures of the scene so we don't forget exactly how the victim appeared "in situ."

I'll tell you, grossest thing I've ever seen, them stakes pushed in through his eyes. That's got to be symbolic some way. Seems to me it's all about seeing something or saying something or both, and this is a symbolic way to stop both things from happening. I write that down, make a note to ask somebody why this apparently ceremonial method applies here. Of course, at the same time, it may not be ceremonial at all; it may be just some sick, violent perp who thought this up just out of cruel meanness.

Then we all help bag up the body to take to Dr. Leon. I don't think he's been dead too long because he doesn't stink that bad yet. I see a little swelling started, but my guess, he was put in that trench late last night or some time early this morning, maybe about when Reggie Gentiles says she heard that heavy breathing. I can't see how he could've been murdered before the crew arrived. Nor do I see how he ended up in that trench, and nobody heard or saw anything except the breathing, which may not even be real. The whole thing's got me stumped already. Got to figure out when he was killed and how he was brought to this mound, and by whom. Right now, it's all a complete mystery.

When we're back in Seminole Pines, just before noon, I decide the first thing is to call that professor from the University. I wrote her name down: Estella Rodriguez. I decide to I call the anthropology department to get her contact information, but they don't want to give it to me over the 'phone. Even when I tell them this is police business and I'm a deputy sheriff in Wassahatchka County, they still don't want to give me out her phone number. So I set up a video conference on face time with the receptionist, so she can see the office and my uniform. An older man with a thin, clean-shaven face and thinning gray hair combed straight back, comes on the phone, and says his name is Professor Bacardi.

"Hello, deputy. What seems to be the issue? We don't usually like to give out personal information about either our students or our faculty members. You look legitimate over the phone. So I'll help you if I can. What seems to be the problem?"

"Well, Professor, does a professor named Toulouse Lavida work in your department?"

"Professor Lavida's been a respected member of this department for almost twenty years. One of the leading experts on Florida's paleoIndians in the world—maybe *the* leading expert. What seems to be the issue?"

"You ain't heard from any of your students or grad students yet this morning?"

"No. About what?"

"Well, sir, you'd better be sitting down. Professor Lavida's body was discovered on an Indian mound here in Wassahatchka County earlier this morning."

He's silent for a moment. "I'm not sure I heard you right, deputy. Could you repeat that, please?"

"Professor Lavida's *body* was discovered at an Indian mound here in Wassahatchka County earlier this morning. We've just been talking with a group of grad students who were out there at the dig site, and one of your professors in the department, Felicia Morgana. You know her, I assume."

He's silent for a moment again. "No, we haven't heard from any of them. Oh, my God! This is terrible! And Professor Morgana—she's not actually a member of our department. She teaches anthropology and paleontology at the Junior College. I think she was there at the mound as an adjunct site leader. I'm not sure why she wouldn't have called us. Oh, my God! I'm assuming natural causes? What, did he have a heart attack? He wasn't really that old!"

I realize suddenly I haven't told him the real reason I'm calling. Now, saying it is awkward. "Oh, no, sir. He was murdered."

He's silent for several seconds. "What? You mean . . . *killed*? Like, ummm, like, foul play? Murdered?"

"Yes, sir. Foul play. Murdered. We're certain it was murder, though I can't divulge the circumstances to you over the phone. I might be able to do that at some point later on, but not right now."

"Good God! Who would want to do such a thing? Oh, my God!" He pauses, then: "Oh, my God! This is absolutely terrible!" I can hear his breathing growing rapid and deep, like he's really, really startled. Little things like that are important. I get a lot out of the sound of people's voices, when and how often they pause, the looks on their faces.

"Well, sir, if I knew who wanted to kill him, I'd have this case all wrapped up already. What I wanted to call you about is this: Wasn't Professor Lavida supposed to be at another site, a . . . ummm . . ." I've got to look at my notes because I forgot the name of that tribe. "At a Tocobaga site south of Sarasota? His students on the site here seemed to think that that was where he was supposed to be until some time today or tomorrow. In fact, that's why I'm trying to get professor Rodriguez's number from you. We wanted to call her to find out if Professor Lavida had been there recently."

Over the computer connection, though it's only a small picture, I can see he's looking not only shocked but, now, also, perplexed. "Why, deputy, that I know of, he had nothing to do with the Tocobaga site. Tocobaga or Calusa, we're not sure. Who told you that?"

"Professor Morgana," I said, "and I believe the students seemed to corroborate that idea. My impression was he was there in some kind of supervisory capacity. Maybe I'm wrong."

"Hmmm. Well, you *would* be wrong about that, deputy. Dr. Morgana is mistaken. Professor Rodriguez may have asked him for some kind of consult, perhaps—I don't know. There's a lot of inter-site support in the paleontology world here in Florida. But that dig is Professor Rodriguez's site, and she's there in conjunction with some grad students from the University of Miami. She's the Tocobaga and Calusa specialist in that part of the west coast of Florida. But that I know of, Professor Lavida had nothing official to do with that site." Then, there's a pause. "My God!" He shakes his head emphatically, "I just don't believe this! What a terrible shock this is going to be for our department! My God!"

"Okay, I certainly understand that. Could I have Professor Rodriguez's number, please? I assume she has a cell number." I hate admitting this in my own story, but I was getting a little annoyed at this man. I could see he was in shock, but he seemed to be getting a little lost, like as soon as he heard that Professor Lavida was dead, he was starting to try to figure out what to do with Lavida's classes. He seemed shocked more than personally grieved, if that makes sense.

"Sure. Yes. Hold on a minute." I see him pull out his phone and start scrolling through it, looking at numbers. "Would you like me to text it to your phone, or just tell you now over the computer?"

"Just tell me now, please. I'll write it down." I don't want to give him my cell number to text me. He can get it easily enough if he wants, but I really don't want him calling a hundred times a day to follow up on where the case is going. So I just jot down the number by hand on my note pad. Within a minute, I've expressed our department's condolences over the loss of their colleague, and I'm on the phone trying to reach Estella Rodriguez. I text her first because I want to face-time her. I want her to see my uniform and badge. I don't get any response to my text, so I just ring her up on the office's land-line.

"Rodriguez." The voice is brusque, a throaty contralto. "Who's this?"

"This is deputy sheriff Denise Sumpter of the Wassahatchka County Sheriff's Department, ma'am. Are you Professor Estella Rodriquez?"

"The same. What can I do for you?" She sounds skeptical, ready to hang up on me. "I'm at a site we're digging. I'm kind of busy."

"I understand, ma'am. You're acquainted, I assume, with professor Toulouse Lavida?"

"Of course." I sense her stiffen up over the phone. Something's up, I can tell. But I don't know what.

"I understand from some of his other colleagues here in Wassahatchka County, that he was, I guess, consulting or something like that, on your dig?"

She's quiet for a moment. Then, she simply says, "Why? What's up?"

"Well, ma'am. Was he supposed to be at your dig site yesterday?"

"He may have been expected, I suppose. Possibly. What's going on?"

I'm thinking, what the hell kind of answer is that? "He may have been expected"? What? "Well, ma'am. I need to know: did he show up at your site, or did you see him any time yesterday?"

She's silent for a moment. "No," she says simply.

"So you didn't see him at all?" I'm repeating the question, I know, but I feel this is crucial. I've got to put Lavida somewhere last night before he showed up dead in a trench at an Indian mound in the middle of the woods in Wassahatchka County.

She's quiet for a moment, then continues in a voice that reflects concern but also confusion. I haven't told her yet that he's dead. "No, deputy. I didn't see him, I assure you. Why? Has he gone missing or something?"

"Not exactly, ma'am. Professor Lavida was found dead this morning, partially buried under some loose earth and debris at an Indian mound site here in Wassahatchka County."

She's silent again for a moment. "I'm sorry. What did you say?"

"He was found dead, ma'am. And it was very certainly murder."

I hear her turn away from the phone and cover the speaker. I can't explain how I know this; I wasn't looking at her. It's all in the sound. I can hear a "Holy shit!" I wait for her to get her shakes under control. "Look," she says, "Who are you really? Is this some kind of sick joke?"

"No joke at all, ma'am. I just spoke to your prefessor Bacardi at the university; he's the one who gave me your number. You may call the Wassahatchka County Sheriff's Office on your own to corroborate all I'm saying to you and to confirm who I am. I'm sorry, but this is no joke and there's no mistake. Professor Lavida has been murdered and was found early this morning lying in a trench at the old Wassahatchka Indian Mound."

I hear a buzzing silence for almost a minute. Then, "Are you still there, deputy? Are you sure it was Toulouse Lavida?"

"Yes, ma'am," I affirm.

It takes her a minute, but shakily she says, almost under her breath, "Good God! Are you *sure?*"

"I'm afraid there's no mistake, ma'am. He was found dead, and we're sure it was murder."

"Who in the *hell* would want to murder Toulouse LaVida?"

A standard question every potential suspect asks, "Who would want to?" Even if, on reflection, they can think later of a dozen people who would love to have been the ones to knock off the victim. "I don't know who would want to kill him, Professor Rodriguez. I'm trying to track his whereabouts the last day or two. I understand from a colleague of his I met at the mound site here in Wassahatchka, one . . . let me see . . . professor, umm, professor Felicia Morgana, that he was consulting at your site. I got the feeling he was sort of in charge of it, at least that's the feeling I got."

Suddenly, her tone changes from shock and disbelief to a kind of aggressive self-defense: "Absolutely not! *I'm* in charge of this dig. And it's not 'professor' Morgana. Dr. Morgana teaches anthropology and paleontology at the Junior College in Tallahassee. She's an adjunct site coordinator—not in charge of anything, really, and certainly not a full professor." Even if you'd never heard full-bore snobbery over the phone, you would have recognized it in this woman's tone.

"Okay," I say simply. "So, Professor Lavida was definitely not at your site yesterday, correct?'

"Yes, deputy," she says, somewhat feebly.

"Was he there any time recently?"

"No," she says simply. "He wasn't." Her voice is a little shaky.

"Why would he have been expected there at all, ma'am?"

She's silent for a minute. "He sometimes consults. You know: helps date strata, shares some expertise on finds."

"For example?"

It takes her a minute to gather herself, but I'm patient and let her have some emotional space. "Well, the site I'm digging is Tocobaga. They were a relatively sophisticated people, deputy—historically speaking, recent. Pre-Columbian, but. not ancient. Not paleo. They wouldn't have had something like, say, massive stone scrapers for processing mastodon kills. If we found one, or found anything else we considered out of place for the site. Professor Lavida would have helped us contextualize it."

"I see," I say. "So, he never even showed up. But were you *expecting* him?"

She's silent again. "Is that what Felicia says?"

"Professor, or Doctor, Morgana? Yes, that's what she tells me." I can almost visualize the smirk or smile that crosses her face, even if we're not on a visual feed.

"Well . . . yes. I was expecting him. But as I say, he never showed up."

This woman's answers, somewhat evasive, are covering up something. In my line of work, you find out that things are usually related by sex, drugs or money, sometimes maybe professional stature. I'm guessing in this case it's sex. Of course, I know it's merely suspicion. But I'm nothing if not direct. So I just ask her directly: "Ma'am, please tell me directly: was professor Lavida supposed to be there because you and him were having an affair?"

"Now, deputy, what makes you ask that?"

"Your whole tone, ma'am. Your evasiveness. The way you pause instead of answering my questions directly. The way your tone of voice sounds more like evading and covering up than like a real desire to answer the questions."

"Well, suppose I tell you it's none of your business?"

"Then, ma'am, I'll tell *you* that this is a murder investigation, and your evasiveness, the fact that you ain't bein' straight with me, tell me that you're my prime suspect."

That seems to have scared her a little. I'm just on the phone, but I can sense things in people's voices, even in their breathing, that the words themselves sometimes conceal.

"All right, then, deputy. Yes, Toulouse and I were having an affair. My husband and I are separated, and Toulouse divorced years ago. And he's a very interesting man—professionally speaking. We sort of fell into this relationship. We work at the same university, and for the time being, neither one of us wanted to become the subject of rumors. I'm still married, although my husband has taken a position at a hospital in Miami, and we're officially separated. The paleontology community in Florida isn't that large—maybe a few dozen people. I doubt anyone would have actually *cared*, but we didn't particularly want to become the subjects of departmental rumors. If it was going to lead anywhere, we'd agree on a time and place to make it public. So . . . we kept it under wraps. I'm sorry, devastated, really, to hear he's dead." Her voice has that damp, quavering sound, like she's talking at the same time that she's been bushwhacked by something she didn't see coming. "How did it happen?"

"I'm afraid I can't divulge details of the death, Professor. Thank you for being up front with me. So he never showed up there. But where exactly are you?"

"About thirty miles south of Sarasota, on a cattle ranch. I was expecting him all day yesterday, and was waiting for him to show up well into the night. But he never showed. Naturally, I was somewhat angry. A little concerned, but mostly, I admit, angry. He didn't show up, didn't call. Didn't answer my calls." As she says all this, her voice shakes perceptibly. I don't think she's choking back tears, but she sounds like the news is beginning to soak in, to become real.

I'm thinking: From about thirty miles south of Sarasota to Wassahatchka County by car—at least two and a half hours, probably more like three, or even longer?

"I see," I say. "Can other people there corroborate your assertion that he didn't show up? I mean, if you were alone in the hotel and he *did* show up, well . . . no one but you would've known."

"I see your point. I'm afraid I can't offhand think of a way to assure you he was never here. None of my assistants would have seen him. Maybe the hotel desk clerks, but nobody else I can think of. We're staying temporarily at a little hotel a bit off the main drag, a short drive to our site. If he went missing in the middle of the night, then I could be the only person who knows he didn't show up where he was expected. Does this make me a suspect?"

Well, she's direct, I'll give you that. "Ma'am," I say, "I don't really know that at this time. I'm just in the process of trying to sort out all the details. Where the man was supposed to be or was expected to be, where he wasn't, where he ended up. Now I know that you were expecting him last night, but that he never showed up and he never called. I want to make sure all that's correct so far."

"So far, that's all correct. Please, can't you tell me how he died?"

"I'm not at liberty to divulge that, ma'am. I assure you, though, it was murder. That's certain."

"Well, then. I guess I'll just have to find out from somebody else." That sounded snooty to me—challenging.

"I guess so, ma'am."

"But if he wasn't here, I'll bet I can tell you where he *was* last night."

"Oh?" I'm a bit startled by this. "And how can you tell me that?"

"He was somewhere in Wassahatchka County."

"He was found dead there, ma'am, but that doesn't mean he was near that mound until the time of death. He might have been anywhere, almost."

"Well, you're a detective, Sweetie. If you found him dead there, then he must have been there last night, eh?"

I don't appreciate that "Sweetie." "Not necessarily, ma'am, not when he was alive, anyway," I say carefully, as if I were explaining something to a school girl. "He was *found* dead here, but no one at the camp site out in Wassahatchka National Forest saw him alive there last night. And there's five people to corroborate that. Moreover, nowadays we have cars and trucks. Who knows where he might have died. For all I know, you killed him in your hotel room yesterday afternoon, drove his dead body up to Wassahatchka, and got somebody, some way, to drag his body into the woods. Maybe you done it yourself. You see? Things aren't all so simple all the time as you'd like to think they are."

"Yesterday afternoon, I was at our dig site, until probably six o'clock or so. That, I can have someone confirm for you."

"Thank you for telling me."

"You're welcome. Anything else you need to know?"

"Did you kill Toulouse Lavida?"

"That's a stupid question, detective. And, No—emphatically, *no.*"

"Then I'll ask another stupid question." She didn't say this, but she didn't need to: I'm guessing that the idea of having her boyfriend working with Felicia Morgana really aggravated her. Jealousy sometimes hangs in people's tone of voice, and hers is dripping with it: "Were you happy that he was working with Dr. Morgana?"

"That's *not* a stupid question. That's a smart question. And, no, emphatically, again. I wasn't happy with that at all."

"Because?"

"Well . . . let's put it this way. It's just too bad she wasn't the one found dead on that Indian mound. Then, you might have had serious reason to suspect me."

Jealousy, then, no question—a possible motive. But it won't be easy to put Lavida over three hundred miles from where he was found dead, the day before he showed up in Wassahatchka.

"Thank you for your time, Professor Rodriguez. I hope your dig goes well today."

"Yeah. Good luck on finding out who killed Toulouse. A bit of advice?"

"Sure."

"Felicia Morgana did it. I'm certain of it."

"You're certain . . . because . . . ?"

"She's a nasty bitch. She's a gold-digger."

"A gold-digger?"

"Sure. Latches onto an important dig with a leading researcher in the field, gets partial credit she doesn't deserve, and probably tries to seduce the man before she decides to kill him. Probably rejected the bitch. Serves her right. Too damn bad for poor Toulouse. But . . . he was weak that way. Never could resist a pretty face."

I decide to end the conversation on a catty note. "Like yours, ma'am?"

"Goodbye, detective," she says, and I just know she punched her "end call" button hard enough to knock the phone out of her hand.

Jake is sitting at his desk. Heard the whole conversation, though not her end of it.

"So, Denise," he says. By the way, he's the only one who calls me Denise. Pee-Wee and the rest call me "Midge." "Let me guess. Professor Rodriguez never saw Lavida yesterday. He never showed up in . . . wherever that is. South of Sarasota? She was having an affair, and she's jealous of Felicia Morgana."

"You got good ears, Jake."

"Morgana's a knockout, Denise. The kind I think many people would be jealous of. So, what do we do now?" Jake has this way of making his eyes go wide when he asks a question. He's got that cute little Errol Flynn mustache. Tell you, I could see the girls this morning at the dig just eating him up while he was standing there. He's a handsome man, for sure. Don't care if he's white and gay; he's a good-lookin' prospect.

"Okay," I say, thinking out loud. "We know, or we think we know, he wasn't at the Tocobaga site down south. I want to talk to Felicia Morgana. Rodriguez seems mighty jealous of her. Afraid Morgana's going to take her man and get partial credit for any major finds at the Indian Mound site. So Morgana's our next target. Then . . . somehow we've got to figure out a way of finding out who's been at that mound before, whoever left them cigarette butts and the empty Bud Light cans. Don't rightly know how to do that yet. Then . . . something's telling me some of them kids have something to hide."

"'Them kids,'" Jake tells me, "are about your age . . . old lady. They're grad students. Personally, I want to know who that heavy breathing was. You know what I think?"

"Course I know what you think, Jake Leon. You think what that one girl heard—what was her name?"

"Ummm . . . Regina. They called her 'Reggie.'"

"You think what she heard was the sound of somebody haulin' that body to the mound to bury it—two-thirty in the mornin'."

"You guessed right."

"Didn't guess, Jake. We're startin' to think alike."

"Must be hanging around the brains of this operation. Seeping into me. Brain osmosis."

Jake's a funny guy.

FATA MORGANA AND A FAIRWEATHER FRIEND

SO, LATER THAT AFTERNOON, WE GO TO INTERVIEW FELICIA Morgana. On the way, Jake tells me an interesting story. He says "Morgana" is the name of a mythical woman from King Arthur days, a sorceress, who could conjure visions in her victims. Those visions were called "Fata Morgana." Things you learn in this business. But Jake was a literature major in college. I was a criminal justice major. Hope this woman doesn't go pullin' no hokey-pokey on us, is all I can say. We got them a camping permit at the County Park, but they ain't done pulled up stakes at the Indian Mound yet, so we've got to drive down that damn long unimproved road again.

We get there and they're all finishing up breaking camp. The mound is taped off as a crime scene. Imagine that! "Crime scene" out in the middle of the Florida pine woods, three miles from the nearest paved road, and the nearest paved road a one lane country farm road. You could be out here days without seeing another living human being, and the world could end and you'd never know it.

We pull up. We brought my old Crown Vic, not Jake's new Challenger Hellcat. That's one damn nice car, but it's a vehicle for good roads. Six point two liter V-8 engine, over 700 horsepower, zero to the next county in half the time it take me to say, "Jake! Slow down!" But he's senior to me by five years in this department, so when Pee-Wee sprung for two new vehicles out of our huge budget, Jake got the new cruiser. We got lots of long, straight roads in Florida. If you're chasin' a perp in a Porsche, you got to have some wheels that got power. Don't know where I got the love for cool cars, but it's deep in my soul, tellin' you.

Kiddin' about the huge budget, just sayin'.

So poor Denise Sumpter gets to keep her ten year old ex-FHP Crown Victoria, 140,000 miles and rust under the floorboards. Ever have to hand-cuff a perp and put 'im in the back seat, all he'll have to do is kick the door out because it ain't held in place by more than duct tape and fishing line.

I'm kidding, but only barely.

But it's good for dirt roads that go from wherever you are to wherever you want to get lost, so we take it down the forest service pathway (ain't really a "road") to the Indian Mound.

They're finishin' packing up. We park, get out, walk over.

"Hey, Felicia Morgana, can we have a word with you?"

She's all sweaty and her hair's disheveled. Looks like crap. But underneath the bed-hair and sweaty t-shirt and muddin' boots, I can see why Professor Rodriguez is jealous. She's one dynamite looking woman. No perfect judge, mind you, but I can tell she's the kind men go boozy-eyed over, and the drool dribbling out of their mouths that they don't even know are open all the way to the ground.

"Yes, deputy," is all she says.

"So, sorry to be messing with you this way when you're having to break camp and you just lost a colleague to something as nasty as this murder, but can we please ask you just a few more questions?"

"Okay. Let me grab a drink. You want one?" I say "no, thanks," but Jake says "Don't mind if I do." Curious thing: Jake's gay, but he can't stop lookin' at this woman. Why's that?

"What can I do for you deputy?" She pops the top off a can of Sprite she takes out of a big cooler, one of those it takes two people to carry. I can see the only thing in it besides cans is melted water. Still, what are you supposed to do out here in the middle of the woods? Jake pops the top on a root beer and it fizzes all over his hands. I can't help laughing. You can tell he's got his eye on this woman, but he's looking a bit silly.

"Thanks for your time. Just following up on some questions we got. Just talked over the 'phone to Professor Rodriguez, the woman from the University who's running that, ahh, Tocobaga site down south of Sarasota. She says our man, Professor Lavida, never showed up there yesterday like she expected him to. You were the one who told us he'd be down at that dig Professor Rodriguez is leading."

"She says he never showed up?"

"What she says, yep."

"That's bullshit. He was down there, I know it. She probably didn't tell you, but they were having an affair. I know he showed up here dead, somehow, but yesterday? He was down at that dig. Or, if he wasn't at the dig, he was with her in the afternoon and they were using the hotel bed pretty hard."

"Actually, Professor Rodriguez did tell us she was having an affair with Professor Lavida. She also said that all of her volunteers and grad assistants can corroborate her story, that she was at the dig until about six in the evening. It's possible she could have killed him, but she would have had to drive a dead man over three hundred miles north in the middle of the night, find this god-forsaken place, drag the body onto the mound, and leave, and none of you reported hearing a vehicle in the middle of the night. All that suggests she's telling the truth."

Morgana looks surprised and peeved. "Well . . . I guess if she says so. Don't trust that woman myself, but if her students are vouching for her being there until at least six, at least that much must be true."

"She also seems to think you were trying to boost up your own professional resume by latching onto Professor Lavida. She called you a 'gold-digger'—increasing your professional cred by getting partial credit for whatever you find at this site. That true?"

She looks at me directly, and doesn't pause for long. She shrugs her shoulders: "Of course it's true. What do you think? I have a Ph.D in paleo-anthropology and I'm teaching freshmen at a junior college. So when the chance came up to co-manage an important site, I jumped on it. Would've loved to use this as a springboard to better professional opportunities. Maybe get on the staff at U.F., Miami, South Florida, F.S.U., Central Florida, Florida Atlantic . . . wherever. Sure I was 'using' Professor Lavida, if you want to put it that way. But it's not like I would've been getting anything for free. Digging out here is hard work. Keeping your files straight, cataloguing artifacts, the whole nine yards. It's exhausting work. Plus, Lavida would probably have dumped most of the writing on me, when it came time to publish our findings. And no shower for four or five days? Good God! I probably smell like a dead armadillo."

"No, ma'am. More dead possum." I can see she didn't like my joke. "Just kidding. Look, blunt question. It helps us with our inquiry. Were you having an affair with Professor Lavida also?"

"Don't mind your asking. He was an attractive man, though nearly thirty years my senior. No, is the answer. I wasn't, and he never sounded me on the subject. Never came on to me. Don't know what he saw in Rodriguez, but he was pretty faithful to her, for whatever reason."

"So, tell me . . . with Professor Lavida gone, will you be taking on sole duties as site manager?"

"A motive for killing Lavida? That's what you're after. The answer is 'No.' This dig is licensed by the federal government—Department of Interior. They manage all National Forest Lands. The university holds the license; they're the ones who applied for it and got the grant for doing the dig. National Science Foundation. I'm just an adjunct added to the project payroll at Lavida's request. I'm paid from grant money, not university money. I'd given a talk at a convention in Louisville on Florida's paleo-Indians that he attended, so he remembered me, called me up, and asked me to help manage the site when he couldn't be here. Now that he's dead . . . well, I'll ask the university if I can manage the site myself, but I'm not on the university payroll, and they want their own people doing the work. Publish or perish, you know. You follow me?"

"I do. You're saying they'd prefer that one of their own department members work the site so they have a chance to get an important publication. Build their, whatever, reputation, I guess. So, you have no connection to the university?"

"Nope. Wish I did. If I did, they'd probably put me in charge out here. Just an underpaid and overworked grunt, an adjunct, like I said. So, you see, now that Lavida is dead, professionally speaking, so am I. I'd get nothing out of killing the man. As to the affair angle, there wasn't one."

"You hear any of the heavy breathing that one girl, Regina, described she heard last night?"

"Nope. Dead asleep."

"Okay. This is my partner Jake Leon, if you remember. Jake, you got any questions?"

"Sure," he says. "You got any idea at all who might've left the beer cans and cigarette butts on the mound?"

"Nope. Doesn't seem it was a grave robber. These aren't graves; they're trash middens. But some people think they're graves, and they dig into 'em looking for Spanish gold—whatever. And they don't find anything except ten thousand year old trash. But they've screwed up the site because they've mixed up the strata. Fortunately no grave robbers here. At least whoever it was, was just out here to drink beer and smoke cigarettes. Don't get it, but there you are."

"How long've you known these grad students?"

"Just met the two girls about a week ago before we all drove out here for the dig. I've known Stan Assice and Tuco Fairweather for almost two years. They were both my students at JC. Came to Tallahassee out of the Army, as I understand it. Took some general classes at the JC, seemed to fall in love with paleo-anthropology. At least Fairweather did. Seemed to really like the ancient Florida Indians. He's a Miccosukee, you know. Why? What would they have to do with this?"

"Don't know. Just following up on all possible angles."

I'm happy with Jake for that question. Shows he's following my advice. Always ask more questions than you have to. Who knows how things are connected? I got no idea where that question might lead; don't see no connection to the dead man, but who knows?

Jake looks over to the four younger people, all sitting around waiting for us to finish talking. Their SUV is packed, and a substantial four-wheel open trailer is loaded with gear. I see other gear in the back of the SUV; the third row of seats is available, but there's barely room for five people. There's a big cargo carrier on the roof, too. How the hell they're gonna get that monster turned around and out of here is more than I can fathom.

I want to talk to them all for a minute before they leave.

"Hey, y'all."

"Hey, deputy," they say. Same mixed-up chorus as before.

"Mr. Fairweather, as I recall?" I ask the Miccosukee.

"I am."

"You know Dr. Morgana from a couple of years ago at the Junior College?"

"Yeah. So?"

"Just asking. Like I tell my buddy Jake here, when you're investigating a strange murder, never know what could be important and what's not. We don't know. She says you came to the JC straight out of the Army?"

"Yes'm. Straight out of the Army. Me and Stan both. Stan was in the Army, too."

"No foolin'? What branch of the Army, you don't mind my asking?"

"Rangers. Both of us."

"Really? The Rangers. They're like, special operations guys. You do special operations?"

"Done a few, yep. But ain't allowed to discuss any of 'em. Clandestine stuff. Stan, he'll tell you the same."

"Did the two of you know each other in the Army?"

"Yep. The whole Ranger Regiment is headquartered in Fort Benning, Georgia. We were in different battalions, so we didn't cross paths very much. But we both did service in Afghanistan—with different battalions, like I said."

"Them Rangers, they're a special bunch."

"We like to think so."

"Tell me. A man mysteriously shows up dead at your work site late last night, and two Army Rangers never noticed it? How can that happen?"

"Wonder the same thing. If I didn't know better, I'd have said that man was planted there yesterday before we arrived. Of course, that can't be because we took a look into the trench Professor Lavida started several months ago, when we came in late yesterday. But you're right. If he'd have come in last night, it would have taken some doing to get past us. I'm a sound sleeper, but Stan here still pops awake at the slightest sound. Ain't that so, Stanley?" He kind of smiles when he says this. Stan doesn't look too happy about it.

"Yep. I guess that's so," Stanley says. "Don't get a lot of really good sleep out on the battlefield in the middle of a mission. Sleep light. Don't want Taliban sneaking up on you in the middle of the night. Know what I mean?"

"So, hate to remind you of anything you'd prefer to forget. But Army Rangers. Maybe you guys did some special operations, you know, 'black ops.' You don't got to tell me about any of it. Just tell me, if you wanted to put a dead man out here, middle of the night, for somebody to find, how would you do it?"

Fairweather looks at Stan Assice, then answers: "I'd take him out first, wherever I found him. Preferably one shot. I never had to move no bodies. But, let's see: Drive the body in part way to where the locals won't hear my engines. Then shoulder him and carry him in some back way, through the bushes. Go slow so you don't make noise you don't want to make. Got to wear night goggles. No flashlights. Dump him, get out of there. Hopefully have a partner to take out obstacles."

Stan shrugs, adds, "I guess that's about how I'd do it, too."

Jake looks at 'em both, and asks: "'Obstacles' meaning people who get in the way? Do you think a woman could do what you've just described?"

It's Stan who answers. "Yes to the first question. And no to the second—not either one of the girls we got here. How much that man weigh?"

I say, "Don't know. Haven't heard back from the coroner yet. Got him right now at the pathologist. I didn't help move him, but our sheriff didn't have no problem. Picked up the whole body bag like it was a bag of jellybeans."

"Your sheriff. That's the really big guy?"

"Six-seven, 320 or so. Yep. He's the one."

"Well, deputy," Stan adds, "I seen some mighty tough gals in the Army. Hate to admit there's some gals are tougher than most soldiers. Male soldiers, I mean. Aren't no women in Special Forces, if that's what you're asking."

"Any in Army Rangers?"

"Yep."

"Any could've moved that man?"

Tuco Fairweather interrupts: "Yep. You get a man across your shoulders, a woman can move more than her body weight. Not far. But she can do it. Some gals are tougher than you think. But like I say, that don't apply to Reggie, nor to Dr. Morgana."

I'm about to ask why he left Becky Rubin out. Maybe he simply thinks the answer is too obvious? But Rubin looks awfully fit to me. But before I can ask, I'm interrupted.

Dr. Morgana sneers, "If I'd 'a' wanted to kill Lavida, I could've dragged his body through the palmettos for a way. Don't underestimate me."

"Make you a suspect," I say.

"Already told you I had nothing to gain," she shouts from where she's sitting.

By this time, it's obvious they're tired and ready to get on. They have to set up camp at the park or else check into my grandmama's motel in town. I look at Jake. We got no more questions.

"Okay. So look, all a'y'all. You stay put in town for a few days. You can camp in the County Park or check into the motel, the Shady Oaks, just on the edge of town next to Mel's gas station. But don't be goin' back to Tallahassee until Sheriff Marion tells you you can. You okay with that?"

"If the law says so," Dr. Morgana replies. The rest just nod, except for the girl they call Reggie, who's asleep in the back seat. They all climb in; Becky is driving. Astonishingly, she backs the trailer perfectly into a little notch between clumps of palmettos, cuts the Land Cruiser sharply to the left, and is out of there on the "road" with nary a problem. Jeepers, I think, wish I could drive like that.

As they drive off it occurs to me I could've asked if she's the one that drove in. But I didn't think to. And it occurs to me that I forgot to ask why Tuco Fairweather left out mentioning Becky Rubin.

"So, Mr. Leon," I say, "Let's go take a look at this Indian mound. See if there's anything we missed."

TRENCHES, CANS, SHARDS AND BUTTS, OH, MY!

SO, PROFESSOR MORGANA AND THE FOUR GRADUATE ASSIS-tants are off down the road, and Jake and me head over to scout around the Indian mound. Professor Morgana says it's an ancient trash midden, not a grave, but I think there's an irony there because for just a while, it *was* a grave—and a modern one. Like my irony.

"What'cha think we might find, Denise?" Jake asks.

"Don't have the slightest idea, Jake. Anything at all that could lead somewhere, let's bag it. We can't dig the mound, but we'll look 'er over pretty thoroughly. You know what I'd *really* like to find?"

"Most useful thing would be his phone," Jake answers. When we bagged up the body and put him in the back of Pee-Wee's Suburban, we found the wallet on his person, apparently untouched, but no phone. "Think we'll find it?"

"Doubtful, Jake. Whoever killed Professor Lavida probably tossed it into the woods somewhere between here and County Road Three. We could search a hundred years with two hundred people and never find it. Sure could be useful to find, though."

"Yep," Jake sighs. "Location history would tell us where he was last night before he ended up dead in that mound. We also might find out who he was talking to Sunday night. But, as you say, it's doubtful we'll ever find it, and even if we did, it'd be all smashed up and we'd get nothing off it anyway."

"Yeah, good luck on us ever finding it and whatever helpful information it might contain. Like, we'd be *that* lucky! In the meantime, let's go over this mound and the trench especially, and see what we can see."

"Roger, Chief Inspector."

Jake likes to kid me about the "Chief Inspector." I ain't no chief of nothin', and Jake has five years seniority on me. But Pee-Wee puts me in charge of murder investigations because it's my thing; I'm good at it.

But at the same time I say that, I'm thinking, I don't have a clue who done this one.

Jake says, "So, Detective Inspector Sumpter, what's your take so far?"

Jake's picked up that "Detective Inspector" from British detective shows. He thinks it's funny. I thought it was funny the first time. Him and Pee-Wee are big British murder mystery fans. Okay by me, but I don't watch 'em. Some of 'em, I hate to say it, I can't understand what they're saying. If they heard me say that, maybe they'd be mad, but it's true. Another thing: any time I watch one with Pee-Wee or Jake, I'm all the time sayin', "What the hell you people doin'? Why didn't you check this?" Like, they just drive right up to a spot where there was a body found, and don't nobody think to park a couple blocks away and check for tire tracks or footprints in any loose soil—skid marks, dirt or sand thrown up on bushes, new tracks or prints on top of older ones, and the like. We had to drive in here, but we parked well away from the mound itself. If anybody'd driven in closer to the mound last night, we wouldn't have obscured their tracks.

Plus sometimes, the whole thing seems phony to me.

There was this one (sorry I'm on my soapbox for just a minute) where the perp killed the victim by drillin' two holes through the wall of a hotel room into the room next door, one hole to see through and one to shoot through, so that's how they killed the victim in the next room and nobody saw 'em go in the room. That's the fakest bullshit I ever heard of in my life. First place, any modern hotel with lots of stories got metal studs in the walls, plus insulation. None of that insulation went flying out into the other room when the drill went through? Drill didn't hit a metal stud? Nobody heard the noise of the drill? Second place, any hole big enough to see through or shoot through, would be big enough to see from the room where the victim was. Third thing: it's hard enough to get a clean shot when you're in the same room with somebody, but in this story, the perp's shooting through a pre-drilled hole and gets a single shot that kills somebody, and he hasn't made any bigger hole in the wall? That's so dumb it makes me want to gag. I watched that, and I was laughin' so hard, Pee-Wee kept lookin' at me sayin', "It's just a show." I said "It's just a bunch of hog poop, what it is." He was aggravated with me, but I was laughin' so hard, Pee-Wee couldn't really get mad at me.

There was another one where the perp wore her work boots over to another farm in the dark of night and got a trout lure, a fly, stuck in her boot sole in all the mud. Only place she could pick that up in her boot was this other guy's barn who wasn't the perp, but was a suspect. All in all it led the inspector to know she was the perp. Now, you ask me, that's the lamest dumb-butt story line I ever heard. Any perp I ever knew would'a' cleaned their boot soles and threw the fly away. You get a trout fly stuck in your boot and don't notice it when you step on concrete? You just leave all the mud in your boots when you go doin' mischief in somebody else's barn? Pure dumb crap. Sorry, but it is. Don't know if America got smarter perps than they do in England or Australia, but Wassahatchka County sure does.

Okay. I'm off my soapbox now.

So, I answer Jake: "Right now, I got two Army Rangers could have done any of the physical part of transporting a body, but I can't see any angle on why they'd do it. They're both graduate students. Way I understand it, a dig like this is a pretty good opportunity to advance in the field—get some experience. Why the hell would they ruin that? Makes no sense. Rodriguez might have some reason, like jealousy, if she thinks Lavida was cheating on her with Morgana, but she's over three hundred miles away. Florida's a damn big state."

"327.7 miles from Sarasota to Tallahassee. I looked it up," Jake says. That's just the kind of thing he'd do! Looks up stuff, sometimes useful, sometimes trivial. "So from somewhere south of Sarasota to rural Wassahatchka County, probably at least 300 miles. A five hour drive, if our perp is Estella Rodriguez."

"Useful stuff, Mr. Know-It-All!" I laugh. But information like that really *could* be useful. "One reason Rodriguez right now isn't at the top of my list of suspects. That's a long way to drive at night with a dead body. And then she's got to find the mound in the dead of night."

"Unlikely, but enough jealousy can be a powerful motive."

"Agreed. So, then there's Professor Morgana. But, again, why? Lavida was her ticket to more higher respect in her field. And neither one of them girls, I don't think, could've carried the body, depending on how far it was. Rubin looks pretty fit, but she ain't big. Judging from what I see right now, Lavida killed himself, which I'd believe except you can't pound stakes through your own eyes when you're drugged unconscious."

Jake just says, "Nope." But he look at me like, 'that's one really disturbing image, Denise Sumpter.' Tell the truth, I can't get that image out've my own head for nothing. That's maybe the most disturbing thing I've ever seen.

We're combing the mound best we can. Jake decides to go down in the trench that's already been dug—where the body was laid out. In a minute he stands up with something in his hand, don't know what. "Hey, Chief Inspector, what do you make of this?" He's turnin' it around in his hand, whatever it is.

"Here, let me see." Its browned and not very big—a flat slab about half the size of the palm of your hand, and slightly curved.

"Pottery?" Jake asks.

"Not sure, Mr. Leon. But I don't think so. This looks more like a piece of skull bone to me, maybe a human skull. Bag it up, take it to professor Morgana, see if she can identify it."

"What you got there, Chief?"

"Well, Pee-Wee already bagged up some cigarette butts and beer cans, but I'm gonna take in a couple extras. If his are missin' fingerprints, mine may have 'em. I'd like to scan around in that trench another minute and see if there's anything else we can find." I take a close-up picture of a cigarette butt planted filter-side down in the weedy soil of the mound.

So I step down into the trench, and we both get on our hands and knees, turning over clods of dirt. Probably all kinds of ancient trash in here, but it's mixed up with clay and dirt and leaves blown into the trench. Truth is, neither one of us has any background in anthropology, so we could look right at something and not know what it is. I pick up a little rock that don't look like nothin', but it seems to have something like the shape of a tooth, so I bag it up. See if Professor Morgana can identify it.

It's about time to haul on outta there. It's getting late and I want to make one more stop before we go back to the station and call it a day.

You'll probably laugh at me for saying this, but on the way out, we seem to take a wrong turn and for about fifteen minutes, we're lost. Not as hard to do in them woods as you might think. You can stand in one place, and it's flat and looks like exactly the same view in any direction you look. Pine trees, some ain't never been cut, palmettos, and scrub oaks and other brush. And forest service roads don't never go straight for who knows what reason. We run right into a dead end with a little clearing of less than a quarter acre, and have to turn around. Somebody's been in here camping, probably illegally. There's a fire pit and near it, some flat spots that look like they're for tents. Kids find these spots and come here back in the woods to make out, smoke dope, drink beer. If I actually saw 'em, I'd bust 'em for possession, but the truth is, I don't really care as long as there ain't nobody getting raped or beat up back here. If some bad shit happened, then I'd really care, but kids bein' kids is kids bein' kids. You were one once, too. But I mentally mark the spot in case I ever have to come back in here again to catch somebody doin' some shit they ain't supposed to be doin'.

Eventually, we find our way out to the "main road," or main dirt track, back onto County Three, and from there back into Seminole Pines. I give professor Morgana a ring, and she ain't at the County Park; she's at my grandmama's motel, the Shady Oaks. So after a few minutes we pull in, say Hi to Doria, the girl at the front desk who's been my friend since Moses' time. My grandmama's in the back as usual, doin' whatever her thing is. She and Pee-Wee are just the same. Don't matter she's an old black woman and he's an older white man. You put people in charge of stuff, and they're all the same. Sit at their desks seems like 24-7 doin' paperwork. I yell out, "Hello, grandma," and she says, "Hello, child," then she pokes her head around the door and says Hi to Jake, too.

"It's all right, grandma. We just got to talk to one of your guests for a minute. Hey Doria, which room is that woman in, probably just checked in, younger, real nice lookin' white woman. She's a professor of anthropology. Need to ask her a question or two."

"This about the terrible killin' happened out at the Indian Mound?" Doria asks.

"Yep, it is."

"Her and that other younger girl'r in room ten, just down the end of this wing." Doria's dialect is pretty local and pretty strong.

In a minute, we're knocking at the door, and we hear a "Who is it?"

"This is deputy Sumpter again. Sorry to keep buggin' you, but we need to ask you a couple more questions."

She opens the door, dressed in clean shorts and a t-shirt. Her hair is wet and it's clear she just got out of the shower. I still hear the shower going, though. "Come in," she says. "Becky is back in the bathroom taking a shower. Hey, Becky!" she calls.

"Can't hear you! Water's running," a voice yells from the shower.

Professor Morgana gets up and pokes her head into the bathroom, obviously to let Becky know we're here.

"Couldn't stand all that grime for another second. We have little pre-packaged bath wipes for out in the woods, but after a day or two of that, enough is enough. Feels good to get a regular shower. So . . . what can I help you with this time?"

I pull out my evidence bag with the flat piece in it that looks like part of a skull bone to me. But with its color and shape, it could be part of a broken pot for all I know. Did those ancient Indians make pots way back then?

I give Professor Morgana a pair of latex gloves. "I wanted to know if you could tell me what this is," I say.

She looks at it, her mouth getting wider by the minute. "Where did you get this?" She says.

"Got it from that trench where we found the body. He could have been practically laying on top of it."

"Oh, my God," she says. Then, she says it again: "Oh, my *God!*" Just like that, with a big emphasis on the "God."

"So?" I ask. "You seem to recognize what it is. Help us out here."

"Deputy . . . Sumpter, isn't it? Well, Deputy Sumpter, this is a piece of frontal bone from a human skull. Down toward the bottom here, you can just see where it starts to raise a little bit above the brow ridge."

"You sure about this?"

"I'm one hundred percent sure. You got this out of the trench?"

"We did."

"Deputy, this has absolutely got to be dated! Did you handle this with your bare hands?"

"Nope. We wear gloves when we're handlin' potential evidence."

"Well, I sincerely doubt this is evidence of anything that has happened in about the last ten thousand years. We really need to send this to the lab in Tallahassee. They have facilities for radiocarbon dating. Without dating it, we couldn't know exactly how old it is, though I can assure you one hundred percent it's no victim of a crime that would fall under your purview. I'd strongly advise you to hand it over to me and let me drive this into the lab tomorrow."

"Sorry, professor. I can't do that. I got no idea how a ten thousand year old bone might figure into our investigation of a two day old crime, but this is going into our evidence locker at the station. Don't worry, I know what ancient remains could mean to your dig. But right now, I just can't hand it over to you. And you can't leave for Tallahassee tomorrow, anyway—maybe not for a few more days. But here, maybe you'd take a look at this, too." I hand her the small rock.

Professor Morgana turns it over in her hand. "My God," she says again. "I've been looking for artifacts like these my entire career. And to have two important human remains just dumped in my lap." She's quiet for a minute. "Well, it's just amazing."

"So this is also human? A tooth, I'm guessing?"

"Oh, dear God, it sure is. I'm not absolutely certain, but this looks like lower left jaw, probably either the seventeenth or eighteenth molar. You can tell by the way the cusps are shaped. See? It would sit in the lower jaw this way." She holds it in her hand, as if her hand were a lower jaw. "Even if this is really old, it's been fairly well preserved. You can see some wearing down, either from grinding on hard foods, or, more likely, chewing on leather to soften it. Likely a woman's tooth, if that's the case."

"You can tell all that just from a tooth?"

"Well, I wouldn't swear to any of it. I'm just talking about patterns. The teeth are numbered, one to thirty-two. The back molars on the top left are fifteen and sixteen, and they bite down on bottom molars seventeen and eighteen. Of course, you can't tell for sure exactly how they'd fit into the mouth of the once living human without having more of the skull and teeth, but you can make reasoned guesses. Like the piece of frontal bone, this really, really needs to be dated. You're sure you found these in the trench?"

"Yes'm', we did. Sort of changes the complexion of this investigation. This will have to go into our evidence locker for the time being."

"Deputy, what could a molar tooth that's likely thousands of years old, possibly have to do with this crime you're investigating?"

"I ain't got a clue," I say. "But it's stayin' with me, or staying with us, until we get this whole thing sorted out."

About this time, I hear Becky in the bathroom turn off the shower. It sounds as if she's getting dried off.

"Hey, Beck? Deputy Sumpter and Deputy Leon are here. Don't come out without being decent." She turns to us. "Neither one of us could stand the grime. Becky doesn't have two dimes to rub together, so I invited her to room with me for a night or two until we can get back on the site, which I fully intend to do now, university license or no. I'll leave that site when they drag me off it."

"Hey, professor," Jake says. "I thought you said these trash middens weren't burial spots? What are human remains doing there—assuming you're right about what these are?"

"Hard to say. Usually, people, no matter how ancient, bury or cremate their dead ceremonially. Very hard to know why human remains, especially ancient ones, would be in a trash midden."

"Cannibalism?" Jake suggests.

"Possibly, but hardly likely. We don't have much here to look at. If we found long bones, they'd likely be cracked open for marrow if it was cannibalism. But even ten thousand years ago, north Florida was a rich environment. It was more open, then. The climate was cooler and drier. There were mastodons on the plains, giant sloths. No shortage of game animals. Those folks had plenty to eat. The reason there's a midden at all is because they were there a long time. I suspect if we could sift even a small part of that mound, we'd find fish bones, fresh water shellfish, God knows what. They camped at that spot and didn't move. Or maybe they camped at it during the same time of year each year, as they moved around their environment to take advantage of different seasonal resources. Who knows? But, dear God, this has just *got* to be dated. I'm itching to get back to that mound."

"But, if there are human remains in a trash midden, they got there some way."

"Of course," Morgana says, "But who knows how? Maybe cultural practices were just wholly different for them. Maybe it was the body of someone who'd been cast out, or the body of a tribal enemy. Who knows? The point is, the whole mound needs to be meticulously investigated, layer by layer, and dated carefully."

Just then, Becky comes out, dressed in clean shorts and a khaki colored t-shirt. You couldn't tell this before when we saw the group at the site and she was dressed in jeans, but it's clear in her shorts that the girl is a dedicated gym rat. She either was a gymnast at some point, or maybe a weightlifter. The muscles in her thighs are pronounced, even small as she is.

"Hey, Beck, look at this," Morgana says, and hands the tooth to Becky.

"Not without latex gloves, please," I caution them.

Becky pulls on a pair of gloves, and turns the tooth over in her hand. "Eighteenth molar," she says. "Lower left jaw. Mesiolingual and mesiobuccal cusps are particularly worn down—likely a woman's tooth. You find this at the dig?"

"They did," professor Morgana says.

She turns to professor Morgana: "Just like . . ." and she pauses just a second. "Just like the one we saw in the lab back in Tallahassee. You know the one—taken from that paleo site near the Miami river."

"Yep," says Morgana. "And look at this piece of skull." For a split second, I'm almost certain I saw a flash of fear cross Morgana's face, as if Becky were about to say something she shouldn't.

Becky looks at it, turns it over. "Left frontal bone. Just above the brow ridge. This tiny spur here would continue down into the orbital bone. You find this there, too?" She looks at me, but I catch a corner of her glance shooting toward Dr. Morgana.

"Yes. It's going into the evidence locker at our office down the road. We'll release it to you, or to the university, for dating when we're done with this investigation."

They shoot strong glances at each other. "Oh, deputy, please release it to me when you're finished. This could make my career. It would mean a lot to me." Morgana is almost pleading.

"I understand," I say, "but we would have to follow whatever the legal protocol would be. I think you said the university holds the license for this excavation? My guess is any artifacts recovered would have to go back to them. But we'll see. I don't know what the legal protocol actually would require. Say, Dr. Morgana," I begin.

"Yes?"

"You said this morning that Professor Lavida invited you to co-manage this dig."

"Yes, that's right."

"He was familiar with the site, then?"

"He started the trench there maybe about three, four months ago, and returned there about a month ago before we got official permission and funds to start the present dig. This mound is locally famous, you know."

"Did he bring you out to look at it before you all started digging?"

"Actually, yes. I said he was out there a month ago—early August. About a million degrees and so humid you could bathe by just standing still. Not the best time to dig."

"Just checking things out?"

"Just checking things out. He said the university was applying for a grant and for a license to dig on national forest land. He was sure both would come through. I jumped at the chance."

"So, you've known about this mound for some time?"

"Well, about a month or so. Sure. What of it?"

"Nothing," I say. "Just trying to get as much information as I can so I can sort things out in my mind. Listen, thank you both for your time. Jake, you have any other questions?"

"Nope," says Jake. "Thanks for your time, ladies."

We leave and get back in the car. Still my old Crown Vic. Anxious to get back into Jake's Hellcat. One sweet ride, tellin' you.

When we're in the car, Jake turns to me: "Did you see that tattoo on Becky's left shoulder?"

"What tattoo? You lookin' at the girls now, Jake?"

"Well, smarty—besides the fact that they're both worth looking at, there was something about that tattoo."

"I saw it, but I didn't really look."

"It was a skull with a 75 on one side and an RGT on the other side."

"Yeah, so? What's that mean?"

"The skull is one of the logos of the U.S. Army Rangers. The Rangers are the 75th Regiment. Usually written 75-RGT."

"How'd you know that?"

"Looked it up on my phone after we talked to the group out at the mound and you found out they were Army Rangers."

"Shit." I say, "Little Becky was a member of the U.S. Army Rangers?"

"Or had a boyfriend who was."

"Lordy, Lordy. What we got ourselves into with this one?"

"Don't know, Chief Inspector. But I'll betcha something else."

"What's that? You gonna tell me them two is lovers? Shit, I spotted that much right off."

"How'd you guess?"

"All the suitcases were on one bed. Only got the one bed to sleep in. Just a guess, but a good one."

"Yeah. And just the way they acted with each other They were very familiar. 'Hey, Beck,' and so on."

"Yeah. Don't make no difference to our investigation, though." And then I pause. "I don't think. Tell you something else. Did you see Professor Morgana just about jump out of her skin when Becky said 'Just like the one,' like she was about to say something she really shouldn't have said?"

"Sorry, Denise, can't say I really noticed."

"Yeah. Well, I'm tellin' you, she did. Just a guess, but . . ."

"You think they've dug at the mound before and found human remains?"

"What I was thinkin', yep."

"Something's going on here, Chief Inspector. Them two are involved in something. Maybe the others are, too. Say, another thing."

"You're going to tell me Becky seemed pretty expert at identifying those remains."

"Yep."

"Way I understood it, she was a, umm . . . what's the word . . . one of those people who restored things in the lab."

"Yeah. A . . . I don't know, lab rat? Preparator?"

"Got to check into them two further."

"I agree."

"But tomorrow morning, first thing, let's check in with your dad and see what he can tell us about the cause of death."

"Deal. We calling it a day?"

"Don't know about you, macho man, but little old me is tired. I need some Willie's gumbo, a cold beer, a Mount Gay rum before bed, and eight solid hours' sleep."

"Mind if I join you at Willie's? Okay to say 'no' if you'd prefer to be alone, or if you and Bell Lake have plans." Bell Lake, Doria's brother, is my boyfriend.

"Bell's workin' at the high school tonight. Join me at Willie's, seven o'clock?"

"Deal."

"Let's get these evidence bags back to the office."

ALPHONSE LEON SAYS THE VICTIM IS DEFINITELY DEAD; MIDGE AND JAKE HAVE A STAKE IN FINDING THE PERP

NEXT MORNING, I GET TO THE OFFICE AT THE REGULAR TIME, about 7:25. Jake's already there. Pee-Wee's already there, too, always the first one there every day, always sitting in his office doing paperwork, on the computer, or on the 'phone.

"That Midge just came in?" I hear him holler from back in his office. You can hear people come in and go out of our office because we have a creaky screen door that slams shut unless you close it really carefully.

"Yep," says Jake.

"Hey, you two. Come in here a second."

We both go in.

"Yeah, boss?" Says Jake.

"So I did a little background checking on our five mound prospectors yesterday afternoon—with Dennis's help." Dennis Martin is another deputy and our computer research genius. "Just calling around, talking to people. According to Professor Bacardi—you remember, the head of the department at the university?—Dr. Morgana is something of a well-known rogue scholar. She's been trying to get a position at the university for several years. She and Professor Rodriguez, the woman at the dig down south of Sarasota, competed for the same job opening about three years ago, and Rodriguez won the position. The two evidently intensely dislike each other. The feeling is, Morgana's out to one-up Rodriguez, show her up, make the university sorry they didn't hire her, etcetera. Evidently she's wormed her way into more than one dig in North Florida. Scuttlebutt is she slept her way into adjunct site manager, though no proof. Just what Professor Bacardi seems to believe people are saying."

"She says they never had an affair," I note.

"Possibly not. Just repeating what I've heard. The point I'm making is that Morgana isn't well-liked or trusted. Seems to be something of a bone-hunter, and has a reputation for not being careful about her time on sites."

"Could be human remains at that mound they're excavating," I say.

"Oh?"

"Yeah, Pee-Wee. Jake found a piece of flat bone, no bigger than half the palm of your hand, that Morgana swears is a part of the, ummm . . . what was it, Jake? The frontal bone of a human skull—and, she thinks, very, very old. It's in the evidence locker, along with a tooth I found, similarly old. At least, so thinks Dr. Morgana."

"My, oh, my! You don't say? I found a similar small, flat piece of bone myself. This could be pretty big, guys. Bacardi tells me many field researchers spend their lives at various digs without ever turning up more than fish bones and occasionally a potsherd or two. If we have human remains at that site that are as ancient as all that, this could be, in the paleontology field, very, very big."

"Reason enough to kill somebody?"

"Don't know. Possibly. Can't see why, though."

"I don't either, Pee-wee," I say. "Right now, I'm just trying to fit together a whole bunch of details."

"Make sure those remains stay in our evidence locker until all this is worked out. When our investigations are complete, we'll hand them over to the university, the licensed entity running this dig."

"Morgana would sure like to get her hands on them."

"Likely. But ain't gonna happen, Midge."

"Say, you know what else, Pee-Wee?"

"Let me guess: You suspect that that one young lady, Becky, was also a member of the Army Rangers."

"How'd you know? Jake's the one who guessed that. She has an Army Ranger tattoo on her left shoulder."

"How'd I know? I talked to the commanding officer of the 75th Regiment. I called to check on the background of those two guys. Got more info than I bargained for. Took me most of the day yesterday to get ahold of him and we only talked for a minute, but he handed me over to some junior officer who told me not only did, umm, those two guys whose names I forget . . ."

"Stan Assice and Tuco Fairweather," Jake throws in. What a memory!

"Not only them, but our 'young' little Becky Rubin was an Army Ranger, too. I just found that out by chance. I ran down our list of graduate assistants at the site, just on the off chance that there might be any other connection to the Rangers, and as soon as I mentioned Becky Rubin, he knew right off who she was. And guess what else."

"Can't guess, Pee-Wee."

"She's older than she looks. This little-girl pigtails look is, in fact, something of a put-on. She's thirty-two years old. Made Captain in the Rangers, led several field operations in Afghanistan. Outranks both the boys, but whether she knew them or not in the Army, I can't tell you. From what I understand, they weren't in her battalion, but there were lots of joint operations in Afghanistan. She could have known them from some mission. Who knows who knew each other in Afghanistan. She's a good five or six years older than they are. She's also an expert marksman—markswoman, excuse me—and holds several black belts in different martial arts. And, guess what else . . ."

"She rates super-high on I.Q. tests," says Jake.

"Good boy," says Pee-Wee. "They don't release specifics, but evidently she scored something like the second or third highest ever on whatever intelligence tests the Army gives these guys. They were willing to share that much, but beyond that, they're very closed-mouthed about where their people have been, what operations they've taken part in, and so on. Got something else for you, but first, how'd you guess about the I.Q. score?"

"Didn't guess about the score," says Jake. "But when our Dr. Morgana showed Rubin the piece of bone and the tooth, she identified both of them right away with really professional detail."

"So, what else, Pee-Wee?" I ask.

"You think she's smart? Well, not only was she a captain in the Army Rangers, but she's actually not a graduate student. She's post-doc."

"Post doc?" I ask. Didn't know what that was.

"She actually has a Ph.D in physical paleontology—human remains, basically. Dennis called the university anthropology department again yesterday to ask about the 'students' and found out that Rubin *isn't* one of them. She's actually in line for a position on the faculty. Sounds like Professor Bacardi wants her on his staff. Sounds like everybody does."

"Wow," I say. "Our girl is full of surprises. Wouldn't that sort of make her and Dr. Morgana competitors?"

"Unless Dr. Morgana doesn't know her girlfriend is post doc in the very field Morgana is trying to establish a reputation in," Jake adds.

"Girlfriend?" says Pee-Wee.

"Just a guess, boss," Jake says. They seemed pretty, ahh, comfy with each other in the motel room. Don't know for sure, of course, but just the way it seemed. Chief Inspector says the same thing."

"He's right, Pee-Wee. All their gear—suitcases, duffel bags, laundry, whatever—were piled on one bed. The second bed was kind of mussed up. Of course, they *might* be sleeping together and no sex is going on, but there were two beds in that room. No reason I can think of they wouldn't be sleeping in their own beds. They were pretty cozy with one another. Well . . . seemed that way, but could be wrong."

"Well, then," says Pee-Wee. "What's your next stop . . . Chief Inspector Sumpter." Seems the whole department has picked up on this

"Chief Inspector" joke. It's getting a little annoying. Maybe subconsciously it's their way of making sure I don't get too full of myself. But I don't mind too much. Underneath their joking, they both know I'm likely to figure all this out before they do. I know I sound like I'm bragging. But it's probably true. Everybody has their strengths, and my strength is putting the pieces together.

"Go see Jake's daddy and see what he says about official cause of death."

"Good move," says Pee-Wee. "Off you go, then. Keep me posted. I'm going to see if I can follow up on Lavida's movements the day before he checked in at the trench motel."

"Trench motel." Pee-Wee's a funny man. What happened to that man ain't funny, but Pee-Wee has a way of making me laugh.

So me and Jake are off to Dr. Leon's office. He runs the clinic in town, but he's also Wassahatchka County coroner and our main pathologist. Not a big, fancy county; budget stretches pretty thin.

We walk in and the nurse-receptionist shows us to the back where the coroner's office is. This early, Dr. Leon doesn't have any patients yet. Most of his patients are kids with scraped knees, teenagers with acne problems, and old folks with broken bones. But this mornin', he's all ours.

"Mornin', Doc," I say.

"Well, if it isn't Chief Inspector Denise Sumpter of the Royal Wassahatchka County Constabulary."

I'm thinkin', they got Jake's dad doin' this "Chief Inspector" thing now? Really? I can see Jake kind of laughing. But there's a difference between laughing because you're having fun *with* somebody and laughing because you're making fun *of* somebody. They ain't making fun. Jake knows me too well for that. Least, I hope he does.

So, what the heck, I play along. "It's me, Doc. This here's Deputy Inspector Jake Leon. What you got for us?"

"Well, Denise," he drops the joking around and gets really serious with us for a minute. "What you've got yourselves here is a dead man, and so far as I can tell, the cause of death is about as gruesome as I've ever seen."

I'm thinkin', shit, don't tell me he was still alive when they drove them stakes through his eyes. That's just too gross altogether. So, I just say, "Cause of death?"

"Well, I haven't gotten a toxicology report from the lab yet; may not for several days at least. But I'll tell you what they're going to find: He had a high level of rohypnol or maybe GHB in his blood stream. Probably enough to paralyze him and knock him out. He was still alive and breathing when whoever it was drove the first wooden stake in, probably, his right eye and then the others through his left eye and his mouth, out the back of his throat. He was killed by the first stake. Went right into his brain, cracked the back of his skull, it was hit so hard, but it didn't go all the way through."

Jake and me are both quiet for a minute. We look at each other with that "What the heck are we dealing with?" kind of look. I don't scare easy and neither does Jake, but this killer sounds like a psycho, for sure. After I compose my thoughts, I try to get focused on procedure. "Where'd the wooden stakes come from?"

"Good question. Each one has a kind of notch on the end—like old-fashioned tent stakes. Usually metal nowadays, but you can still find wooden ones. Used to stake down the corners of the tent and the guy-wires that hold up the top."

"Tent stakes?" Jake says.

"Well, tent stakes or something pretty similar. They're clearly stakes designed for holding down a line. Might be garden stakes, you know, for holding down those support wires that hold small trees up."

"So, he was actually killed by those?"

"Yep, the first one, I'm pretty certain."

"So, Doc," I say, "We know those stakes didn't go through the back of the skull. Found that out when we moved the body. But was there anything identifiable on the stakes when you took them out? Extracted them from his . . . uhhh . . . face, I mean?" I'm trying to establish whether he was actually killed at the site. If the stakes killed him, that tells us the murder weapon, but it doesn't tell us where he was murdered.

"Like what?"

"Well, something that might show us where he was killed. Like, if there was oil or grease on them, maybe he was killed in a garage. Not sayin' that's where I think he was killed, but that's for an example. A particular color of clay? A particular fragment of leaf we could have identified? Anything."

"Nope. Both the stakes had blood and brain material, but nothing else I noticed, though I'll take a closer look now you mention it. Can tell you, neither stake penetrated the back of the skull. The stake in his mouth went through the back of his throat and hit the second cervical vertebra, sometimes called the Axis bone. But didn't break the skin on the other side at the back of his neck."

"Any guesses as to time of death. Doc?"

"Well, hard to say for sure. Rigor mortis is usually pretty complete by, say, eight to ten, maybe twelve hours after death. So when Sheriff Marion brought him in, he was stiffer than a board. That says he'd been dead at least, close guess, twelve hours. When I saw him, the blood around his face was completely dry."

"Will the toxicology report help any?"

"Well, a toxicology report can help some. While the person is alive, they metabolize the drugs in their system, but that process stops when they're dead. If we know the amount that would have put him out and the amount left in his system after he died, we can make a pretty accurate guess as to how long he'd been out when he was killed. However, that doesn't do a lot for precisely specifying time of death."

"How long before we have any reports from the toxicology lab?"

"Wow. Well, deputy Sumpter, that could take a while. This isn't a crime detective show on TV. A good toxicology test performed by a competent member of CAP, could take several weeks."

"CAP?"

"College of American Pathologists. Look, I'm just a country doctor. I can tell you basically what's going on, but the real details will have to wait on somebody with a whole different level of skill from mine."

"But you've told us a lot, Doc. We know what killed him, know that he was probably out from the effects of drugs, and we know he'd been dead for about twelve hours, give or take, when Pee-Wee brought him in—maybe six to eight hours when we found him in the trench. That tells us a lot."

I turn to Jake. "You got any questions for your daddy?"

"Well," Jake muses, "not a lot. One thing: Any signs of what the perpetrator might have used to pound the stakes in?"

"No idea," says Dr. Leon. "Anything from a rock to a hammer. A microscopic analysis might pick up something—particles of rock, discoloration from a steel hammer. But I haven't gotten that far."

I understand Jake's question: if we knew the tool, then we could look for it in someone's possession. But this is a dig site, so everybody's going to have access to picks, shovels, whatever. So I turn to Jake: "We could go visit the hardware and garden store up on First Street; see what they have in the way of garden stakes, and see if they have any recollection of any of our trenching crew buying some."

"Gonna need to get pictures of our group of suspects. But, you know, Midge, . . ."

I finish his thought for him: "It might not be any of them. I know. This is a tough one, Jake. But at least we've got somewhere to start. How about you head over to the motel and get a picture of the two women, and I'll head down to Lake Park and see if the two boys and that other girl, Regina, are camping out. Then you and me can head down to Pruitt's Hardware. Good a way as any I can think of right now to get rolling."

IF A PICTURE IS WORTH A THOUSAND WORDS, THEN HOW MUCH ARE FIVE PICTURES WORTH?

ABOUT TWO HOURS LATER, JAKE AND I ARE AT SEMINOLE Pines' version of a hardware and garden store—not your big box Home Depot or Loewe's like you might have in your big city, but a little mom and pop owned and run by locals: Pruitt's Garden and Hardware. That store has everything from screws and nails to potted plants and fishing equipment.

I know the boy behind the counter. I say "boy" just out of habit—not to diminish anybody. He was a year ahead of me in high school, and for a while I had a crush on him. He was tall and athletic then, and now he's still tall, but you find out in life that what was "athletic" in high school is pretty well short of being athletic in a major college or in he pros.

Silvio was a star on our basketball team, but no college recruited him. He went to The University of Florida and walked on, but he sat on the bench for two full seasons before leaving the team. In two seasons he scored two points, had no rebounds and no assists. In the meantime, he wasn't the greatest student in the world, and he left before getting his degree, joined the Army for two years. From what I heard, went to Afghanistan.

Should've stayed in school, for sure—made himself a life with his mind and his learning. But kids— they get seduced into thinking they're better at their chosen sport than they really are. You always read about the high school stars who made good; nothin' wrong with that. But Silvio's like the vast majority who don't. Nothing wrong with dreaming big, but you've got to have a realistic view of the world, and of yourself. You're only one of *hundreds of thousands* of kids who dream big.

Sometimes life makes me a little sad. Silvio had every egg he owned in one basket, and he worked at it. But it wasn't to be.

So now Silvio is helping customers find what they need in this crowded maze of a little store. Narrow isles choked with wheelbarrows, rakes, stacks of bagged garden soil, rows of tools like hammers and saws, hundreds of pull-out plastic drawers with nails and screws and hinges. Could probably build a house and plant a whole garden out of what you'd find in this little store. Silvio knows where every damn kind of nail you could imagine is located. Paint is in isle three; glue across from the ceiling paint. I guess that's a kind of success, too. Don't need to be a star to be a good person and do good work in life.

"Hey, Silvio!"

"Well, if it ain't Denise Sumpter. You ain't growed an inch since I saw you last. Look at you! Look good in that uniform, you do. Did they have to run it through the wash to shrink it a little before you could wear it?" He laughs at his own little joke. Silvio's maybe six-four, so he's more than a foot taller than me. He was always a bit of a joker, but he never meant any harm by it.

"No, they didn't. They actually had my size, believe it or not. You know deputy Leon?"

"Last I saw you, deputy Leon, you was sitting in that hot Dodge of yours behind the Hardee's sign where it leads out of town on County Two." He laughs again.

"Hello, sir," says Jake, real polite. "Don't recall that I ever had to pull you over."

"Don't speed, least not in city limits," says Silvio, and laughs. "One good thing about havin' a job, you can get your own wheels. Got mine not but a month ago. She's used, but she's cool. Put mags on the back. She'll put ruts in the asphalt, you floor 'er. But you'll never see me doin' that." He laughs again at this.

"Yep," says Jake. "Never seen you speeding. Doesn't mean I think you drive everywhere the way you drive in town."

"Well," Silvio smiles, "You see me speeding, you give me a ticket, then. Hard enough to keep up with payments, though, So I don't need no tickets!" And he laughs.

I interrupt this car talk. "Glad to see somebody I knew in school doin' so good for himself."

"Well, ain't what I was aimin' at, but can't always hit what you're aiming' at, know what I'm sayin'?"

"I do." And Jake nods along with the comment. I can see him looking around. He wants to go check out the garden equipment, see if they sell the kind of stakes that were driven through Lavida's eye sockets. But Silvio ain't quite done tellin' me about his life. He was always chattery in high school, too.

"Mr. Pruitt, who owns this store, is gonna give me a raise soon— making considerable above minimum wage. I come in every day so regular, almost feel like I own the place. Mr. Pruitt worked out a deal with me where he withholds some of my salary and invests it in the store, so's I become gradually a part owner. Own about five percent right now. How you doin' in the sheriff's business?"

"Doin' all right. That's why we're here, Silvio. Investigatin' that murder took place up at the Indian mound. You heard of it?"

"Murder? Holy shit. Who got murdered?" He looks startled when her hears this. Something in his demeanor seems a bit . . . worried? Maybe I'm reading it all a little wrong. I get a lot from watching people's reactions. But I don't always know how to interpret them.

"A professor from the university."

Silvio's quiet for just a few seconds. Shakes his head. "Ain't heard nothin' about it 'till just this second. How's that brought you around to Pruitt's Hardware and Garden?" There's something I think I detect in

Silvio's tone, a slight twist of his lip that tells me there's somethin' going on, but I don't know what it is. Don't know for sure if I'm right. But I put it in the back of my mind for thinking about.

"Man killed had wooden stakes drove through his eye sockets. Want to know where the perpetrator got them stakes."

"Jesus! You ain't messin' with me, are you?"

"Nope. What you got in this store in the way of wooden stakes?"

"Well, for whatever help it's like to give you, I'll show you. Come on this way."

He walks from in back of the cash register down the central isle, out the back door to the covered patio area where the garden equipment is stacked or shelved.

"Got these," he says, and he pulls a wooden stake out of a clay pot. "These is used to anchor down ties if you want to stake up a young tree while it's getting rooted.

What he pulls out of the pot is dead-on *exactly* what we're looking for.

"Well," says Jake. "Found a source for our murder weapon— or weapons."

"Yep, I say. Don't mean they were bought here. But these are exactly like the ones killed the professor. Hey, Silvio," I take out my phone. "Gonna show you some pictures. Tell me if you ever seen any of these folks before, okay?" I slowly scroll through the pictures on my phone and bring up, first, Becky Rubin.

"Nope. Can't say I ever seen her," says Silvio.

Next I show him a facial of Felicia Morgana. "Ooh! She's a hot one! Ninety percent sure she's the one bought them stakes."

"Ninety percent?"

"Closer to a hundred. Remember her pretty good. Talked to her for a few minutes."

"And then?"

He shrugs. "Then she left."

"That's it? She left?"

"Yep."

I sense there's something Silvio Treadwell isn't telling me.

We show him pictures of Regina Gentiles, Stan Assice and Tuco Fairweather. He says he doesn't recognize any of them.

"No memory of any of these, eh?"

"None of them come in the store," he says, but he looks nervous. My experience tells me that if I press him on it too hard, he'll clam up. He might just be nervous because the stakes he sold to Morgana could have been used in a murder. Lots of things probably buzzing through his mind. When people aren't sure of their footing, they tend to clam up. I'll give it a shot, but I ain't hopeful.

"You're looking nervous, Silvio. You sure you never seen any of these folks in here?"

"Just don't want to miss somethin' I should remember. Never been asked no questions about a murder before." He pauses a minute, then: "Hey, don't know whether to mention this or not. But figure it can't hurt. That murder happened out by the old Indian mound, right? Think that's what you said."

"Exactly. There is, or was, an anthropology dig goin' on there—university people."

"Don't know nothin' about the archaeology, but I been out that way once or twice myself. You know old Mr. Bass?"

"Umm . . . not really. That old man they call 'Skanky'?"

Silvio laughs. "He's the one." He pauses. "You know he spends a lot of time out at that old Indian mound?"

"No, I didn't know that. What does he spend time out there for?"

"Don't know. Used to visit the graveyard, too. Somebody told me once he likes to commune with the spirits." He laughs at this.

"No way. Who told you that?"

"Think it was Mr. Pruitt himself, or maybe somebody else. Don't want to get nobody in trouble, but you might want to go check him out. Just sayin'. Tryin' to be helpful."

"Know where we could find this guy?"

"Best I know, lives in a little shack next to the abandoned sawmill."

"Thanks, Silvio. You've been a great help. Jake? Any questions?"

"Sure. So, Silvio, that cap you have on. 199th Infantry Brigade. You were in the army?"

"Two years. Spent a whole year in Afghanistan. Worst damn place you ever seen. Wished I'd never had no part of the U.S. Army."

"Didn't have a good experience in the Army?"

"Hated the Army."

"Couple other people at the dig site were in the Army. Army Rangers."

"I wasn't no Ranger. Them are the real soldiers. I was just a grunt wanted out from the minute I got in."

"But you wear that Army cap."

"Sometimes I forget I have it on. People who come in here like it. They respect the Army, sometimes even thank me for my service. Don't have to tell 'em I hated the Army. They never been to Afghanistan. They never been shot at. Never had to shoot back."

"Tough go of it over there, I take it?"

"Might say that."

"Thanks," says Jake.

We thank Silvio for his time and head out.

In the car, Jake looks at me: "Kind of narrows things down a bit, don't you think?"

"Well, Jake, yes and no. Remember, the stakes Morgana bought could have been used for staking down the tarp they put over her work table. Wish I'd paid more attention to their campsite before they pulled it all up and packed it away. If it was her, IF, she must've bought quite a few, so somebody else could have used several to kill Professor Lavida. Or the stakes used to kill him might have been bought by somebody else at some other store."

"Still," says Jake, "We've got somebody at the scene of the crime who might have bought either the murder weapons, or stakes exactly like the murder weapons."

"At the scene of the crime, yes. Or . . . maybe. We still don't know for sure where Lavida was killed. None of the stakes driven into his skull went through into the dirt beneath. He could have been killed on the moon, for all we know, and his body transported to the site."

Jake looks at me and smiles. "Learnin' a lot from you, Denise. I think maybe people have a tendency to make things too simple. Woman buys wooden stakes doesn't equal woman is the murderer who used exactly the same kind of stakes. True enough. Still, we don't want to overlook possible connections, eh?"

"Course not. All part of the puzzle, Jake. This probably makes Morgana a suspect. But we still don't know where Lavida was killed, and especially *why* she would have killed him, if she did. Motive is what trips me up on Morgana. Lavida was her ticket to a higher-class professional career. Why kill him?"

"Because he wouldn't cooperate? Wouldn't speak up for her on the faculty, maybe?"

"Well . . . maybe. But she's the one he asked to be adjunct site manager, remember?"

"Yeah. I do. Damn. So, where to now?"

"I say we go pay a visit to this guy. Damn. Forgot his name."

"Bass."

"Yeah. Mr. Bass. Shack next to the old sawmill."

"Figure he may have seen anything?"

"What I'm hoping."

And off we go.

BASS FISHING, OR, HOW TO CATCH... NOTHIN'

STANFORD "SKANKY" BASS LIVES IN A CURIOSITY SHOP OF AN old shack. It was built—mostly by him, as I understand it—near an abandoned sawmill, so half of it at least was built of "borrowed" materials. It resembles more a collection of sheds and lean-tos than an actual house with a front door and rooms inside. How he managed to evade county building codes and ordinances I have no idea. I think he never claimed the property as an actual residence—had it registered as a utility shed, so it didn't have to meet livability standards. But he lives there anyway.

When we arrive, we catch Skanky in the middle of deep-frying some fish in an old, converted oil drum he's repurposed as a large deep-fryer, with a burner taken off an old gas grill set up beneath. He's clearly old, skinny, stooped and white-haired, but with the darkest skin I've ever seen. I'm pretty dark myself, but he's even darker than I am. He has a cigarette mostly burned hanging from his lips. I look for blue beer cans, but don't see any. An ancient-looking red pickup truck sits in the yard, or the dirt and weed-covered pair of ruts that serve as a driveway. Oddly, the truck looks pretty clean, some corner of my mind notes. I'll file that away for further investigation if I need to.

We pull up in Jake's Hellcat—damndest badass patrol car that's ever boasted a bullbar, as I've said before. We get out, and Bass turns around and looks at us with something far less than concern in his eyes. Gutted and beheaded bass go from a bowl of mixed flour and cornmeal, plop into the hot oil. He's mixed up some hushpuppies which he plops into the hot grease from a knife blade, rather than forming them into balls, so the hushpuppies came out looking more like big Cheetos than like traditional round hushpuppies. He doesn't seem to care one way or another whether we're there or not. He's concentrating on his lunch.

"Hey, there. You Mr. Stanford Bass?"

It takes him a while to answer. "Who's askin'?"

"Me. I'm Deputy Denise Sumpter of the Wassahatchka County sheriff's office. This here's Deputy Jake Leon. We're here to ask you a few questions, 'f you don't mind."

"I s'pect it don't really matter whether I mind or not, now do it? Already know my name and where I live. What more you want to know?" He's tending his frying fish with a long pair of tongs. Every once in a while, he turns a hushpuppy. At no time while we're talking does he neglect his frying.

"Like to know if you ever visit the big Indian mound off the forest service road comes out on County Road Three. You know the place?"

"Sure do. Go up there all the time."

"Been up there recently?"

"Been up there just a few days ago. Plan to go back soon, too."

"What you go up there for?"

"Now, what you want to know that for? What business you got prying into a man's private affairs? I go up there for my own reasons."

"There was a really bad murder happened up there just two days ago. Really bad. Man stabbed through the eyes with massive wooden stakes. Nasty. We need to gather as much information as we can about what went on there. If you've gone up there recently; maybe you saw somethin' would help us find out who done the crime."

He pulls out a golden brown hushpuppy, then another, then another. He's silent while he's working. Out comes one fried fish, then another, then another. There's enough in his fish fry to feed ten. It's probably meant for his dinner as well as his lunch.

"Let me set this aside to cool." He sets two bowls on an old card table spread with an old, torn sheet, one bowl piled with fish, one with hushpuppies. Good enough table cloth, I suppose. "You gon' ask me questions, then you gon' join me for lunch. Don' git enough company during my meals. Got iced tea, fried fish, hushpuppies, and blackberry cobbler for dessert, you ain't too full by then."

"We didn't come to take your lunch, Mr. Bass."

"Didn't say you did. You see how much I got here?"

"Well, sure. I figured you was cookin' for lunch and dinner both."

"You figured wrong, deputy. I knowed you was comin', so I cooked for three or four. Thought maybe that big sheriff a' yours was comin', so I cooked an extra bunch."

"You knew we was comin'? How'd you know that?"

He looks at me like I got sawdust for brains and I'd have to take up practicing dumb full time to get any worse. "I got the sight, a'course. Got the sight. And besides," he laughs quietly, "besides, that young fellah at the hardware store called me a half hour ago, told me you was comin'."

"Didn't even know you had a phone out here."

"Got an old one, one of them has a rotary dial. Old as I am, but it works. Now, you gonna sit down and have some lunch, or you gonna jaw at me all day while the food's gettin' cold?"

We sit. I have to admit, the fish and hushpuppies really do look scrumptious—a perfect golden brown, very crispy, just inviting us to eat. Gotta say, after I took one bite, I never had a better fish fry.

"Where you learn to cook like this?" I ask. Jake, who hasn't said a word, and who looked just a little skeptical at first, has bitten into a hushpuppy and is chewing away happily. I can see Mr. Bass has chopped some scallions and added them to the mix, and just a touch of sugar.

"Awfully good, Mr. Bass," Jake says. Then he crunches into a big piece of fish, taking the meat and the crunchy coating off the bone carefully. It's perfectly cooked.

"Course it's good," Mr. Bass says. "Caught the fish down at the lake just this mornin'. Cleaned 'em, beheaded 'em, skinned 'em. Fresh as can be. Frying mixture as old as the hills: flour, corn meal, salt, corn starch, pepper. Couple other things I ain't goin' to say. Spices, you might say. Best fish fry you ever tasted."

"I'm convinced," I say. But, we're here on business, so in between bites, I talk and he answers. "I guess you don't got to tell me if you don't want to, Mr. Bass, but how come you go out there to that old Indian mound in the first place?"

"I'll answer your question," he says, "but you just leave it be, if I tell you." He pauses a minute between bites. He eats slowly, almost as if contemplating bites.

"There's spirits up there, deputy. You might not believe it. You can believe what you want. But there's spirits up there, and I can hear 'em. I go up there to listen. You learn a lot from them old spirits, if you got the patience and know-how to listen. I listen."

"What do they tell you?" Jake asks.

"That's my business, deputy," he replies. "Just things about the spirit. Things that's eternal. Ain't all here in this world, you know. There's another world, a better one—you can believe it or not, whatever you like. But them spirits choose people. God knows why they chose me. But they talk, in a language that ain't no words. It's just pure understandin'. Like feelings, only not exactly feelings. It's like, just . . . a presence in your soul, is the only way I can describe it. Now, I know you won't believe a thing I said. But it's all true."

"I see you smoke," I say.

"Sure do. Been smokin' since I was ten, twelve years old. Ain't never done me nothing but good. The spirits like tobacco smoke. So I smoke up there at the Indian mound."

"Do you share your cigarettes with the spirits?"

"Course I do. Who wouldn't? Them Indians, they invented tobacco, you know. Wouldn't have tobacco if it wasn't for them Indians. Best contribution ever was to civilized life, tobacco."

I shoot a look at Jake. That explains the cigarettes thrust butt-first into the mound. He looks at me, still chewing fish. He knows what I'm talking about.

"You wouldn't drink beer out of a blue can, would you?" I ask.

"Only beer I drink," he says. "And, yes, I share some of it with the spirits at the mound. Them ancient Indians, they had tobacco, but they didn't have beer—not regular barley beer, barley and hops. They had corn beer, but ain't the same. You can make corn beer, but best thing to do with corn mash is to make whiskey."

"I see," I said. "So, Mr. Bass, here's the big question: You seen anything up there at the mound that's suspicious, unusual?"

"Course I have. You wouldn't 've come here if there hadn't been nothin' goin on up at that mound. There was a murder up there. That's what you're here investigatin."

"We're on the same page so far, sir. But you haven't told me what you've seen up there."

"Lots of goin's on shouldn't be goin' on at all," he says, looking down at his food with a shake of his head that conveys a wagonload of unhappiness.

"Like what? Can you be more specific?"

"Like diggin' into that mound for starters. That's an ancient Indian site. There's a couple people buried there, and their spirits still live there. They're peaceful now, been peaceful for thousands of years, but them people gone diggin' up there, and they disturbed that peace."

"Have you seen anything else, other than people digging?"

"Never said I seen anybody digging. They wasn't digging when I was up there. They done all that before, maybe a month or two ago."

"So, you've never actually seen anybody up there?"

"Oh, I didn't say that. I seen people up there. But they didn't see me."

"When did you see people up there at the site?"

"A couple of times. A couple weeks ago; no, it was only a week ago, even less, when that one gal planted something up there, don't know what it was."

"Planted something?"

"Yep. After that one man dug that trench, or him and his assistants did. Then, a couple weeks later, that gal I said come back and put something in the trench."

"Put something in . . . like what? A body?"

"Nah, nah, nah." He laughs. "That body—that's the victim you want to know who killed 'im. Nah. I'm talkin' about something else, somethin' smaller, like she carried in her pocket. Don't know what it was, but I seen her put it in the trench. I looked later because I thought she was putting garbage in the trench, but I couldn't seen nothin."

"Could you identify that 'gal' if you was to see a picture of her?"

"Yep. Sure could."

So, out comes the phone, up scroll the pictures, and Stanford Bass looks at them intently. I'm expecting him to point to Felicia Morgana, or maybe Becky Rubin. But he doesn't. He points to Regina Gentiles. I ask him again, and he points to her again. "She's the one I seen drive up there a couple days ago. No doubt about it."

I look at Jake and he looks at me, and his face shows surprise just like mine.

"Were you out there two nights ago?"

"Don't go out there at night."

"Not ever?"

"Nope. Not ever. Camp at the campsite at night, but not out to the mound."

"So you wouldn't have seen anybody transport a body in? Any foul play of any kind?"

"Nope. Only things I saw were that man and his assistants just after they dug that trench. Knew they done it, but didn't see 'em actually doin' it.

But they had shovels, picks and the like. That was maybe two months ago. And then just three days ago, now I think about it, that gal I showed you drove up here by herself and put something in the trench."

"How do you get up there?"

"Drive my old truck up to the campsite about a mile or two from the mound, then walk through the woods."

"How come you don't drive up to the mound site itself?"

"Ain't right."

"Ain't right? How come?"

"Just ain't right. Told you there's spirits up there. They like peace. Like a good smoke, too. But they don't like cars. Don't like noise. Don't like digging, neither."

"How long's it take you to walk there through the woods?"

"About an hour. It's a good walk. But it's peaceful and solitary. Ain't no cars, no roads, no people. Snakes, occasionally. Armadillos. Possums sometimes up in the trees. Seen deer. But that's how it should be. Never no people."

"How'd you ever find out about this mound in the first place?"

"Heard about it years ago from somebody, can't remember who. That mound been there since as long ago as you can get. Got trees growing on it, now. Then, I found it about thirty years ago walkin' through the woods. Looked for it almost two years before I found it."

"And you've visited it ever since."

"Like I told you, go to visit the spirits."

"But you've never seen anything connected to the murder of the man who was killed up there, or killed and put there?"

"Can't help you there. That man was killed: he the one started that trench?"

"I believe he was, yes. Him and one of the women I showed you— and maybe one of the young men, too. Can't say for sure."

"Well . . . spirits be happier when they're all dead."

"Oh? You know this for sure?"

"Yep."

"You didn't help the spirits out, now, did you?"

He looks disdainfully at me. "You mean did I kill that man. No, I didn't. Told you, I never go up there at night. Spirits don't care it's night, but rattlesnakes do. They come out at night and hunt. Got rattlers out in them woods big 'round as your arm, and longer than you are tall."

"Hmm. I guess. Deputy Jake, any questions you can think of I missed?"

"You said you put in at a campsite about a mile or two from the mound?" Jake asks.

"Yessir, I sure do. Camp there most times I go to the mound. Sleep overnight in my truck, go to the mound first thing in the morning."

"That little campsite, sort of circular, surrounded by palmettos, maybe just a bit off the old forest service road that goes up to the mound?" Jake asks.

"You set up a tent? Build a fire?" I ask.

"Nope to the first. Yep to the second. Build a fire, but ain't got no tent. Sleep in the bed of my truck. Don't want to be down on the ground where them rattlers are prowlin' around. Cook my lunch or breakfast on that fire. Bacon cooked over a campfire, then taters browned nice in the bacon fat, coffee made in an old-fashioned coffee pot. Cast iron pan and metal coffee pot both near about sixty years old. Got 'em both when I was twenty-seven. Served me ever since."

"Ever seen anybody out there?"

"Nope. But there's been other people there."

"How you know that?"

"Somebody put a tent up there once. Maybe more'n once. Don't know. Used my campfire site, too. I burn old sawed pieces abandoned from he sawmill. Burn great. Them others burned natural logs that didn't burn completely."

"Ever seen any cars on that forest service road?"

"Yep. Seen that big van, or SUV they call it, from the university. That's the one the man drove who put that first trench in. Spirits be disturbed, telling you. Then, same van, or one just like it, the one them people drove to the site. Saw some teenagers' car in there once about ten years ago. Smokin' dope." He begins to laugh at this.

Jake is quiet for a minute. "Can't think of nothing else to ask, Deputy Sumpter. Can you?"

"Actually, yeah. You said you went fishing this morning."

"Yup. Sure did. Had to get lunch for us."

"But you didn't know we was coming here this morning."

"Sure I did."

"Oh? How'd you know that?"

"You're detectives. Knowd you'd find out who been up to the mound, and you'd be out to see me. I know."

"But how did you know we'd be around *today?*"

"Ain't hard to figure. Heard about the murder. Lots of people know I go out there. Didn't figure it would take you long to get around to me."

"Nah. Mr. Bass, you're messin' with me. Come on. How'd you know we'd be around to see you *today?*"

"Got the sight, deputy."

"You're evading my question."

"Bullshit I am. I left cigarettes there. I left a couple beer cans there— offerings. I seen them folks digging, or seen what they dug. Been goin out to that mound for thirty years. Why would it take me any trouble to figure you'd be out?" He's laughing.

"Okay. You got the sight, as you call it. Anybody help out with that sight?"

He starts to laugh. "I was about to put the extra fish in the freezer when that young fella from the garden store called. So instead of freezing 'em, I decided to cook 'em up. If you showed up, I'd give you lunch. Best fish you ever ate. If you didn't show up, I'd have dinner made. Ain't hard to figure." He starts laughing.

"Last question. You didn't kill that man, did you?"

"You asked me that already. Answer's the same: Hell, no. Spirits thank me if I did, but I didn't never kill nobody. Don't like killin'. Like my peace and quiet."

Jake and I thank him for his time, then we leave.

REGINA, OR, IS IT SHREWD TO HAVE 'TUDE?

WHEN WE LEAVE, JAKE ASKS ME: "I ASSUME WE'RE GOING TO go see young Ms. Gentiles?"

"Well, I'd guess so. But there's something I want to do first."

"Hmmm. Let me guess. You, umm, think she probably planted those human remains in that trench?"

"What I'm thinking, yep."

"So, let me see: What would you want to find out first?"

"Let me know when you get it."

A minute later, he says, "Well, the obvious thing I can think of is, if she did plant those remains, where did she get them?"

"Precisely. I mean, maybe if they're really old, she got them from some dusty store room in the university paleontology department. I'm betting she does restoration work, but I mean to find out for sure. Or maybe she's faking it and they're not really old. I don't see how she'd be able to get away with that, or what her point would be, but I am assuming that Mr. Bass is telling the truth and he saw her there putting something in a trench. Now, how all that might be related to our murder, I have no idea."

"Call Dr. Bacardi at the university first?"

"I'd say so, yep."

A few minutes later, we're in the office and on the phone with Dr. Bacardi, who's making himself very accessible in the course of our investigations.

"Hi, Professor Bacardi?"

"Yes?"

"This is Denise Sumpter. I'm the deputy who's conducting the investigation into the death of Professor Lavida."

"Yes? Glad to hear from you again. Sheriff Marion has mentioned you. He thinks highly of your skill."

"Oh, thank you. He's a good sheriff. So, tell me, do you have a graduate student named Regina Gentiles?"

"Umm, let me think . . . Yes. She's one of Toulouse's proteges, I believe."

"Would she do reconstruction or restoration work, whatever you call it, in the university's paleontology lab?"

"Very likely."

"Do you have human remains in that lab?"

"We do, some dating back almost 40,000 years. But those are from Asia or Europe."

"Would you have human remains from the Americas?"

"A few, but not many. American Indian tribes are mostly very, very sensitive about disturbing human remains that are found on this continent."

"But you might have some?"

"We probably do, in fact."

"Is there a protocol for how you treat those remains?"

"Well, yes. Once in a long while companies dig up something in the course of construction. When they unearth human remains, we're asked to place those remains for safekeeping in our store rooms until they're reclaimed and re-buried by whatever tribe claims them. It's a function of NAGPRA—The Native American Graves Protection and Repatriation Act. I think it was passed in 1990. In Florida, the tribe is usually the Seminoles or the Miccosukee. I have to say, though, that despite their claims, it's unlikely any ancient remains are directly related to them. I understand the law, but . . . just saying."

"Because?"

"The Seminoles and Miccosukee are both related to the Creek nation, and they originally came from Georgia and Alabama. It's possible there were some in North Florida a very long time ago."

"So, it's possible you might have a few remains stored away somewhere that haven't been claimed?"

"It's possible. The Indians are very protective of their ancestor's remains, as I said. Sometimes, researchers want to test for age and DNA results before they apprise the tribal governments of our finds. It's not, strictly speaking, the way things are supposed to be done, but research and tribal rights, when it comes to ancient remains, almost always clash. But we respect the Indians' right to claim ancestry, so most of the time, the remains will go back to tribal authorities almost as soon as they're discovered."

"Would Ms. Gentiles have had access to any such remains, if she worked in the restoration lab?"

"Sure. She would have had access to anything in our stores."

"Do you keep careful catalogues of your remains?"

"Oh, for God's sake, of course!"

"Would you be able to check if any are missing?"

"Well, I could have someone do it. We have probably over a thousand fragmentary remains from all over the globe."

"Could you check for me, then, please, and give the office a call when you find out?"

"Sure. Anything else?"

"I think that'll do it."

So, naturally, later that afternoon, the sun beginning to set, we go to the campground at the County Park to talk to Regina Gentiles. She pronounces it Hen-TEE-lays. The big university SUV is parked in the space in front of her tent. We find her sitting at a picnic table at her campsite, her tent set up and cooking gear on the table. She's working on something. It looks like a bit of bone fragment. She sees us pull up, but turns back to her work, measuring and cataloguing her specimens.

"Ms. Gentiles?" I ask.

"What do you want? Have you figured out who killed Professon Lavida yet?"

"No," I answer, "but we wanted to ask you a few questions related to that investigation."

"I'm kind of busy right now."

"I can see. But it's important we talk to you."

"Why?"

"To clear a few things up. We can talk here, or we can escort you down to the office. Prefer it be here."

"Suit yourselves, I guess." She motions to the bench opposite hers at the table.

"I'll get right to the point, Ms. Gentiles. We have a person who goes out to the Indian Mound frequently, who can supply a positive ID, and saw you—yes, you—at the Indian mound about three days ago. He says you were putting something in the preliminary trench dug by Professor Lavida's crew a few weeks ago."

"You're bullshitting me. I was out there all by myself."

"Oh," I say, surprised that she's fallen into so obvious a trap, "so at least you admit you were there."

"I was. But that witness you mentioned? That was a lie."

"No, it wasn't, Ms. Gentiles. There is a real person, though I'm not going to reveal his identity, who goes out to the Indian Mound frequently, who saw you there and saw you put something into that trench."

"It's that old man, that guy who listens to spirits. I know all about him. He's a crackpot."

"Hmm. How do you know about that old man?"

"Everybody connected with that mound knows about that old man. He's the one showed Professor Lavida where it is. He goes up there to 'commune with the spirits.'" She says this latter with a sneer. "Aren't any spirits there. Just trash in the midden and animal bones."

"What did you put in the trench, Ms. Gentiles?"

"Don't know what you're talking about."

"From what I understand, based on what Professor Bacardi at the university and others tell me, trash middens rarely if ever contain human remains. And yet, we have a positive, professional identification of two pieces of human remains from that trench: a piece of a skullcap, and a molar tooth. Now, I ask myself how it might be that a trash midden would have human remains in it when normally they don't. And I have somebody who can identify you as the person he saw depositing something in the trench. One plus one, in my experience, equals two."

"So, you're saying I put some old human remains in that trench?"

"You understand my math perfectly well, Ms. Gentiles. But I'm asking. Did you?"

"No."

"You used to work in the reconstruction lab at the university, didn't you?"

She pauses. "I did. I still do."

"There are, as I understand from Professor Bacardi, thousands of fragments of ancient human remains in the vaults there."

"You've talked to Professor Bacardi?"

"Earlier today."

"Ah. So, what did he tell you?"

"That you have ancient remains from, and I'm quoting him, 'All over the globe.' He says they're carefully catalogued."

"They are. I catalogue them myself."

"Would professor Bacardi be able to find any drawers with missing samples?"

She looks nervous when I ask this. "Look, deputy, we have thousands of partial remains, from loose teeth to long bones to skull fragments. Pieces sometimes get lost. Honestly, I doubt Professor Bacardi would be able to identify anything as missing, even if there *were* any missing."

"Well, we're going to find out, because I asked him to look."

"Fine by me."

"We may send the samples we confiscated from the crime scene to the lab to have them dated, and perhaps to extract a DNA sample."

"You do that."

"I'll let you know what we find out."

"You do that."

"Why would our witness positively identify you as the person he saw show up at that mound after the preliminary trench was dug, and put something in the trench?"

"You'll have to ask him that."

"You know we're going to find out the truth, don't you?"

"When you do, let me know what you've found out."

"We will, Ms. Gentiles. Oh, and for the next week or so, we'd appreciate it if you didn't leave Seminole Pines."

"Got work to do. I won't be going anywhere for a while."

"Deputy Leon, you got any questions?"

"Sure. Ms. Gentiles, what kind of restoration work did or do you do at the university?"

"Mostly human remains. I piece together skull fragments, try to see what ancient people looked like."

"So, you'd have experience piecing together loose bits of bone?"

"Yep."

"So, if a box or tray, or wherever you keep these samples, had a lot of pieces for you to reconstruct, you could easily remove a piece, couldn't you?"

"I suppose I could. Why would I?"

"Well, we don't know. Just asking questions. That's it from me, Deputy Sumpter."

With that, we leave. In the car, Jake asks me: "You think she's lying? That she put those bone fragments in the trench?"

"Ninety percent sure of it," I say. "What I can't figure out is, why would she? Who's she working for? And how does this tie in with our murdered man?"

"Well, then, she's lying. But why? What the hell's going on here?"

"Oh, my God! Did you see how nervous she looked when we mentioned having asked Professor Bacardi?"

"I guess. I'm not so keen as you are on reading people's reactions."

"Thanks. It's just things, some subtle, some not. But I'm certain she's lying about putting those remains in the trench, even if I haven't got a clue as to why. But we'll figure 'er out, don't worry."

"Well, hope you, or we, figure it soon. I want to know myself." With that, it was off to dinner at Willie's.

THE BOYS IN THE HOOD

THE NEXT MORNING, JAKE SEES ME COME IN. HE'S AT HIS DESK filing the requisite reports. I appreciate him doing that. He looks up at me, one hand on his computer and his fingers laced through a mug of very dark-looking coffee.

"Where're we off to today Chief Inspector?"

"We ain't talked to the two boys yet," I answer. "What's their names? Stan and Tuco. We need to go talk to them. And you'd better hold on to that coffee cup; you spill that on your computer, I'll have to start filing reports on mine. And the department will have to save up the next ten years, likely, to get you a new one."

He smiles. Carefully lifts his cup. Takes a sip. "Dennis Martin special. Measures twice the amount of coffee you need and then puts in half the amount of water. His version of espresso, except you serve it in mugs. Have a cup. Put hair on your chest and the spirit of love in your heart."

"Don't need no hair on my chest and cain't have no more love in my heart than what I already got. But pour me a cup anyway."

He does, and I take a sip. If this stuff put love in your heart, we'd all have the love of Jesus and we'd be singin' Kumbaya 'til God turned the lights out. As it is, I think it's more likely to be used for road fill.

So after a cup and a half, me and Jake are off to talk to Stan Assice and Tuco Fairweather. In fifteen minutes, we're through town traffic—in Seminole Pines, two stoplights and a merge sign where Main Street merges onto County Two—and pulling into Seminole Lake Park. We pass the campsite where Regina Gentiles has her tent, but neither she nor the SUV are there. There's a tent a few spaces down where the two young men are batching it.

Tuco is standing in front of a little gas stove set up on the picnic table, and Stan is sitting eating the remains of what looks like a mess, but I assume is probably fried potatoes mixed with scrambled egg. We park in the camp space's spot and get out. It's Stan who speaks first.

"Hey, there! It's deputy . . . uhh, I forgot your names."

"Denise Sumpter, and this is Jake Leon."

"Well, deputies Sumpter and Leon. Have a seat. Chef Tuco here has just finished making a splendid camp breakfast of bacon bits, fried potatoes and scrambled egg. I think there's coffee coming up. Hey, chef! Got any extra coffee?"

"We've had some," I say. The truth is, I'm barely holding down the jitters from Dennis Martin's road-paver special. "We just dropped by to ask you-all some questions. I see you're having breakfast, so you shouldn't be too busy."

"Just busy eating Tuco's delicious cooking. It actually *is* pretty good. Looks like a mess, but it's just fried potatoes and scrambled egg, mostly. Was only two strips of bacon, so he chopped them up to make the grease for frying breakfast. Damn good, if you ask me." He's talking between mouthfuls, so I assume he actually means what he says.

Tuco sits down opposite us with his own plate, a mound of the same breakfast mixture piled on it. He hasn't so far said a word.

"So, gentlemen, good morning. A few questions while you're finishing up your breakfast."

"Sure, Stan says. Shoot."

"So, you two were in the Army Rangers."

"Special Forces," says Stan. "But don't like to talk about it. That gig's in the past—for me, anyway. Like to leave it that way, if you don't mind."

"Can't do that completely, Mr. Assice. Can't do that. Got to ask you: You could have easily carried Professor Lavida's body a way through the woods if you'd had to, couldn't you?"

"Carried my buddies off the field on a few occasions, through some pretty rough terrain. With their packs on. Yes. Could have, but that don't mean I did."

"Did you? Did you cary Professor Lavida's body from somewhere else and set it down in that trench?"

"Nope. Where would I have carried it from?"

"That's one thing we're trying to figure out. Had a dead body in that trench day before yesterday. Don't know how it got there. You-all were the only ones out there, you two, Professor Morgana, Regina Gentiles and Becky Rubin. There you all were with a dead body in a trench; the body wasn't decomposed or chewed on by critters. Professor Lavida'd been killed by two stakes driven through his eyes—grotesque and awful. None of you heard another vehicle come in. Somebody has to have carried that dead man from somewhere nearby, no more than a mile or two, and put him there, and done it the night before you called us out there. Had to. Unless the whole lot of you are in on it, some one or two of you have killed that man somewhere else and carried him there and put him in that trench. I don't know who did it or why, but I'm gonna figure it out, guarantee."

"Sure hope so," Stan says, and smiles.

"Mr. Fairweather." I turn to Tuco, finishing off his own cooking in great mouthfuls, eating like he's half starved.

"Yep?"

"You're kind of a silent one, aren't you?"

"Speak when I got something to say."

"You're a Miccosukee, right?"

"Full blood, so they say."

"The Miccosukee—are you familiar with traditional Miccosukee burial beliefs?"

"Pretty much, yes."

"Has Ms. Gentiles told you that human remains were found in that trench, and I don't mean Professor Lavida. I mean ancient remains. Deputy Leon here and I found part of a skull cap and an ancient molar. They're in our evidence locker at the office. Were you aware that they'd been found in that very trench?"

He looks neither startled nor aware—I can't really read his reaction. "Heard of it. Becky found that long bone, probably a femur, part of a femur, in that same trench."

I'm caught by surprise. So is Jake.

"I'm sorry. What? A long bone? Becky Rubin, you mean?" I shoot a glance at Jake. This is getting stranger by the moment. Neither Ms. Rubin nor Professor Morgana mentioned that. But I suddenly remember Morgana's suppressed look of worried surprise when, as I now believe, Becky Rubin was about to mention that very bone and then switched up to something about the Miami River.

"Yeah," Tuco continues, somewhat low-key: "She didn't want anybody to mention it. I think she thinks it's her ticket to some big publication. Fame and glory and a tenure track position, you know? It's only a partial bone, but it was found in that same trench. Ought to be given to the Seminoles or us Miccosukee for burial." Stan is looking across the table at Tuco with a "What did you have mention that for?" Look in his eye.

"I can promise you," I say, "that if those bones belonged to an ancient Indian, they'll be turned over to the proper tribal authorities. Are you sure it was human? I mean, a long bone—could have been an animal bone, couldn't it? In a trash midden?"

"Becky seemed pretty sure it was human," Tuco affirms with a shrug. "Probably a femur—only partial, but the head of the bone where it joins the hip, the 'neck,' and part of the shaft, about six inches, were all more or less intact. Becky is pretty expert at bones, so is Reggie. They seemed sure it was human. And what do you mean 'if'? The bones were found in an Indian mound. Whose else would they be if they're as ancient as that mound is?"

"What if they weren't actually from that mound. What if somebody put them there?" I ask, thinking of what Stanford Bass revealed about Regina Gentiles. Evidently, this part of the story is completely alien to him; his eyes widen in surprise.

"What in the hell would anybody do that for? That makes no sense at all."

"Well, we don't know. But we have reason to think that that's what happened."

"Where the hell did you pick up that little piece of information?" Stan asks. There's a sort of combative edge to Stanley Assice's voice—maybe the product of too many missions in Afghanistan?

"Doesn't matter," I say. "All I'm saying is, if those are Indian remains, I'm sure our department will honor tribal customs and turn them over to the Miccosukee or Seminole authorities for burial—or the university will."

"So, they may not be Indian?" Tuco asks.

"It's possible. We don't know."

"Wow. That's totally freaky. Who would do that?" He looks at Stan. "Hey, Stanley, you suppose that's what Reggie had in that little velour bag she didn't want us to see?"

Stan just shrugs. "No idea," he says.

"Little velour bag?" I ask. I'm thinking, she's been to the mound before, a few days ago, and she has a velour bag that may have other remains in it. Maybe she was planning to plant more?

"Yeah. We saw her put a little velour bag in her backpack. It looked kind of like what you'd put jewelry in. I thought maybe a boyfriend had given her something, like a necklace, maybe. We teased her a little about it, but she wouldn't tell us what it was. Just smiled and said it was her secret."

I'm trying to keep my eyes from going wide. I'm astonished that nobody has said a word about this before now. "Why in the heck didn't you say anything about this before now?"

"Didn't know it was important," Tuco says, shaking his head. "How'm I supposed to know a girl's velour bag might have important evidence in it?

I mean, I didn't even know you were thinking human remains might have been placed there in the trench."

I see his point. Sometimes in the middle of an investigation, you lose a little perspective on your circle of suspects and witnesses. There's no reason for Tuco Fairweather to have thought there was anything suspicious about that velour bag. If he's telling the truth, he had no idea the site may have been seeded with those remains.

I decide on another tack. "So, Mr. Fairweather, can you see any significance to the way Professor Lavida was buried? Two wooden stakes, one through each eye, and another stake through his mouth?"

"Don't know, deputy. My thought is that it might be a symbolic way of . . . ummm . . . well, making sure he can't see or speak. You know? Whatever he's seen, he's being punished for it. Plus, he's being prevented from speaking. Tell you one thing, it ain't Miccosukee. That's not tribal custom."

"Mr. Assice? Any thoughts on the matter?"

"I'd say the same as Chef Tuco here. Sounds like somebody was symbolically making him blind and stopping up his mouth, keeping him from speaking. Or, just as likely, somebody was trying to make it *look* like a symbolic killing."

I was actually thinking exactly the same thing. These people are way too sophisticated to believe in such ritualistic mumbo jumbo.

"So, you were in the Army Rangers, too, weren't you, Mr. Fairweather?"

"Second Battalion, seventy-fifth Regiment. Yep. But like Stan, I don't really care to talk about it. I'm still getting over Afghanistan. May never really get over it as long as I live."

"I'm so sorry to have to pry, but we have a tough murder to solve, and I need all the information I can get. If I'm stepping over the line here, just try to understand me. I need to really understand all you people. So . . . if I may ask, 'get over' what, exactly?" I'm asking because I want some read on whether Tuco Fairweather or Stan Assice has flipped—you know, gone over the edge. Maybe one of them, or both, is or are acting out some strange—I don't know—some strange compulsion of some sort. An act of vengeance against society, maybe? Or maybe some kind of perverse form of atonement? I don't know. I'm not a psychologist. I just want to know as much as I can—see if anything clicks for me.

Tuco is silent for several minutes. I leave him that way. Then: "You have a tough murder to solve. Yeah, I guess it is. I have a few of my own, you know. A few murders."

"You want to tell me about it?"

"No. But I will. Just a little. I was Army Special Forces. So was Stan. I was a marksman. Could take out a target from over four hundred yards, easy. Nine hundred if I had to. Distances like that, so many things come into account. Not many can shoot accurately that far, no matter how good the gun. Gravity. Wind speed and direction. Spindrift. Even Coriolis effect. Doesn't have to influence the shot a whole lot. Just a little bit, and the head you're aiming at you miss. Didn't miss often, but I missed that once."

"And?"

"And I hit a little girl standing beside the target—an Al Quaeda chieftain. Would have been awful enough for her if I'd hit the man. See a bullet come through his chest. But I didn't. Little girl—maybe eight or ten? I don't know. Could see her perfectly through the scope—black hair curling from under her hijab; dark eyes in her brown face. I was eight hundred yards away up in the rocks. Village far below me—over eight hundred yards by line of sight, but a good twenty meters at least below my position. Very remote. Snow-capped peaks in the distance. God, Afghanistan can be so beautiful! Tried to take the man out by drone half a dozen times, but kept blowing up civilians' houses. So they got me up there—dropped me four miles from the target in the snow and rocks. Make sure we got the guy. I got him, all right, but only on the third shot." He's quiet for a moment. "Got the little girl on the first. He was holding her close. We forget our enemies are people like us, you know? Got families. Kids. Wish to God, just wish to God all the killing would stop. Couldn't take no more." He's quiet for another moment. "I'm out of it now."

"Thank you for telling me." At that moment, I just couldn't see Tuco Fairweather as a murderer. Maybe, but that sort of story just leaves you devastated. To have to live with that! I couldn't imagine him deliberately pounding wooden stakes through the eyes of a man drugged and helpless on the ground.

"And you, Mr. Assice? Anything you can tell me about your experience as a Ranger?"

"Special Forces." He says this firmly and deliberately. "And, yeah, I could tell you all kinds of things. But some of 'em I'm not allowed to tell you anything about. I did some special operations. Took out high value targets. Captured some high value targets. Things get rough out there, deputy. Like Tuco says. Sometimes innocents get in the way. Take them out, too. It happens. Tell you, though, we were the best—better than the Navy SEALS, my honest opinion."

"Anything specific you can tell me? A particular mission, maybe?"

"Don't know what that would have to do with your murder investigation."

"I don't know, either. Just trying to understand my pool of suspects."

"So, I'm a suspect?"

I appreciate these men's service, but sometimes in questioning, you lose your patience with people's reticence. "Oh, for God's sake, Ranger. Of *course* you're a suspect. You're *all* suspects. You, Tuco here, Dr. Morgana, Regina Gentiles, Becky Rubin. Dead man shows up out of nowhere. Was supposed to be somewhere else. What the hell? Either one of you killed him, or more than one—maybe all of you." I stay quiet for a moment to calm myself. "Look: I need to know as much as I can. Anything you can tell me at all will help."

"You mean, is there anything I can tell you about my Army past that will make me seem unbalanced, like Army life pushed me over the edge. Make me seem crazy—a guy that will kill a man by driving spikes through his eyes. Well, here's what I got to tell you. If that man was a target, and if my CO told me to make it look like a ritual killing, I could have done it.

Sure. I've done worse, or, maybe, just as bad. But there wasn't no orders to kill Professor Lavida. I'm actually sorry he's dead, and I've seen more dead people that you'll ever have any idea. I didn't kill him, and I don't know who did."

"The night before Professor Morgana found the body and we showed up, you guys said you'd been partying pretty hard. Last night before the real work started. You drink a lot that night, Mr. Assice?"

"My share."

"More than his share," Tuco Fairweather adds. "He drank more than anybody. Kept chasing shots of bourbon with cold beer. Well, cool beer. Coolers keep the beer cold for a few hours, but not forever."

"So, Mr. Assice was pretty well wasted?"

"He was falling-down drunk."

"And you?"

"Drunk, but not falling down."

"Regina?"

"She drank a beer or two. But that's all. A little tipsy. She's not a hard drinker."

"Becky Rubin?"

"Hah! Becky. Little Becky Rubin. There's more to that girl than meets the eye. She wasn't putting 'em away like Stan, here, but she tipped back a few shots and chugged a few beers. Strange, though, she never showed any effects. Or, maybe she did, but I just didn't notice it? She's a tough little character. Like her, our Becky. Wish she'd give me the time of day, but I've tried and she don't want nothing to do with me. You could say she ain't as pretty as Reggie, but she's got her own brand of hot—my opinion." Then, after a second, he adds, "Kind of like you, deputy."

I appreciate the compliment, but I ain't about to get friendly with a suspect.

"Did you know that Becky Rubin was also Army Rangers?"

Stan looks at me like I'm crazy. Oddly, Tuco Fairweather looks down at his plate. I'll file that away in my mind, see what comes of it later.

"You're out of your mind, deputy," Stan says. "Becky?"

"It's Captain Rubin. She's thirty-two years old—old as Dr. Morgana. She's also a post-doc. Has her Ph.D in vertebrate paleontology. She's a genius. And an expert markswoman. And she's led field operations in Afghanistan."

Stan looks stunned. He's staring at me like I was crazy. Stan just says, "Becky? Our Becky? Pigtails Becky?"

"Yep," I say.

"You're putting us on, right? This is some kind of psychological ploy, isn't it?"

"Nope. Ain't putting you on at all. And if it's a psychological ploy, it ain't comin' from a practicing psychologist. Ain't no tricks. I'm telling the truth. Becky Rubin is Capain Rubin. She's a good six or seven years older than either of you. She's not a grad student. She's a post-doc—post doctoral. She's also a combat veteran. How did you-all not know any of this?"

They're silent for a minute, processing what I've said. Then, it's still Stan who speaks. "Wow. This is a bombshell. She sure carries off the giggly little girl routine pretty well. Maybe she's an actress, too, huh? God, Becky Rubin! I thought she was maybe a year or two younger than I am. She sure doesn't look any thirty-two. Not, I mean, that thirty-two is old. Just . . . well, she looks so young. And a combat veteran, you say?"

"Yes. That's what I said."

"Jesus holy prophets. I'll be damned. And a post-doc? What the heck is she doing on this dig?"

"Don't know. Thought you might be able to tell me."

"Must be doing some kind of research project. Has to be. Obviously has to do with paleo-Indian research. Got to be some big article in *The Journal of Vertebrate Paleontology* or somewhere similar. I'll be damned. Tuco, you know anything about this?"

Tuco is silent for a few seconds, as if thinking through an answer. I file this away in the back of my mind, maybe something to follow up on later. These people keep secrets—all of them. "God, no," he says. "I thought

Becky was my age, and a grad student like me." He switches topics quickly: "I tried to move on her, you know, but she wouldn't have nothing to do with me. Thought I was a reasonably good-lookin' guy. Income from the Army, good prospects in school. You know. But couldn't get her interested."

"Might not have anything to do with you," I tell him. But I don't elaborate.

"You going to ask Becky about her Army background?" Tuco asks. He looks at me fixedly when he says this.

"That's my business," I say. "We'll follow up what we need to follow up on in the course of this investigation. Deputy Leon. You got any questions?"

"Sure. Thanks, Deputy Sumpter. Do either of you two guys know a Mr. Bass? Old African-American fellow, goes out to the Indian mound frequently?"

"Heard of him," says Stan. "Not really," says Tuco.

"Would I be correct in saying neither of you has ever seen him out there?"

"That would be correct." It's a muddle of two voices overlapping, but that's the upshot.

"Mr. Fairweather, what would your reaction be if you knew there really were Indian remains in that mound and that members of your own team were planning on seizing hold of them for their own benefit, without regard to tribal custom or professional protocol?"

"I'd expose them," he says."I'd expose them to Professor Bacardi, the dean of the School of Paleontology at the university, and I'd let authorities know at both the Miccosukee and Seminole headquarters."

"Even at the possible cost of your own professional and academic career?"

"Absolutely."

"Would it make you mad enough to kill?"

Tuco answers up promptly and directly, his eyes right on Jake's face: "Yes, it would make me angry enough to kill. But I wouldn't. You know, I understand fully the need to take samples, to try to understand the age of these remains. I understand the paleontology, the science, very well. But regardless of its importance, it doesn't trump people's deeply held religious beliefs and feelings. I'd ask, even plead with, tribal authorities to allow the team to do its studies before returning the remains to their rightful ancestral owners. But I wouldn't kill over it. I'm not killing *anybody* anymore over *anything*. Period." That was delivered with emotion and emphasis, and seems to be Tuco's last word.

"Thank you. Gentlemen. Another thing. If you found a part of a long bone, like a femur, in a mound like this, how likely would it be to be by itself, without the rest of the leg? The rest of the body?"

"Don't know how that could happen," Stan answers.

"Because?"

"Well," Stan muses, "I'm just a grad student. But this is the way I'd see it. It's a burial, right? You find broken or disarticulated bones out in the open, or maybe in burials that are thirty or forty thousand years old. Perhaps a river has cut a new channel, or there's been an earthquake, or subsequent human activity has moved earth with remains in it. You see? But this is a midden. It's been undisturbed for ten or maybe twelve thousand years. Very possibly even more. Generations of trees have grown on it, died and spread their seeds. There's never been any subsequent settlement. No earth moving, no rivers cutting new channels. How would the bones just disappear?"

I really liked that question from Jake. It corroborates what Mr. Bass was telling us about seeing Regina Gentiles planting something. Of course, it's *possible* that digging the trench itself separated bones that had lain in the mound for thousands of years, but I'm thinking all the bones in that midden are plants. Can't figure out why, though. My head's buzzing over that.

I feel like there's probably something we're missing, but I decide enough is enough. Time to move on. I want to have another chat with Dr. Morgana and Dr.-Captain Rubin.

"I can't think of anything more, Chief Inspector," Jake says. He's taken to calling me Chief Inspector openly, even in front of suspects and witnesses. I kind of don't like it—but I kind of do. I haven't made up my mind on it yet.

"Gentlemen," I say, "You all stick around for a bit. Give it at least a few days. You-all okay for funds?"

"University is still paying for us to dig, even if we're not—Chief Inspector," Stan half sneers. Jake smiles when he says this.

Jake and I head out the way we came.

In the car, Jake is quiet for a minute, and then looks at me. "Sorry about that 'Chief Inspector' thing, Denise. I wasn't thinking that we were talking to actual suspects. I'm just so used to saying it."

"It's okay. Let it go. We got to figure this thing out, Jake. What's your take so far?"

"What's yours?"

"Ohh-noo, buddy boy," I laugh. "I asked you first. What're you thinking?"

"Well, I'll be damned if this hasn't got me stumped. Okay, so, let me run down the list: Tuco Fairweather, No. He seems too genuine to me. Was surprised that we'd found bones and the bones might have been planted. Didn't *seem* like he had any idea about Becky Rubin. But I don't know. I think he might be hiding something. Stan, kind of the same thing, though I get more a sense that he's holding back. Wouldn't talk to us at all about any specifics in his Army background. Right now, I'd have to say my suspicions lie in the direction of Dr. Morgana and Becky 'Mystery Woman' Rubin. Don't know what their motive is, but there must be some reason they'd want Lavida dead. I just don't know what the hell that reason is. And as for Reggie Gentiles: she's lying about planting those bones. Maybe she had some big scheme going, Lavida discovered it, and she decided to kill him to shut him up. But that doesn't explain how the hell he ended up there in the first place. And somehow, I also get the feeling old Mr. Bass is mixed up in this. He isn't telling us everything, either."

He stops, so it's my turn. "About my take. So here's what I'd add. If it's one of the girls, I think it's two of them. What I mean is, I think they'd have to be working together. I *think*. Even Becky Rubin would have to have help . . . I *think*. But when she came out of the shower, did you see those legs on her? She's lifted weights. And she's a martial artist. Maybe she'd have strength enough to move Lavida on her own. As to Gentiles—more going on there than she's let on, but we'd have to have the whole story of why she decided to plant those bones there. And Mr. Bass? He's our wild card. He knows this whole area like the back of his hand. Could have had that body hid somewhere close by and none of the team would've known about it. Now, what do we need to know? What do you say?"

"Well, other that who done it. We need to know where Lavida was when he wasn't down south with Professor Rodriguez at another dig. Where the hell was he? I mean, he had to be *somewhere* nearby. But who saw him? Who was he with? Why wasn't he where he was supposed to be? What the hell's going on there? Jesus, Denise, my head is spinning. I'll help all I can, but I'll confess I'm just blown away by this mess."

"Me too." We're driving out of the park, past Becky Rubin's camping spot. Still no SUV; still no Becky. "Hey, let's make a quick drive up to the mound. I'll bet our Ms. Gentiles has made an unauthorized visit."

"Well, okay . . . but if we want to catch her there, you'll need to step on it."

We're in Jake's Challenger Hellcat, so it's not a problem stepping on it.

THE WOMAN ON THE MOUND, OR, JUST SO YOU KNOW, YOU REAP WHAT YOU SOW

JUST AS WE'D EXPECTED, WE FIND THE BIG LAND CRUISER, minus its trailer, at the Indian Mound. The Challenger isn't too quiet, bumping along on these potholed, sandy, muddy, narrow forest service roads, so she must've heard us coming. But it doesn't seem to have dissuaded her from doing whatever she came out here to do.

Regina Gentiles has crossed the police tape and is standing on the mound, looking down into the trench.

We park and get out. She looks in our direction, but doesn't move.

"Ms. Gentiles," I call out. "You're in the scene of a crime, across police tape. You need to get out of there right now."

"Can't. I've lost a tooth."

"I'm sorry?" We're walking closer, so we're right at the police tape when the conversation resumes.

She doesn't move from where she's standing. I can see by the dirt on her knees that she's been down on her hands and knees in the trench. She's holding a little velour bag, like a small purse.

"You need to get out of there, please, Ms. Gentiles. You're not allowed to be in there. This is the scene of a crime. If you don't get out now, I'll have to arrest you for trespassing and interfering with a police investigation. Now, come on down from there and come talk to us."

"Shit!" She says, very emphatically. "I had another tooth, and now I can't find it."

"Another tooth? You mean you planted another tooth?"

She seems exasperated. "Oh, for God's sake, deputy. You know the answer to that."

"Please come down from the trench and come talk to us, or I'll have to come in and get you."

She seems grumpy and pissed, but she comes down. It's vertically only a few steps down—the mound is high, but the trench is down toward the bottom. She scrambles some on the loose gravel and sand. "Am I under arrest?"

"No. Not yet, anyway. So, plain English, what were you doing up here?"

"Trying to find that other tooth."

"Okay. What tooth, please?"

"The other molar I planted along with the one you found."

"So, you planted them?"

"Just said I did." She's standing with us on the right ride of the police tape, which she's just ducked under.

"Is that together with a partial skullcap and a partial femur?"

"Exactly," she says. "This'll really screw me over for any advancement in the program. I'll probably get kicked out. Damn it! Never should have agreed to do this in the first place. Stupidest thing I've ever done." She's crying.

"Okay, so you planted the bones. You lied to us before. Don't appreciate that. Did you plant them for yourself? For who?"

"You haven't even figured out that much?"

I'm pretty pissed at that question. "No, I haven't even figured out that much. Too many people involved, you see? So, who are you working with, or for?"

"Professor Rodriguez."

That one startles me. "Professor Rodriguez?"

"Of course. Who do you think?"

"Okay," I say, "Professor Rodriguez. But what's her game? What was her plan?"

"It started out as a joke. She told me to take a couple of old bones from our collection, mostly from ancient Siberian deposits, and plant them in the trench Professor Lavida had already started. She was messing with him. I don't think she thought he'd take it seriously. Then that damn ignoramus Becky Rubin found that long bone she wasn't supposed to find, and you two found the skullcap and one tooth, and now it's all blown out of proportion. Becky wasn't even *supposed* to be up at the mound until Lavida arrived. He was supposed to *be* there when the discoveries were made. That was the joke. But Plucky-Duck Rubin just had to go and scout out the mound the evening we got there—the evening before you guys showed up. And she found that femur. Shit. Ruined the whole damned thing!"

"Why didn't you tell us all this before? Why didn't you just *tell us* what was going on with the skullcap and the tooth?"

"And screw my chances for advancement in the department? Do you *know* how rare jobs are in paleontology? Do you *know* how hard it is to get research grants, teaching positions, museum curatorships?" She's almost screaming, very agitated. "This is an easy field to fall in love with, but a damn hard field to find jobs in. Besides, you think I was crazy enough to implicate myself in Professor Lavida's death?"

"Hmmm," I say slowly, "So, how exactly does planting bones in a dig implicate you in Professor Lavida's death?"

"Well, how the hell should I know? *You're* the detective. I'm doing something surreptitious and dishonest, and Professor Lavida suddenly shows up dead in the trench where I planted some bones. Then I lie to you about it the first time you ask. If I were you, I guess I'd think maybe I'd done it."

"Okay, and how would you have done it? Where was Professor Lavida the day before he was murdered and the night he *was* murdered, when he was supposed to be way south of here at another dig entirely? Where was he, and how did you get him from there into the trench?"

She just stares at me like I'm crazy. "How the hell should I know? I don't know any more about where he was or who killed him than you do. I know *I* didn't do it."

"And we should believe you because . . . ?"

"Because I'm an honest person." As soon as she says this she laughs at herself. "Like, you're really going to believe *that* now that I've lied to you about the bones I planted. It's just, the thing is, I really *am* mostly an honest person—most of the time." She laughs one of those laughs that's full of despair. "God, have I ever screwed up."

"Well, I guess I'll agree with you on that one. So, I'm going to ask you one more time, and you be straight with me, you hear?"

"Yeah, sure. Whatever."

"The night Professor Lavida was killed, did you see or hear anything, *anything at all*, unusual? I mean, except for the heavy breathing you said you heard?"

"No, and that's the honest to God truth. No cars, no bushes rustling."

"If somebody was being murdered up on the mound, that would have made a lot of noise. Or if they were being dragged up there. You didn't hear anything?"

"No, I really didn't. Just the breathing."

"And you went back to bed?"

"Yep."

"If I remember right, Becky Rubin said she'd gotten up to pee, too?"

"Yeah, just like me. She'd had a few beers. More than me. I don't really like beer that much. She had more to pee out than I did."

"So, remind me: did you go in the same spot, the same general location?"

"No, no. I peed in the bushes near the tent. She went out by the SUV. Peed on the other side opposite the camp. More private, I guess."

"So, she got up to use the toilet, but you didn't actually *see* her?" I'm wondering if Rubin was up to something and used going pee as an excuse for being out of sight for a few minutes. It's reaching, but no reason not to at least ask.

"Yeah. Well, I don't usually watch people when they pee, you know?"

"I guess I see your point on that. Okay, so . . . Have you thought any about how Professor Lavida wound up dead in the trench he and his team had dug a couple months ago? How did he get up here? Who would have a reason to kill him?"

"How he ended up there, I have no idea. Who killed him, I have even less of an idea. Who had a motive? That's what you detectives want to know. Hell, these days, some people kill just for the shit of it—don't need no motive, no more'n I need another hole in my head."

"So, who might've had a motive to kill him?"

"Oh, my God, deputy, I don't know. I know I don't. With Lavida dead, and now I screwed up with this planting the bones joke, I'm pretty screwed. Lavida was my major mentor, the man who headed my doctoral committee. If I can't get Rodriguez to plead for me and take me on as a protege, then I'm as shit outta luck as you can get."

"How about Becky Rubin? Would she have any motive you know of?"

"Nah. She's in the same boat I'm in. A grad student needing a major professor. Your committee's got to be headed by one of the full professors on the staff. I think Lavida was her major professor the same as mine."

"Maybe not. Did you know she was doing post-doc work with Lavida?"

"I'm sorry, *what?*"

"Becky Rubin has her Ph.D in vertebrate paleontology."

"What the *fuck?* My *God*, that's crazy! How come she never told me?"

"Can't answer that one for you, Ms. Gentiles. But she actually is post-doc. If she is, then what would be her relationship in your department with Professor Lavida?"

"Don't know. He might have been co-authoring or sponsoring some sort of specialized research. Maybe he's fast-tracking her to a position on the faculty. I don't know. Jesus, I can't believe this! I can't figure why she never told me!"

"Did you know she's also ex-Army Rangers?"

Reggie is quiet for a moment. Her eyes are going wide. "You must have the wrong person. How can Becky Rubin be an ex-Army Ranger and have a Ph.D in paleontology? She's only my age. I thought she was younger than me."

"How old are you?"

"Twenty-seven. Twenty-seven in about two weeks, anyway."

"Becky Rubin is at least five years older than you are."

"My God! Little Becky is over *thirty?*"

"Yep. And she's actually led teams in the field, like, patrols or whatever. I don't know those details."

"My God, that's so weird. It's like, she's all the time giggles and bounces. She sure disguises her past well."

"Is there any reason you can think of that Professor Lavida's death would benefit her?"

She thinks for a moment. "No, not that I can think of."

"She wouldn't stand a better chance to get a position on the faculty if he were dead?"

"No, why would she? He was her supervisor. He's the one who spoke up for her, tutored her, helped her publish—same as me. Even if she's post-doc, she's not on the faculty yet. That just doesn't figure to me."

"How about professor Morgana?"

"Oh, please! Morgana's a fraud. Her plan is to sleep her way to the top. Lavida is just another conquest."

"I'm sorry. Say that again?"

"Just another conquest? Lavida's just another man she's using to get what she wants."

"Why do you say that?"

"Oh, for God's sake, deputy—what is it? Sum-thing?"

"Sumpter. And this is Deputy Jake Leon."

"Deputy Sumpter, if you have eyes in your head, you've had a look at Felicia Morgana. She's beautiful—a real 'looker' as they say. And let me tell you, she doesn't mind using her looks to get what she wants. She's had Lavida on her hook for the better part of a year."

"You're sure of this?"

"Oh, my God! Nothing could be more obvious! You haven't figured out *that* much, yet?"

"Stop being insulting, Ms. Gentiles. I can still run you in for trespassing, obstructing justice, perjury, and probably a couple other things I can't think of right now." I say that pretty forcefully. She's being a pissant, and I don't appreciate it. "You forget, I'm not a member of your department, and I never knew your professor Lavida when he was alive."

"Yeah, okay—sorry."

"So, when you say she's had Lavida 'on her hook,' do you mean she's had an affair with him?"

"I'd mean exactly that. She has a legitimate Ph.D in vertebrate pale-ontology, but she's not the brightest bulb in the paleontological heavens. I doubt she's published anything. Even little old me has her name as co-au-thor on a study of midden remains—along with about ten others, I admit. Part of a team. Morgana is a bone-hunter, pure and simple. Wants some big find that'll make her famous. Sleeps, or slept, with Lavida to get him to make her adjunct site manager on this dig."

"She says she got the job because he heard a paper she presented at some conference."

"Oh, for God's sake, what *pish!* My God. Donald Duck could sub-mit a paper proposal for some conferences. She probably did submit such a proposal, and probably did present. 'The Need for Human Remains in the Context of Paleo-Indian Middens,' or some such malarkey. She prob-ably had three people listening to her present. There are always people who present just to see their names in the list of speakers, who don't really contribute a damn thing to the field. She's obsessed with human remains. Florida middens don't have them, or I don't know of any that do. The schools that put on conferences will sometimes take almost anybody just to make their advertising bulletin sound impressive. Lavida made her adjunct manager, but not because of any paper she presented."

"So why did you ever agree to this 'joke' as you call it, that Professor Rodgiquez was playing on Professor Lavida?"

"Oh, my God. It just sounded funny when she asked me. She likes to tease Lavida. They're kind of like rivals, you know? But they're friendly rivals. They both focus on paleo-Indians, and both are interested in Florida in the period of earliest habitation, when there were still megafauna around for people to hunt—like mastodons, giant sloths, and whatnot. It's an exciting time in pre-history. Did you know Florida was much larger then than it is now? The ice caps had taken up a lot of water, and the shores had receded several dozen miles further out than what they are now. This patch of pines and palmettos where we're standing was once open or semi-open prairie. A little like parts of East Africa. How cool is that?"

"Yes, I do know that. So, the joke?"

"Oh, yeah. Well, she thought if she planted some human remains in the midden, she'd see if he'd bite. He wouldn't have. The joke's got 'Rodriguez' written all over it."

"But what if he'd fallen for it?"

"Nah. One, he probably wouldn't. Two, she was going to call him after the first day's digging. She's way too professional to let something like that go on. If he published on those remains, he'd be ruined. There are a few genetic markers that distinguish those bones as east Asian, not paleo-Indian, although they're similar. She wasn't out to ruin her colleague's career. She's a pistol, but not evil. She asked me to help, and I said okay. It was fun. Kind of a girls' thing—putting one over on the Big Man in the department."

"Doesn't sound like he'd have appreciated it."

"Oh, you don't know the half! Lavida once put parts of a Greek funerary urn in an Atlantic coast dig Rodriguez was on—sort of making it look like the Greeks had sailed to America in the years BCE. Those two have had this thing going on for years. They always fess up. 'Got one on you,' you know?"

"Were they in a romantic relationship?"

"Lavida and Rodriguez? Oh, hardly. At least . . . I don't *think* so. He's a batch, swings with the younger chicks, you know what I mean? Gets it on with some of his grad students. Not supposed to, but Bacardi looks the other way. Lavida publishes more than everybody else put together, Rodriguez included. Can't afford to lose the golden goose that helps get your department accredited. Besides, honestly, Professor Lavida is pretty circumspect about who he sleeps with. He doesn't flaunt it. Rodriguez is, I think, happily married to a nice señor—chief of orthopedic surgery at University Center Hospital in Miami. Come to think of it, he's in Miami and she's in Tallahassee. Hadn't thought of that. Maybe they're separated?"

"Hmmm," I say slowly. "Do you know Professor Rodriguez has already admitted to having a running affair with Toulouse Lavida?"

Gentiles looks surprised, but not terribly surprised. "Well, can't say I'm not at all surprised. I didn't think she would be his type. My impression was, he went after the younger ones. But . . . doesn't really surprise me all that much, come down to it. He's a kind of horny old bastard. Rodriguez, the old rival and friend—guess it makes sense, now I think of it. I guess maybe he had better taste in women than I gave him credit for."

"Did Professor Lavida ever approach you with a proposition?"

"He hinted once, but, as I say, he's not really pushy about it. He could tell I wasn't interested, and he backed off. I thought it might impact my career here, but I got an A in his class and a strong recommendation to serve on this dig and co-author on publishing the results. So—no harm done. If other girls want to sleep with him, that's their business."

"Deputy Leon? Questions?"

"Can't think of a lot to add, Deputy Sumpter. I just want to make sure of a couple of things. So the night of Professor Lavida's murder, you say you heard heavy breathing?"

"Yep. Sure of it."

"Could it have been people carrying a body?"

"Well, yeah, I guess. It's pretty hard work, and it's hot, even at night."

"You say you heard nothing else at all mysterious?"

"Nope."

"No noise up on the mound, or by the trench?"

"Nope. Just an armadillo."

"Ah, oh. So you heard an armadillo. How'd you know the noise was an armadillo?"

"Shined my flashlight over here and saw it scamper away."

"When you shone your flashlight on the mound, did you see the trench?"

"Oh, no. It's a big mound and a small trench."

"Could people have been up on the mound, or in the trench, and scared the armadillo?"

"Oh, sure, I guess. Well, that is, I didn't think of that. I guess something must have scared it. I didn't even think about that."

"Okay. And you're sure you heard no vehicles?"

"Yep. That one I'm sure of. You don't even hear trucks out on the highway, but that's about two, three miles away as the crow flies. This mound is pretty off the grid, so to speak."

"All I got," says Jake. "Deputy Sumpter?"

"Okay, Ms. Gentiles," I say, "You listen to me carefully. This mound is off limits, absolutely, tooth or no tooth. You need to stay off this mound and stay away from this area. You also need to tell Ms. Rubin, who found that long bone, that it's a plant."

"Oh, My God! No. Don't make me do that! She's such a . . . such a prick. I mean, for a girl—woman. She seems all giggly and cute, but underneath she's a killer. She'll spend the whole dig making fun of me for being Rodriguez's dupe."

"Well, if you don't, we will. We'll have to let her know that long bone is a plant, and needs to be returned to the university collection. Eventually, the skullcap piece and the molar we found will also need to be returned. When we no longer have use for them as evidence."

"Well, you go ahead and tell her, then. But please, tell her it was Professor Rodrigueze's idea. I was just a little puppet."

"Have it your way," I said. Then we watch her get in the big Toyota and followed her out onto the highway.

CHAPTER TWELVE
WEDNESDAY AFTERNOON

IT'S ALL LOVE AT THE BURGER BUTT DINER

HEADING BACK TO TOWN, JAKE AND I TALK.

"Hey, you know, Jake. We're kind of going about this wrong."

"How d'you mean, Chief Inspector?"

"Well, think about it. Except for Stanford Bass and Silvio Treadwell, we're concentrating mostly on the people who were *at the scene*, trying to figure things out."

"What's wrong with that?"

"Nothing so far as it goes, but it's leaving something out."

"Explain, please. Your loyal partner, supporter and coffee-toter is interested to know."

"Okay, well, look at it this way, coffee-boy." I see that one makes him smile. "We have five people—Morgana, Rubin, Gentiles, Fairweather and Assice, who all arrived at the dig site together, and all of whom were there together throughout the night, except for a beer run. And Morgana and Assice were back by seven-thirty. Later, Assice was dead drunk, or so he says; Gentiles got up to go pee in the middle of the night, etc. Now, none of them drove back down the road in the Land Cruiser. The others would have heard it, right?"

"Right."

"Also, if they came in with the body in the truck or in the trailer, somebody would have seen it. I mean, it's not like you can hide a 180 pound dead man in a pile of tents, equipment, food, water and stuff, now can you?"

"Okay," Jake nods.

"Well, okay. So, what does that mean?"

"The body didn't come in with them. Either that, or it did, and they're all in on it."

"Right! I'm thinking the 'all in on it' scenario is pretty far out there. I can't see any advantage to Lavida's death that sews them all together."

"Neither can I." Nice to see Jake agrees with me.

"Okay. So, if the body didn't come in with them, what does that tell us?"

"That it came from somewhere else. And since nobody heard wooden stakes being pounded, that means he was probably murdered elsewhere."

"Right! We're thinking alike, Mr. Leon. And if he was murdered somewhere else, then . . ."

"Aha! I see the light! There's got to be somebody *outside this group!* Got to be. Why didn't I see it before?"

"Because it's so obvious. I didn't think of it 'til a while ago while we were talking to young Ms. Gentiles. There's got to be somebody who transported Lavida to the spot, maybe after killing him along this road, or, no, more likely, in that camping spot that Mr. Bass uses. Somebody killed him there, or near there, hauled his body through the woods in the middle of the night, deposited him in the trench, then took off."

"So, our murderer may not even be one of these five?"

"Maybe not. But I think at least one of them, maybe two, were in on it somehow, for reasons I don't yet know."

"Hey, anyway, if Lavida was killed off-site, so to speak, there probably would have had to be somebody else to carry the body, or help carry the body, to the trench, eh?"

"Yeah. I'd think so. Then, the person among the five who's the co-conspirator goes back to bed in camp, and the other person, the mystery outsider who'd been holding the body, scoots through the woods after they've transported the body to the mound and planted it in the trench, back to the other campsite, the one Bass uses, gets back in his or her car or truck, and drives away, leaving the co-conspirator at camp to wake up the next morning and 'discover' a dead Dr, Lavida. Yeah?"

"God! Awfully damn complicated, Denise. But, yeah. So, we need to figure out who the other person is. Right now, I'm thinking the only person who knows those woods well enough to negotiate them at night is Mr. Bass."

"So far as that goes, I agree. But is his belief in spirits reason enough to kill Lavida? He seems too old and frail to be a part of this murder. Plus, there'd have to be somebody to carry the body up to the mound—somebody who *bought into* his notion of the sanctity of those spirits."

"*Or* somebody who teamed up with Mr. Bass but killed Lavida for an entirely different reason. Maybe it *does* have to do with the spirits he believes are in the mound that he doesn't want disturbed. But," he pauses, "I agree with you. Bass doesn't seem murderous. And if he were, why would he kill Lavida and not target anybody else in the group? They're *all* responsible for digging up the mound."

"Well," I pause a minute and let things sift through my mind. "You know, we have three ex-Army Rangers or Special Forces folks in this affair. I'd think any of them could have negotiated the woods at night. Eh? These folks are super-highly trained. Somebody's the insider, and somebody is the outsider. Got to figure all that out."

"How the heck do we do that?"

"We keep asking questions 'till something cracks. Right now, we need to go find those two women, Rubin and Morgana. They haven't told us the truth. Neither one of them."

It takes about twenty-five minutes for us to drive back down the forest service road, out onto County Road Three, and into town. There, Doria Lake at my grandma's motel where the two women are keeping each other company, tells us they're having a late afternoon coffee at The Seminole

THE INDIAN MOUND MURDER

Pines Bar and Grill, a fancy name for a greasy-spoon joint. I call it the Burger Butt.

It don't take us three seconds to see 'em sitting together. I'm not in the best of moods, knowing they've both concealed evidence and lied to me, so I don't even ask their permission to slide in right next to 'little' Becky Rubin and across from Dr. Morgana. I can feel Rubin bristling because I've invaded her space, but I don't particularly care. Jake is standing next to the table. He's way too polite to slide into the booth next to Dr. Morgana.

"Why, gosh sakes, what a pleasure it is to see you, Deputy Sumpter," Morgana says. Sarcasm is dripping from her lips like viscous spit. "You're certainly welcome to join us, and thanks so much for asking! Why don't you slide right into the booth next to Ms. Rubin—Oh, excuse me, Captain Rubin. Did you know she's Captain Rubin? She's ex-Army, and also a black belt in several martial arts. Becky, darling, please don't kill deputy Sumpter here. I know she seems to be acting rudely, but I suspect it's just in her primitive nature—maybe in her jungle instincts, you know?"

Why is it that with some white people, there *always* has to be a racial element to their threats and complaints? This is sure a different-sounding Felicia Morgana. But I decide to come at both of them directly. "I don't appreciate being lied to when I'm in a criminal investigation, Dr. Morgana. Actually, I don't *never* appreciate being lied to, *especially* when I'm in a criminal investigation."

"Oh? Did I lie to you? Dear me! Why, I must search within myself and see if I can find some reason to feel sorry, because right now, I don't feel sorry at all."

"Look, *Doctor* Morgana, I ain't in the mood to trifle with you right now. You ain't feeling 'sorry right now,' but you'll be damn sorry when I charge you with obstruction of justice, and impeding an ongoing police investigation, *and* perjury. They're all serious crimes, and you need to *listen*—you and Captain Rubin here." I look straight at Rubin. She's fuming, but she evades my direct stare. "You need to listen to me, and you need to answer up straight."

They're both silent. So after a few seconds I go on. "You, *Doctor* Rubin, are a post-doc student at the university. I get the sense Professor Bacardi is trying to recruit you because you have a reputation for intelligence and ability, though it *ain't* showed so far in the way you've evaded my questions."

"Yeah, I'm post-doc. So?"

"So, you never told me that. You let me think you were a grad student like Stan Assice and Tuco Fairweather."

"Don't see what difference it makes."

"All the details make a difference. Can't put a puzzle together so the picture makes sense unless you have all the pieces, now ain't that right?"

"If you say so."

"I do say so, Captain-Doctor Evasive-Action Let's-Not-Tell-the-Truth Rubin. I'll tell you what else: You never mentioned you found a human long-bone at the mound the evening you got there."

"Didn't see a reason."

"There's always a good reason to be forthcoming with the truth, *missy*." That catches her by surprise, and I see her bristling more than ever. I've ticked her off. Too bad for her. "Do you know why it would have been a good idea to tell me? No, don't answer, because you don't know the reason, though now I do. If you'd told me, it might have been easier for me to figure out that they were plants. That bone you found was a *plant*. It's about twelve to fifteen thousand years old, but it came from a dig site in Siberia. It's not paleo-Indian. It's Siberian. Probably belonged to some hunter or huntress during the days of the Bering Land Bridge."

I actually see her coloring. And her 'I'm very pissed' face looks more pissed than ever. I can see she's holding it in, just ready to grab the knife on the table in front of her and stab it right into my heart. I can see Jake hovering very near, his hand not too far from his sidearm.

"So who the fuck planted it? Lavida wouldn't. Must be Assice or Fairweather, or maybe gentle Reggie Gentiles. I'll figure it out."

"Maybe you will, but you'll take no action against any of them, whoever it is. If you do, you'll answer to me—directly."

"Oooh. Scary shit, that. So, the little black detective girl knows about the Bering Land Bridge? Didn't think you'd made it that far in school."

"Yeah, well, Captain *missy*, I made it a lot further than that. I made it far enough to know you have combat experience, for which I along with the rest of the country thank you from the bottom of my heart. I mean that. I respect your service. I *don't* respect people evading my questions, and I *don't* respect people withholding evidence from me."

"Didn't know that bone would be important."

"Yeah, you didn't. You thought it might be your ticket, probably along with Dr. Morgana here, to a nice career at the university. So, tell me, is Professor Bacardi grooming you to take a position at the university?"

"Of course he is. I'm a genius. But you have a couple of guesses wrong. First, I have, or had, no intention of publishing with Dr. Morgana here. She's an idiot and can barely spell her name right, nonetheless actually contribute to a professional publication. Which leads me to number two: her plan is to sleep her way into the department and use her supposed 'good looks' to win over the gents' hearts. That included Professor Lavida before he was killed, which she revealed to me privately."

I'm a little surprised, but only a little. Dr. Morgana's face falls like all the muscles and connective tissues suddenly dissolve into air. It's half slack-jawed shock, half voiceless anger, and all bitterness at this heartless betrayal. Talk about being thrown under the bus! Morgana looks like the bus has just run her over, backed up and run over her again.

"Well, while we have Dr. Morgana in a state of shock, I'll ask her a question or two." I look across the table at Felicia Morgana. "Your erstwhile partner in crime here, Captain-Doctor Rubin, seems to have thrown you under the bus. But you know, she hasn't told me anything I haven't already figured out. Namely, that your assertion that you hadn't had any relationship with Professor Lavida was a flat-out lie. You had, and you know what else? Little Becky Rubin here is right: you were, probably still are, trying to sleep your way into the department. Does that include sleeping with any-body else? You were trying to cozy up to Rubin here. Why? Because she's right? Because she can write a good paper and you can't, and you needed her as a means to get your name in the limelight?"

Morgana is quiet for a moment. Her jaw is set stiffly, but her whole face is quivering, and there are tears beginning in the corner of her eyes.

"Yeah," Rubin goes on, "She was going to seduce me, too. Thinks her supposed good looks are enough to manipulate *anybody*. Problem is, I don't go that way. I like the *guys,* pure and simple. Good ole American farm girl. Except I can kick any ass I want to kick."

Morgana is crying, but trying to hold it back. She's obviously pow-erfully hurt and in a state of shocked betrayal. "You . . . nasty, . . . *nasty,* . . . DIRTY, . . . little bitch. *Bitch.*" Then she loses it and screams for the whole restaurant to hear: *"Bitch!* I don't know how I'm going to do it, but I swear to God, as I live, I'm going to get you back for this. We were going to publish *together,* become famous *together,* write the definitive book of paleo-Indian remains *together.*"

"Oh, for God's sake, Felicia," Rubin spits out, "Don't be such an idiot. *I* was going to do the writing, *I* was going to publish, *I* was going to do all the work that took brains and ability. You were going to ride along on my coattails, supposedly making me happy, and put your name on the publica-tions next to mine because you'd made a few random, useless suggestions here and there and slept with me. My God, you are such a ditz."

It's time for me to break into this little spat: "Anybody else you've slept with, Dr. Morgana?"

"Oh, shut up, detective." Saliva spews out across the table as she turns to me. Her speech is angry and a spray of spittle is jetting out from between her very white and very straight teeth. "I sleep with who I want to sleep with. For whatever reason I want to sleep with them. Women have been acquiring power that way for generations beyond numbering. We have a male-dominated hierarchy to contend with, if you haven't noticed. Given what you *do* notice, which isn't much. I doubt your senses are that keen.

At least I have the physical equipment, like *beauty,* for example, to be able to do it. Not like little plain-Jane Army bitch Captain Kick-Your-Ass here. I doubt she could seduce a lump of asphalt into lying down on the road."

Rubin laughs loudly at that. "You'd be surprised how hungry some men get for a little feminine attention. Never slept with anybody under my command, but I've seduced a few higher ups in my day. Some men like a woman who has actual *strength.*"

"Oh, well, whoop-de-doo. So you've seduced a few 'higher-ups' out in the field. To a starving man, even dog-food looks good. Even a pile of dog puke like you is going to be able to seduce *somebody.* I suppose a few balding, droopy-eyed, limp-dicked, half-blind little Napoleons *have* slept with you. I mean, why not. They couldn't handle a *woman.* What you know about sex wouldn't fill up a three-by-five index card."

"Okay, girls," I say loudly. "Now, listen. *Listen,* both of you. First, that broken part of a femur needs to be turned over to me, or to the Sheriff's Office. It's right on the corner of First and Magnolia, a half mile past downtown. Second, Dr. Morgana, when you've had a chance to settle down a bit, you need to explain to me your relationship with professor Lavida, which you lied about."

"Oh, detective," she snarls. "Do for God's sake shut up with your patronizing attitude. I don't need to calm down. Sure, I had, was having, a relationship with Professor Lavida. He was a sweet, attentive lover. Not very enthusiastic, a little too brainy for my taste, but he had his points. Of course I was cultivating him in the hopes he could benefit my career. For God's sake, what do you think? I'm not some celibate nun, you know. I get what I want how I want. But the fact I was sleeping with him doesn't mean I killed him. Why would I? That makes no sense. I'd gotten him to make me adjunct site manager at the mound. He'd promised me, *me,* not our Rubinesque little Army firecracker here, that he'd help me publish an article or two. I'd do my share of the work. You forget, I *am* a Ph.D in human paleontology. I actually *did* write a dissertation. I'm not nearly so helpless as Rubinsky here seems to believe."

"Probably had your boyfriend at the time do most of it for you," Rubin snarls.

"Don't kid yourself, sweetie. Jeffrey was helpful, but not *that* helpful."

I'm not sure she realizes what she just said, but it doesn't surprise me that part of her dissertation would have been written by her supervisor, whoever that was. Professor Bacardi, maybe? Good looks can go a long way. For a second, they're both quiet. I need for us to get ready to go. We have other things to get accomplished. "Dr. Morgana," I say, "Any other affairs you've had that bear on this investigation, I need to know about?"

"Interested in joining the queue, are you?" She's pretty snarky when she gets her dander up.

I laugh. "Not on your life. But I have a murder to solve. Right now, both of you two are high on my list of people of interest. You're sharing the spotlight as my two favorite suspects. Now, Dr. Morgana: You seem to like to sleep around a lot to advance your career. Okay by me, if that works for you. But if it overlaps our murder investigation in any way, you need to let me know about it."

"My private life is private, detective. But . . . if I feel anything bears on your investigation, I'll certainly let you know."

"Thanks." And as I'm sliding out, I politely nod at both: "Ladies. Good day to you both. Oh, Jake, Deputy Leon, do you have any further questions for these two women?"

"You know," Jake says, "For once I don't think I do have any further questions. But . . . maybe I do. Wait. Professor Morgana, do you ever drive the Land Cruiser?"

"No. That's Becky's job. She knows how to maneuver that sucker pretty well, even with the trailer on it. I'll give her that much. Why?"

"You helped load it, though, right?"

"We all helped load the van and trailer both."

"Ahh, of course. And Dr. Rubin—Captain-Doctor Rubin—is that right? You all helped load?"

"Yes, that's right. Of course. What does that have to do with anything?"

"Just asking. Just making sure of things. No unusual packages or bundles?"

"You mean, like an insensate man? No. Anybody would have noticed that."

"Yes, of course," Jake says. "Of course. Just following up. The night before you discovered the body in the trench, Regina Gentiles says she heard some heavy breathing. Neither of you noticed it?"

"No," they say in a discordant semi-unison.

"Ahh. Yes. Good. Okay, then. And it was you, Dr. Morgana, who discovered the body?"

"It was. I've already said all this."

"Right. Right. Just following up."

"And, Dr. Rubin, you were up at the same time as your tent-mate, Regina Gentiles, going to the bathroom?"

"Yep. Beer goes in, pee comes out. It's of the way of nature."

"Quite, yes, it is. And you went behind the truck or van, whatever?"

"SUV."

"Okay. SUV. So, is that right?"

"Yep. That's right."

"And you're sure you didn't hear any heavy breathing like Ms. Gentiles said she heard?"

"I'm sure."

"Were either of you with Professor Lavida when he started that trench a couple of months ago?"

"Yes, I was," says Morgana. "We've told you all this already."

"And you, Dr. Rubin?"

"A couple months ago? I think I was helping write up a short field report for Professor Rodriquez. Got my name on it as co-author. Build up your cred, you know?"

"Well, sure. Of course." He turns to me. "Chief Inspector? We ready to call it a day here?"

"I think so." We turn to leave, but Rubin follows us out.

We're getting into the car when I feel a strong hand grab my shoulder. "You need to get your hand off me, Dr. Rubin."

She takes her hand away from my shoulder, looks me in the eye, steam almost visibly spewing out of her reddened ears. "You listen to me, deputy. You might be in charge of this investigation, but investigation or not, you ever call me 'missy' again, I'll kick your face off. You won't know what hit you. I'll break every damn bone in your little body, you hear me? It's *Captain* Rubin. Or, if you have to go by academic honorifics, *Doctor* Rubin. It's never 'missy.' I wouldn't even let my daddy call me that."

"Noted," I say. I can see I riled her. My intention, but I can see underneath her barely suppressed fury, she's very, very dangerous. The 'Captain' seems to mean a lot to her. I watch her walk away, and I can see a suppressed power surging at every step.

When we're back in the car, Jake turns to me. "Seems like you riled up our little 'missy.'" He smiles when he says that. "But I'd take her at her word, Denise. That young woman will spend her life behind bars before she'll be talked down to that way."

"Seems I riled her a bit. Yep. But don't you worry, Jake. I'd take her down some way if I needed to."

"Oh, I'm sure of it. I just wouldn't want to see the two of you go at it. I like my partner, I do, and Army Captains with multiple black belts in all kinds of martial arts scare me. Personally, I wouldn't want to take her on without my Glock and some backup. She's dangerous, Denise. Really, really dangerous. Anyway, what did you make of our interview with our two 'lovers'?"

Even as he says that, I see Morgana walk out of the diner, heading toward the motel at a brisk walk. Rubin is following her—at a distance. Neither of them has transportation other than the Land Cruiser the whole group came to Seminole Pines in. If Rubin is going to be kicked out of the room, she'll have to call Gentiles to come pick her up, or else walk all the way to Seminole Lake County Park. It wouldn't be too far for her—about five miles along paved roads. But nobody would want to do it in the grow-ing summer heat.

"Well. It's clear Morgana was using Rubin for her own purposes," I say. "But Rubin wouldn't sleep with her, I mean in the sexual way, I don't think, just to get out of the tent and into a soft bed. She's tough—that much I can tell. What would she get by cozying up to Morgana?"

"Don't know, Chief Inspector. I don't think she *would* 'cozy up' to Felicia Morgana. She may have acted nice just to get in the room and get a shower. On the other hand, Morgana was the site manager. I don't know exactly what that entails, but I take it she was the 'superior' at the dig site, at least when Lavida wasn't there. Maybe that means any published work to come out of this dig would have Morgana's name at the top? Doesn't seem like Rubin would have handled that well. It doesn't seem she'd need Morgana for much academically."

"Hmmm. Yeah, I agree. She seems easily capable of spending a while in a tent, but, then, she may have been tempted, like you said, simply by the nice motel bed and a shower. Or, maybe she was trying to get something out of Morgana."

"You think maybe they were both in line for the same faculty posi-tion?" Jake asks.

"Exactly what I was thinking. Though my impression is there really wasn't much actual competition there. Seems Rubin is the real deal, whereas Morgana is a wanna be. Still, they *may* both have had ulterior motives for seeking each other's company. Not absolutely sure."

Jake muses: "Did you see how furious Morgana was at what Rubin said about her writing ability?"

"I did. She, I mean Rubin, seems a bit on the ruthless side. Do you know what I think?"

"I sometimes know exactly what you think. But in this case . . . what do you think?"

"I think we need to call her commanding officer later, see why she was discharged. She's pretty tightly wound. Like she could explode at any second. Betcha what you want she's been disciplined for violence against somebody or other in her time in the Army."

"Let's find out," says Jake.

"Yes," I say. "Let's."

And we head back to the office.

A COMMANDING VOICE

"HEY, PEE-WEE," I SAY AS WE'RE WALKING IN, "ANY CHANCE WE might ring up Becky Rubin's ex-commanding officer? We might not be able to find out, I don't know, but I'm betting she's been disciplined for something or other. She's wound up pretty tight, if you know what I mean." It's getting late, but I'm anxious to get this done.

Pee-Wee gives me the number. When I call, I get some assistant, a young man who introduces himself as Corporal Stanislaus. I explain who I am and what I'm about. I try to get connected with the commanding officer of Becky Rubin's outfit, but evidently he doesn't do a lot of phone interviews. I'm put on hold about a dozen times, but within an hour I'm actually face-timing with the commanding officer of the Seventy-fifth Regiment, U.S. Army Rangers. By now, it's dark outside. I really appreciate him talking to me at what must be his dinner time.

"Hello, Sir. Thanks for talking with me." He's in plain khakis, with one of those flat-topped Army hats.

"I've only got a minute, but always happy to talk to law enforcement. I understand from Corporal Stanislaus that this is about one of our own, an Army Ranger?"

"Yessir. So, I'm a deputy sheriff investigating the murder of an anthropology professor at the university here."

"Yes? I've talked to your commanding officer, your sheriff, I mean, before."

"Yes, I know. But this is more specific. Three of the people on the dig are ex-Rangers." I tell him their names. When I mention Becky Rubin, I can see him, even over the poor reception with face-time, look up grim-faced. "It's particularly Captain, Rubin I'd like to talk about."

"What do you need to know?"

"She seems a very, very intense young woman."

"I remember her well. She's somewhat famous in the Rangers."

"I see. Good famous or bad famous?"

"Both, deputy."

"What do you mean?"

"Captain Rubin was an excellent soldier, in many ways. Loved competing with the boys. And she was damned good at it. Just as tough as most of them and smarter than almost all of them. Graduate of West Point, whole thing."

"Really? That's impressive."

"But she took everything to the next level. There was something in her that was super, super competitive. She loved to beat people—at anything. She earned the highest rating in Ranger school on her academics, got three martial arts black belts, was second in the marksmanship class, passed every physical just short of Special Forces."

"Just short of Special Forces?"

"Yes. Right. All positions in the Army are open to men and women alike. All of them. Even the Special Forces are open to women. But so far, none has ever passed the physical tests for Special Forces."

"I see. I assume Becky Rubin tried."

"Yes. Three times. But she failed on upper body strength every time. Very hard for women to do. No knock on women, just a different physiology. Its too bad. I think it made her a little bitter, but she survived."

"And."

"Well, she made Captain, but not Special Forces, was shipped to Afghanistan, and led several operations into Kandahar. On one occasion, she lost two men to sniper fire. Deadly accurate shooter got both men in the head. No good shooting the body armor. Got two of her men dead in the face from close to four hundred yards. Becky's lieutenant spotted the perch the shooter was using, and Becky took three men with her to take the guy out herself. He was perched in a tree in front of a rock face, a cliff. Very hard to see. His clothes blended in perfectly with both tree and rock. But from about a hundred yards, she spotted him and took him out."

"Sounds like good soldier work."

"Oh, it was. Brilliant. But about a thousand yards from the tree was a little field, some kind of grain, and a pen with goats and a little two-room shed. Becky found it, and inside was a woman and three children. Becky questioned them about the man through an interpreter, but they wouldn't talk. The interpreter, who's a native Afghan, simply told her they were probably Taliban or Taliban sympathizers. She shot all of them right there in the hut. Seemed cold-blooded as you can get. Her junior officer reported it to the base commander, and she was sent back home where there was an Article 32—a military probable cause hearing. She wasn't absolved, exactly, but there were mitigating circumstances. Basically, severe PTSD. She'd been in the field two years—very tough stuff. You get inured to gunfire and death, especially the death of the enemy. She was sentenced, if you want to put it that way, to three years of psychological therapy for PT. Half way through she surrendered her commission. She left the army, dropped out of therapy, and has led her life ever since as a civilian. She was, at the time, only twenty-seven years old."

"Never any civilian follow-up to her crime?"

"No. I know this is hard to grasp from a civilian point of view, but technically, there was no 'crime.' The people really *were* Taliban sympathizers. The woman wouldn't talk. The hut was jammed with munitions. The woman actually tried using the children for a shield—ruthless in her own cruel way. Becky never should have shot, but there were small details that made it seem in a military hearing as if there were sufficient mitigating circumstances so as not to bring court martial charges."

"So, Captain Rubin was a bit on the ruthless side?"

"Could seem that way—to a civilian. Look, deputy, I'm not going to tell you your business. But please don't make judgments about the military unless you know it intimately. Afghanistan is a tough place. It's a guerrilla war. The Taliban are an organized force and they have the support, express or tacit, of much of the Afghan population. It's very hard leading operation after operation after operation, winning every single encounter with the enemy, only to find yourself no further advanced than you were a year or two years before. Somehow, we're always winning the battles but losing the war. When Captain Rubin lost those two soldiers, she was on her own with two companies of U.S. Army Rangers helicoptered deep into Taliban territory, looking for a major target, a Taliban leader. The woman wouldn't talk. The shooter was dead. Feel awful about the kids, but absolutely nothing one can do now. It's a terrible shame. She was a good soldier."

"Mind if I ask who the junior in command was who was with her?"

"Actually, I do mind. And, no, I don't know. And no, I wouldn't tell you if I did. No use bringing somebody else into your criminal investigation who has nothing to do with it. There was probably an NCO there and a few PFCs. The captain doesn't just go into an enemy compound by herself."

"But you'd describe her, at the time, as troubled?"

"That much I'll answer. Yes. She'd seen a lot of combat against a tough, disciplined and determined enemy. Sometimes things just boil over; you lose your sense of perspective, detective. She went to therapy and now she's a civilian. End of story."

"Well, thanks very much, Colonel."

"You're welcome. Can I tell you one more thing, please?"

"Shoot. Or, I mean, go ahead."

"I said Captain Rubin was, or is, very competitive."

"Yeah?"

"She's also a trained killer, Deputy Sumpter. She's very, very dangerous, and not a woman to be crossed. I'm serious. There are a hundred ways in which she could kill you, and every one would end up with you being just as dead. She doesn't like to be trifled with. That was a big, big element in her psychological exam."

"I actually know this."

"Well, good. Pursue your investigation as you see fit, but please note that on a basic, primordial, almost animalistic level, Captain Rubin is a powerful bomb that can exlode violently if she's handled the wrong way."

"Thanks, Colonel," I say. "Goodbye."

"Goodbye," he says.

I turn to Jake, who'd heard the whole conversation on speaker. "So, what do you think, Mr. Leon?"

"I think another visit with Ms. Rubin is in order."

"I'd say so, too."

WHO'S IN COMMAND?

NEXT MORNING EARLY, JAKE AND I ARE OUT AT LAKE PARK, parked in back of the University SUV just out of the roadway. Regina Gentiles's tent is pitched under a broad-armed pine tree, and the picnic table and outdoor grill are opposite under the shade of the same tree. There's no sign of Gentiles, but Rubin is in shorts and a t-shirt, seated at the picnic table having coffee.

We get out and she greets us—in her way. "Well, if it isn't deputy What's-'er-name and Assistant deputy What's-'is-name. Can't seem to get rid of you folks. What the hell you want this time?"

"Just a few more questions, Captain Rubin. And Deputy Leon here isn't my assistant; he's actually the senior deputy between us two. I'm just the chief investigating officer. He's here to keep me on the straight and narrow."

"Whatever you say. Look, I'm enjoying a cup of coffee and this glorious moment. So can we make this quick?"

"Sure, Captain. We'll make it as quick as we can. You seemed a bit short with Doctor Morgana last time we talked. You might say that, from her point of view, you kind of threw her under the bus. Why is that?"

"Well, that's one interpretation. The truth is, deputy, Dr. Morgana is a ruthless gold-digger who doesn't mind using her sexuality to get ahead. She actually came onto me, trying to arrange some kind of deal where I'd do most of the work—the analysis, the writing—and she'd give me the benefit of her 'experience' and site management, plus a little lesbian action on the side. I wasn't interested in the latter, and the former was really no deal. She's trying to get on the faculty at the university and feels she ought to have the inside track on the next available opening. But she doesn't. I do. I'm a better analyst, a better site worker, and a much better writer than she is. I've been published in the PAAS—*Proceedings of the American Anthropological Society*. She never has, although she's tried."

"So all those plans are off off the table now, I take it?"

"Yep. Rebecca Rubin and Felicia Morgana are no longer associated, except that we have to finish this particular dig together—unless one of us walks off."

"What were you hanging with her for in the first place?"

"A shower and a soft bed. Been a while since I was in the field in 'Stan, you know?"

"We talked to your commanding officer at Fort Benning. He told us about your shooting incident in Afghanistan."

She's quiet for a minute and looks away. "The woman and her three little Talibrats?"

"Yes. The woman and her . . . children."

"Rather not talk about it."

"It might be pertinent to this investigation."

"Why? Because you figure if I'd callously knock off a few bratty little enemy rugrats I'd just as callously knock off a professor in the Anthropology department at the Big U?"

"Something like that, maybe. You don't seem to be especially concerned about the deaths of those children."

She's silent for a moment, staring into her coffee cup. "They were the enemy, Deputy. Simple as that. Feel bad for the kids, but the woman wouldn't tell us where the leader was, and she tried to use the kids as a shield. And I swear to God, at the time I thought she was strapped to a bomb she was about to explode." She lapses into an agitated silence, turning her steaming coffee cup in her hands. "What do you want me to do, deputy? Commit fucking *suicide?* Is that how much regret you want me to show?" Her voice is rising and she's clearly extremely angry.

"No, I don't think suicide is . . ." She cuts me off.

"Appropriate? Not what you were suggesting? There's never an *end* with you people. You fucking civilians. God *damn* you people." She slams her cup down hard on the table. Coffee splatters out. I can see anger shaking her whole body. And . . . shame? Hurt? Fatigue?

She goes on, spitting out her words in an angry, whispering hiss. Barely able to control herself. "You think of three little kids in Afghanistan that were between me and the completion of my mission. To you, it's just the kids. But you forget the mission. It's *all about* the mission. The mission is why you live. So three kids stand in my way, and I can leave them alone and skulk away with my tail between my legs and radio my base commander and tell him the mission has to be scrubbed because some Taliban mama won't talk to me and she's hugging her three children who are already so fully indoctrinated in Taliban bullshit that they might as well be full-fledged fighters. You ever been shot at by a six year old?"

"No," I say. "Been shot at, though."

"Not the same, sister. Not the same. You think of kids here, they're children. Innocents. Over there, you'd better watch out. You see a kid playing in the mud in the street, she's there so you'll stop your vehicle so the Talibads can tick off an IED planted right under your Humvee. You send some kid into the other room in an Afghan hut so you can chat with mom or dad, and they'll either come around behind your back with a Kalashnikov, or else scoot across the road to warn their local commander that the Yanks are parked across the street and are easy targets. You think I'm just callous about those kids. I'm not. I just spent two years there getting properly indoctrinated in the tactics of a defiant, resourceful and utterly ruthless enemy. I lost at least *two of my men* because of Afghan children. One time, before the incident you're talking about, was to a little four or five year old girl who came with a bouquet of flowers. My man stuck his arm out the window of the Humvee, took the flowers, and she tossed a grenade in through the open window. One man dead, one seriously wounded. The seriously wounded man is still in Walter Reed, minus a right arm and a right leg. The girl ran back to her hut and the whole family was long gone by the time we brought machine gun fire on the place."

"Sounds like an awfully rough life, Captain. Look, I'm not here to diminish your service or to question your devotion to duty."

"No," she interrupts. "You're here to question my sanity, to find out whether I'm just looped off enough to do in my chief professor. And don't fucking *patronize* me. Don't shit on me with your 'your fine service to our country' crap. 'Stan wasn't about our country. 'Stan was about the Army, the mission, your buddies, and the people that as a commander you're responsible for."

"Didn't mean to patronize, Captain."

"Yeah," she snarls. "You know what you *really* want to know? You *really* want to know whether Afghanistan turned me into an animal, a voracious, vicious killer who loves the hunt, loves to burn people, loves to blow apart human bodies with high-velocity five-point five-six millimeter business ends."

"Are you that animal? Do you love to do that? Dream about blowing people away?"

She stares into her coffee cup, reaches down the length of the table to the pot sitting on the propane camp stove perched on the end of the table. She grows quiet, calms. "What do you think?"

"I don't know," I answer. "I haven't got you pegged as a wild, uncontrolled killer who kills for fun."

She's quiet another minute. "Well, you probably got me wrong. I got used to shooting at the enemy. You got an enemy—shoot 'em. It's an easy process, deputy. It's basic, animalistic and simple. You have a mission, there's an enemy to overcome, and you go after the mission, most of the time by sweeping away some bad guys." Then she lapses into silence.

"But that's Afghanistan."

"Yep. That's Afghanistan. Problem is, you come back home and the rules are all changed. Nothing is simple. They make you an enemy of *yourself*. That's why so many ex-soldiers commit suicide. They're used to killing the enemy. But the system, it makes *you* your own enemy when you get back."

I'm really at a loss for what to say. I didn't expect this conversation to take quite this turn. "Is that why you turned to Anthropology? To escape your past, I mean?"

"Nah. Or maybe yes, sort of. I turned to Anthropology because I want to use my brains for something other than leading men into battle. Had enough of that shit. Battle is shit, you know that?"

"I guess so, if you say so, Captain."

"Yep. I do say so. I turned to Anthropology because physical anthropology is fun. It's comforting. I get to glimpse a whole other human world of a long time ago when there weren't any societies at all, not big, organized ones. There weren't vast, arcane systems of rules and expectations. Just people, good people, living off the beautiful land. Wish to God, wish to *God* I could've lived then. Wish to God I'd been with those people who built this mound. I would've had peace." She's curled over her coffee cup now, speaking low and silently. Almost in a whisper.

"Was Professor Lavida the enemy?"

"Huh? God no. What makes you think that?"

"Didn't say I thought it. I'm asking."

"No, then. He wasn't the enemy, You're putting everything now in military terms. You're still patronizing me, deputy. You need to stop. No, Professor Lavida wasn't the enemy. He wasn't my base commander, either. He was my mentor. He was the guy fixing to give me a hand entering the academic community."

"So, no reason to kill him."

"None whatsoever."

"You sure you didn't know either Stan or Tuco in the Army?"

She's quiet. "Yeah, you're right. I lied about that. Not Stan. He was special forces all the way. Crazy fucker, Stan. Tuco was special forces for a while, but before that he was regular Army Rangers. He was on that mission with me, the one where I shot the woman and the three kids. He was in the hut."

"Was he the one that reported you to the base commander?"

"Yeah, I think so. But I'm not sure. Doesn't matter. I wouldn't hold it against him. His duty to report malfeasance."

"Kind of odd, its seems to me, that you were in Afghanistan with Tuco Fairweather, and that you ran into him again here in Florida, attended the same classes, even."

"Not so odd, Deputy. We're both, by chance, from Florida. He's from the Miccosukee Rez somewhere down south, and I'm from the town of Live Oak, maybe forty minutes from here, forty-five—whatever. He was a good PFC—very dependable, very brave. Even in the Army it was clear to me he had a crush on me. He never said anything about it. He was a good, loyal soldier. Very skilled, very calm and level-headed. To be a woman commander leading a bunch of men, keeping all that testosterone channeled in the right direction, it's a tough job, know what I mean? Tuco never once pushed it, pushed the boundaries. Once I had my incident, I was gently put on enforced leave, sentenced to psychological therapy until such time as I was deemed safe. When Tuco's stint was up, he left the Army and looked me up. I think he feels like he's my guardian angel or something. He's also in love with me."

"Do you love him?"

"Don't know, Deputy. I don't really know what that word means. People use it all the time. I don't know what it means. Don't know if I've ever felt that for anybody, even for myself. That part of me seems gone, empty—if it was ever there."

"Why did you lie and tell me you didn't know either of these men?"

She looks at me straight. "Are you kidding? You're investigating a *murder* and one of your suspects is a crazy Sheila who bumped off a woman and three little kids, which I knew you'd find out, and Tuco is about as sane and decent a human being as you'll ever find of those who have served their country in war. And you think I want you to associate him with *me?* I *know* he had nothing to do with that murder. Nothing. I'll do what I can to protect him. Not mentioning it to you was another of my growing list of mistakes."

"Why didn't you corroborate Regina Gentiles's report of heavy breathing?"

"Didn't hear it. I'm mostly deaf in my right ear. Firing a weapon close to my right cheek. Messed up my hearing. Mostly all I hear when it's otherwise quiet, is a constant ringing in my ears."

"What's with the pigtails? I mean, you can wear your hair any way you want, of course. But such a little girl type of style. I don't get it."

"I don't either. Seemed as far different from my Army persona as I could get. If I were to psychoanalyze myself, it's sort of the furthest I could get from my previous life, my former self."

"Okay. So nothing out of the ordinary that night at the camp?"

"Not so far as I knew. Tuco was asleep, probably snoring. Stan was asleep, I assume."

"Why do you say you assume?"

"Because he and Tuco were bunking together. I heard Tuco snoring. I know he snores. Couldn't tell whether there was one guy snoring or two. Like to wake up the dead."

"Wake up the dead. Interesting turn of phrase." She says nothing, but acknowledges with a head nod the irony. "So, did Tuco drink as much as Stan?"

"Probably not. But, you know, I think Stan's a bit of a showman when it comes to his drinking habits. He made a good show of being drunk as hell, but I don't think he holds his liquor as well as he claims. He actually dumped out a perfectly good can of beer when he thought nobody was looking."

"Hmm. Really?"

"Yep. Really. The man's got a reputation to protect. But I think he went to bed on more like three beers, not the six pack he's claimed."

"Hmm. Not so drunk, then?"

"Oh, I don't know. He was probably a bit drunk, sure. He just sells himself as a party animal, and the truth of it is, he's much less able to hold his liquor than he claims. He'd have to alter his whole macho mystique to let on that he isn't quite the drinker he wants everybody to believe he is."

"Okay. So, he was definitely not in your outfit in the Army?"

"Nope. Truly. No kidding this time. Anyway, I don't think he especially likes me. I'll tell you what, though, he's sweet as heck on Morgana."

"You know this because?"

"Oh, for goodness' sake, Deputy. Any woman can tell a man who's lost his wits over a woman. He drools like a hot St. Bernard around her. If you want a crazy ex-Army, Stan is pretty nuts. Not a murderer, I don't *think*. But whatever he tells you, you need to take with a grain of salt. He's . . . I don't know . . . very secretive."

"Is that so?"

"Well, seems so to me. Of course, no telling. I'm just trying to be helpful this time. Get you off my back, honestly."

"Could'a done that first time around."

"Could'a. Okay. But I wanted you to steer in any direction other than Tuco Fairweather. He's a really solid guy, Deputy. I'm used to bodies. But not in civilian life. You arrest people for murder here. Don't want any part of that, you know?"

"Why do you think we'd have steered toward Tuco?"

"The stakes in the eye sockets and in the mouth. It seems symbolic. You saw nothing, and now you cannot speak. Sounds like a defense of the spirits in the mound, an Indian thing, you know? Sorry, but I'm kind of ignorant on Miccosukee rituals and practices. But that old man, he's part Miccosukee, and he goes there to speak to the spirits. I thought maybe only the privileged are allowed to commune with the dead. Maybe, I thought, in digging up this old mound, we were disturbing the ancient spiritual world.

Okay, sounds goofy. But as soon as I'd seen the method of murder, my thoughts went right to Tuco. But he swears he had nothing to do with it, and I believe him."

"That old man? Mr. Bass? He's part Miccosukee?"

"Sure is. He was out there the day before we arrived. I happen to know because Tuco went to visit him—an old family acquaintance, I think."

I'm a little stunned. Keep asking people questions, and eventually something breaks. Why didn't she or anybody say all this before? Why are people so damn stubborn about withholding information from the police?"

"Well—nice to have all this come out three days after the murder took place. Deputy Leon. Do you have any questions for Captain Marvel?"

Jake Laughs, but Captain Rubin doesn't. "Sure. So, Captain Rubin, what makes you say Stan Assice is 'crazy'? I think I'm quoting you there."

"All kinds of behaviors. He seems so calm and rational. He's not really that interested in Anthropology. The bones do nothing for him. He just decided to take some courses because he knew Tuco in the Army and Tuco was taking courses with Dr. Morgana. He met Morgana one night at some sort of student-faculty party an the JC, and Stan was hooked. Decided to enroll at the U on the new GI Bill, see if he could meet up with Morgana."

"I'm confused. She doesn't teach there."

"Yeah, but Tuco said she was applying and had gotten this site manager thing, and Stan figured she had the inside track on a new job there, so he went right for the University enrollment. In the meantime, he enrolled in her class at the JC."

"So . . . Tuco thinks Morgana had an inside track on an opening at the U?"

"Yeah. So he thought. But believe me, the University wouldn't hire her. She's a clunk. She can teach lower level courses, but she's hopeless as an actual publishing scholar."

"But she published her dissertation, didn't she?"

"Pfffft! You don't *publish* dissertations. The University binds them and shelves them, as if they were 'publications,' but they're not. It's a common myth. She didn't even write most of hers. I think her chief professor wrote most of it for her."

"Who might that be, do you know?" Jake asks.

"Don't know for sure. Bacardi, maybe?" She answers that way, as if her answer were a question.

"Thanks. All I have for now."

"Thanks, Captain Rubin. That's all for now," I add. "We appreciate your help. And thanks for being more forthcoming this time around."

"Don't mention it."

"We'll look into all this further. Oh, and say, one more thing:"

"Which is?"

"You said you were trying to protect Tuco Fairweather?"

"Yeah? So?"

"And you called him a sane and decent human being."

"He is. I wish I were as sane as he is. He's a good man."

"Trying to protect a 'good man.' Sounds like love to me, Captain."

She's silent. We turn and retreat to the car, get in, and pull away from the campsite.

In the car, Jake turns to me: "Hell of an interview, that one. Think she's telling the whole truth this time?"

"I think so, Jake. But I'm getting jaded, you know? I don't know if I completely believe anybody any more, not completely. More or less, I do. Do you?"

"I feel about the same. Your nuance detectors are better than mine, I'll admit, but she sounded sincere and honest to me."

"Yeah, but then, she probably sounded sincere and honest back in the motel room too." I smile, to let him know I'm messing with him a bit. I'm not scolding.

"Yeah. Well, this time around, we got some good information. So . . . Can I guess where we need to go to next?"

"Where do you guess?"

"I'd go back to Mr. Bass."

"Yep. He wasn't telling us everything. And after that?"

"Ummm. We need to talk to Stan Assice again."

"Yep. And who's left?"

"Umm . . . back to Dr. Morgana, I guess."

"Yes indeed. And one more person."

"Regina Gentiles?"

"Nope."

"Umm . . . Professor whats'er name? Rodriguez?"

"Nope."

"Okay. I'm missing something, then."

"We need to go pay a visit to Professor Bacardi."

Jake seems surprised. "Because?"

"Because Rubin seems sure Morgana believes, or believed, she had the inside track on a new faculty position. But Rubin seems sure she herself is the faculty on-deck. And Professor Bacardi is the key figure in all this."

Off we go for some lunch.

BASS FISHING: IF THEY NIBBLE, CAN YOU HOOK 'EM?

THIS TIME WE CATCH STANFORD BASS SNOOZING ON HIS front "porch," a make-shift awning made of an old canvas tarp spread over a frame hammered together inexpertly from loose pieces of lumber.

Stanford Bass makes the most out of the pieces left over at the abandoned sawmill. His whole house is a tribute to that abandoned mill. I doubt he's ever once applied for a building permit to make all the additions he's made to his sprawling, ramshackle house. It spreads like a strange, cancerous shanty: here a covered porch, there a bathroom addition that's really an open pit toilet (and highly illegal in Wassahatchka), and over there a "utility shed" with an ancient washing machine attached to a hose that, when it empties, spills out directly onto the greasy dirt next to his house. The same ancient red pickup truck, old but well-kept, sits in the rutted patch of dirt that's Stanford Bass's front yard and driveway.

I'm not sure why the county commission has never seen fit to cite him for about every building site infraction imaginable, but they haven't. Or maybe they have, but "going after" Stanford Bass just makes no sense. He has nothing with which to pay a fine, he'd simply be out on the street if the commission decided to bulldoze his house, and there's no worse publicity for a county commission than ousting a quiet elderly citizen from his home, especially when he's doing no one any harm.

Thus, I guess, the shanty stays. Besides, the old sawmill is off the beaten track a ways, and Stanford Bass's shanty is out of sight from the main road about two hundred yards off. Out of sight, I guess, means out of mind as far as the county commission is concerned.

I honk the car horn and see Stanford slowly wake up from his beer-induced afternoon nap. He shakes his head to wake himself, slowly and shakily stands, and a blue beer can falls off his lap.

We get out of the car. "Why, hello, there, Mr. Bass. Sorry to wake you from your nap." He's very groggy, and doesn't seem in a good mood. No fish fry this time around. "See you had a little liquid cheeseburger for lunch today."

"Ain't no liquid cheeseburger. It's a light beer. But you don't need to worry about me. I *never* start drinking before I wake up in the morning. What you want this time? Thought I satisfied you folks last time you was here. What you want?"

"We'd like to ask you a few more questions, Mr. Bass. You weren't entirely forthcoming last time we talked."

"How's that?"

"You didn't tell us you were part Miccosukee, for one thing."

"Yeah? What of it? What's that got to do with anything? My mama was half Miccosukee and half African. My daddy was half African and half white. I'm all mixed up. But, yeah, my mama was pretty faithful to her Miccosukee roots. Spent part of the time on the reservation. She took me to the casino where she worked a few times. Lived there when my daddy was in jail."

"Your daddy was in jail?"

"Possession and distribution. Meth, smack, weed . . . whatever. Yep. The man liked to make people happy. Dealt out back of the casino. Got caught, got sent up. Mama raised me partly on that reservation."

"You familiar with Miccosukee funeral rites? I'm specifically thinking about ancient burials in that mound."

Now he's awake and looking at me steadily. "Shouldn't mess with them spirits. That mound is rich with spirits."

"Okay, okay. I got the spirits thing. But what spirits would be in an old trash midden?"

"Listen to me good, Deputy . . . what's your name, again?"

"Sumpter. And this is Leon."

"Okay, Deputy Sumpter and Deputy Leon. You need to listen to me good. That mound goes back to the beginning of time for people on this *whole continent*. That ain't old like Rome is old or Egypt is old. What's ancient Egypt? Like a few thousand years old? That mound in thirteen, maybe fourteen thousand years old. It's a trash midden. But that's because nine, ten thousand years ago, hunters stayed there and threw their trash on a grave they didn't know was there. They's a couple in there, maybe a whole family. It was a grave before it was a trash heap. Them spirits just wants to rest. Let 'em rest. Shouldn't never, never disturb them people resting in the earth. *Never.*"

"Did you kill professor Lavida for digging into that mound?"

Now, he looks steadily at me. "Nope," he says plainly, "I did not."

"Know who did?"

"Nope."

"Could it have been Tuco Fairweather?"

Now he's silent for a moment. "I don't know, deputy. Don't know. I don't think so. Tuco's a good man. He don't do that sort of shit. Killin' people? That shit ain't Tuco Fairweather at all."

"So you have no idea who might have killed professor Lavida?"

"Got no idea." He says this, but he turns his head slightly away from me when he speaks.

"I think you're lying, Mr. Bass."

"Then you're gonna have to find out."

"Why don't you just tell me what you know now?"

"Told you all I'm gonna tell you."

"You glad that professor is dead?"

"Don't give a shit about that professor. He been diggin' in the mound, he got what was comin' to 'im."

"Did you know the bones found in the trench in that mound were planted?"

"I'm the one told you that."

"You're the one who told us you saw someone putting something in that trench. You didn't say it was bones. But it was."

"How come?"

"It was that young woman, Regina Gentiles. She was seeding that trench with ancient remains from another part of the world. It was supposed to be a joke. It went badly wrong."

"Hmmmff," he snorts. "Them bones is fakes then. I mean, real bones, but not from the ancient people lived here twelve, thirteen thousand years ago. Them ain't the people was buried there. The people was buried *there* are deeper under the mound."

"How do you know that, Mr. Bass? Come on, really? You just can't know that."

"But I do know that, Deputy."

"How can you?"

"You can believe me or not, whatever you choose. But them spirits has spoke to me. They's spoke to me because I listen and I believe in 'em. They don't want to be disturbed. Sometimes, they give me visions. It was a man and a young woman. Ancient folk. Big game hunters. There used to be mastodons here, and it was more open country. He got gored by a mastodon, and she buried him there. Years later, she was married to another man and she died in childbirth, and her family or clan, maybe ten people, most, buried her with him. All that was so long ago, seems like the dawn of time. People was new to this continent."

"You can't know all that."

He just looks at me steadily, a little defiance in his eyes. "Know what I know."

"You just made up a story to go with that mound, that's all. The anthropologists say that trash middens rarely have human remains."

"They'd be right if'n it was only a trash midden. But like I say, it was a grave site before it was a trash midden. You don't know how old this mound is. It was a trash midden nine, ten thousand years ago. But it was a grave a thousand, maybe two thousand years before that. You think back two thousand years, that's the time of Christ. Rome. That's ancient history for us. For the people who made that trash heap, the grave was so long before their time, they didn't know it *was* a grave. They were descendants of the people buried there, though."

"You seem to know an awful lot about this site for a man who isn't an anthropologist."

"You don't need degrees from a university to know things. I read a lot. You see? You don't know that about me. I read stuff all the time. How I know about trash middens; how I know about the history of ancient Florida."

"But the gravesite under that mound. You just can't know that."

"Seen it, deputy. Seen it. Went out there once years ago, many years ago, just to be by myself. Like to be by myself. Took my cold six pack and my cigarettes, and just sat in the woods, lookin' up through the pine trees. A thousand generations of pine trees grown up on that mound, grown up all around us in this forest. Long time ago, long before white folks come or black folks, either, this forest had burned over and regrown a thousand times. I was listenin' to the wind, the trees, lettin' them tell me their story. I was lying back in the mound, smokin' my cigarette, and then the voice come through. I was a little scared at first, but then, I wasn't. The voice was the young woman who died in childbirth. Later her beau spoke to me, too. 'Let us drink,' they said, so I poured out a beer onto the mound to let 'em drink. After that, and that was thirty years ago, after that I made it a duty to come once a month or so. Listen to their stories, share a cigarette, pour them a beer. That's how I know all I know. I know you don't believe in no spirits, deputy. You're like most folks nowadays. Don't believe in nothin'.

You go ahead. Believe what you want. The spirits spoke to me, and I got to honor that."

"You say Professor Lavida got what he deserved."

"Yes, I sure did. Ain't sorry he's dead."

"Would you kill someone to make sure that mound stayed undisturbed?"

He just looks at me. "Maybe."

"What if bones actually were found. They'd be returned to the Miccosukee for proper burial. What's wrong with that?"

"The folks in the earth here ain't Miccosukee. They're far, far older than the Miccosukee. They're ancestral to all the American Indians in the East. There's groups that came in later on, sure, came into the country twelve thousand years ago, ten thousand years ago. But the people in that mound were here a thousand years before that—before what they call the Clovis people. This is their resting place. Time passes like magic for those who are dead in the earth. They'll speak to you. But they're tied to their remains. Just bad, bad medicine to disturb them."

"So, if you didn't want them disturbed, why did you show the mound to Professor Lavida in the first place?"

He hangs his head a bit when I ask. "Didn't think he'd go way out there to start diggin'. Needed the cash at the time. Ain't proud to say that. But they paid me. Sometimes got to supplement Social Security."

"Was anybody else with Professor Lavida when you took him out to see the mound?"

"Yeah. That other professor."

"The woman? The nice looking woman, dark hair, fair skin, really good looking?"

"Yeah, her, too."

"What do you mean her too?"

"I mean what I say. Her too, and Lavida, and that other professor."

"Know his name?"

"Nope. I think it was Jess. All I know, and ain't too sure of that."

I was thinking hard, but I didn't know any Jess. "Was this Professor Jess a man or a woman?"

"A man, an older man. Older but not old. Kind of Spanish looking, if you know what I mean. Had a kind of funny name, too."

"Bacardi?"

"That may have been it, I think. But I don't rightly remember."

I'm thinking. It makes sense that Professor Bacardi might have come out here with Lavida and Morgana, but I can't see what that has to do with anything. I know Old Man Bass is holding out on me, but pressuring him will likely get me nothing.

"Deputy Leon? Any questions?"

"Hmmm. So, Mr. Bass, have you been out to the mound recently, within the past several days?"

"Not real recently, no. There's police tape up around the mound. Can't go there."

"The police tape was put up only three days ago, sir. How'd you know that?"

Bass looks stubbornly tight-lipped. "Must'a' forgot that."

"Mr. Bass, you're not being at all forthcoming with us on everything."

"Look. I done told you the most important things. There's spirits don't want that mound disturbed. That's as simple as I can make it for you. But I didn't kill that professor, Lavida, and I don't know . . . for sure . . . who did."

"You don't know *for sure?*"

"What I said."

"Well, that means you have some suspicion."

"Could be."

"Well, then . . . who do you *suspect* killed Lavida, and why do you suspect that?"

"Ain't sayin'. Ain't goin' to be blabbin' my big mouth seemin' to accuse people when I ain't got real facts to back it up. You go ahead and ask all you want, but I ain't sayin' nothin.'"

THE INDIAN MOUND MURDER

"Well, then, you've seen something that makes you suspicious. Could you tell us what you've seen?"

"Ain't sayin' nothin' about that, neither. Just them people, that department, anthropology, that's a den of iniquity. Ain't nothin' goin' on there is right like it should be."

"What makes you say that?"

"Just what I seen. What I figured."

"Now we're back to being the mysterious Mr. Bass, again."

"Guess so."

I break in. "Mr. Bass, please. We have a murder to figure out, and it's very confusing, and it has a lot of moving parts. You'd help us out so much if you'd tell us what you know."

"Don't know nothin'. Already said that."

"What you suspect, then."

"Tell you what I suspect? Tell you that, and you'll go off and arrest somebody didn't do nothin'. I ain't gonna do that. I'm just telling you I got my private suspicions, but I ain't got nothin' to base 'em on except a feeling, pure suspicion."

"But suspicion based on what?"

"I ain't sayin' no more. Already said too much."

"Please?"

But Stanford Bass is resolutely silent.

"I could arrest you and take you in to the station, you know."

"You do that. Go ahead. Just feed me and give me a place to make my water, I'm fine. Can't be no worse than what I made for myself here."

"You'e very frustrating, Mr. Bass."

"And you-all's annoying as hell."

"I guess we are. Well, we'll be back in touch if need be."

"Go ahead and do that. I ain't goin' nowhere except to jail, maybe."

"Okay, last time, then: You have suspicions, but you're not going to share them?"

"That's right."

Chapter Fifteen

"Are your suspicions based on actual evidence?"

"Not what you'd call evidence."

"Are your suspicions based on what the spirits have told you?"

He stands up, looks straight at me, and gets up and walks inside. An old door scavenged from somewhere and ill-fit to the doorframe it fills, closes creakily, and we don't see Stanford Bass any more.

A NICE SPOT IN THE WOODS

WHEN WE LEAVE, JAKE AND I STRIKE UP A CONVERSATION.

"Frustrating old codger, our Mr. Bass. What do you think?" Jake asks.

I have to think out my answer. "Well, yes. But I can't tell whether he's frustrating because he knows something but isn't saying, or because he really doesn't know anything but has 'suspicions' as he put it, based probably on some supposed vision from the spirits. If his 'suspicions' are based on what the spirits told him, they ain't worth a damn thing."

"So you think maybe he's yanking our chain just to yank our chain?"

"Don't know," I say. "Maybe. He don't seem the type. What I think is, he's got real suspicions, but they're based on only, maybe, fleeting glimpses of things. For example, he took Lavida, Morgana and Bacardi out to the mound together."

"Yep. With you so far."

"What did he see? Did it look to him like something conspiratorial was going on? Maybe nothing overt or obvious, but something subtle, something that in his mind has proven to be grounds for this suspicion of his. I don't know, Jake. But what I'm thinking is, this is looking more and more like we've got to have a word with Bacardi. What drives me nuts is, I can't no way think of a reason he'd want one of the stars in his department killed. That doesn't make sense."

"Well, we don't know that he *did* want anybody killed. But if he did, sex or money. Money doesn't seem to be an issue because all these people exist on university salaries and federal or private grants. Gotta be sex, and to my mind, that puts Morgana right at the center of the wheel. I'm betting, just betting, she's got a hand in this murder. Wanna know my theory?"

"Can I guess your theory?"

"Be my guest."

So, what would Jake be thinking, I ask myself. "Here goes: Morgana bumps off Lavida to make room in the department for herself. Maybe she knows that Rebecca Rubin has the 'inside track,' so to speak, on any new positions, so she has to make room for herself to fill a vacancy left when somebody already in the department dies. A lot of death and plotting for a damn university faculty position that doesn't pay all that much in a really competitive 'publish or perish' environment."

"People want different things. But, yeah, that's my theory. Tell you what else . . ."

"Can I guess the what else?"

"Be my guest again, " Jake laughs.

"The 'what else' is that Morgana is like the outsider looking in. She has real intellectual pretensions, but she's had no luck really making inroads into the professional community. Maybe she's just not good enough, like Rubin says. So she gets frustrated teaching lower level classes year after year, and she decides her ticket into the big leagues is to bump off a big leaguer. Eh?"

"You're pretty good at guessing somebody else's theory. But I can tell you don't really buy it." He's quiet and smiles at me, a genuine smile. "Go ahead. You won't hurt my feelings. What's wrong with my theory?"

"Not a thing, movie star." I call him that sometimes because he looks so much like an old-timey movie star. Some people say he looks just like Errol Flynn, but I've never seen a movie with Errol Flynn, just Internet pictures. Looks like him, sorta. But he's got a thin mustache, slick hair that's always got a curl down on his forehead, and deep blue eyes. I guess lots of women would call him handsome, and I guess I see it. Not my type, though. Besides, he's gay, so he don't go out with women.

So, I continue: "Ain't a thing wrong with your theory. But several things are blocking my way. If Morgana is guilty of murdering Lavida, how'd she get that body to the Indian mound? How? When?"

"Don't know.

"She'd have to have had some help. Tuco Fairweather? Stan Assice? Professor Bacardi? Maybe even Becky Rubin?"

"Yep. That body in the trench is a big problem. I figure they just have to have brought it in with them."

"But, if that's what happened, then how come nobody else noticed it? That would mean the whole lot of them are guilty. But what *sense* does that make? Like we said before: there's an outside person, and right now, that means either Rodriguez, who seems to have an alibi, our friend Stanford Bass, or Professor Bacardi. Unless there's another person involved in all this we haven't met before."

"Any chance the murderer, if it is Morgana, could have killed Lavida and brought him in the day before the group arrived together?"

"Maybe, Jake. Maybe. But these woods are filled with coons, coyotes, hogs . . . How come the body hadn't been disturbed by critters?"

"Well . . . if it wasn't the day before, then he *has to* have been put there that night. Night time. Somebody familiar with the woods. I'm believing right now it's Stanford Bass."

"Yeah. Maybe. But a frail old man, to move a body who knows how far through the woods? Does that figure to you?"

"Okay," Jake nods his head. "That leaves Bacardi of the people we know. But what the hell does he have to do with this? There's somebody else. Rodriguez has an alibi."

"Somebody else. Somebody else. But who?"

"You're the brains of this outfit. Who do you think?"

"We're both the brains of this outfit, Jake. It's a team effort. You know where we ain't gone yet?"

"Where ain't we gone?"

"We ain't taken a look at that camping spot off the forest road yet. We were just out there by accident that once. Let's go out there and take a look and see what we see."

"Well . . . okay. What do you expect to see?"

"Don't expect nothing, Jake. Just hoping we can find something that will help us. Don't got no idea what that might be."

"I know what you're thinking. Don't see why I didn't see it before."

"Okay, smart boy. What am I thinking?"

"Unless I miss my guess, you're thinking that that camping circle was used as a staging ground, best term I can think of, for whoever was out there that night to bring in the body. That was where they brought the body. Then, whoever, moved the body to the Indian mound from there. It's about two miles through the woods. Could'a' worked."

"Well, well . . . looks like great minds are thinking alike, my man!" I high five Jake in the car. "I don't know that we'll find anything to link that campground to anybody, but it's worth a try. We ain't exactly getting too far just interviewing our suspects."

So we drive out County Road Two to single-lane County Road Three, then off the paved road onto the forest service "road." Some of these forest service roads that haven't been used in a long time, not used regularly, anyway, are hard to find. County Road Three in Wassahatchka County is itself a pretty lightly used road. We drive off into the trees headed for the Indian Mound, looking for the turnoff to the campsite. It's hard as heck to find out in the woods—just a narrow, rutted track around a bend in the forest understory, all palmettos and scrub oaks. If you didn't know it was there, you'd easily miss it. But we find it without passing it up. I think to myself, I'll have to flag this turn so it's easier to find next time around.

We drive a way along a rutted pathway, hardly a road, palmetto fronds brushing against the car, feeling the springs bottom out of the old Crown Vic as we lurch through ruts on their way to maturing into ravines, and sliding through wet spots of red clay, slick as a bowling alley. But in ten minutes, we're there. I park on the "road" without driving in. I don't want our car treads obscuring anything that might be vital to our investigation, even though our car's tracks will be there from our accidental visit before.

We both get out, though neither of us has room to fully open their door. Once out, Jake looks at me across the top of the car. "What we looking for, Chief Inspector?"

"Anything, Jake. Just anything. Tire tracks would be useful. Might tell us who's been out here. Cigarette butts, beer cans, the leavings of modern humanity—anything we might be able to link to any of our suspects."

"Of course, anything we find could'a' been left by somebody else. Teenagers sometimes use this little clearing to hang out. Smoke dope, shoot up, mess around."

"They do, they do. But I don't think there have been any out here recently. The only person's been out here that I know of is Mr. Bass, and he's not telling us anything. Didn't tell us he's seen anyone out here."

"True enough. Alrighty, then . . . lets get to it. How about I start to the right and go counterclockwise around the circle. You start at the left and go clockwise?"

"Deal. Just remember, anything transportable, pick up with latex gloves and put in an evidence bag. Here," and I give Jake a couple of large plastic bags, no different from plastic kitchen storage bags, though a little bigger.

"Deal, Chief Inspector. Damn, I hate these things." He's pulling on the tight gloves. Can't say as I blame him for hating them.

I walk slowly around the site. It's not really very big—just big enough to park a car or two and put up a small tent. It doesn't take me long to find out at least part of what I'm looking for. Tire tracks. Fresh, or reasonably fresh, and not obscured by our own tracks from two days ago. The red mud is dried, but we've had no rain all week, so, lucky for us, they haven't been washed out. I carefully take out my phone and snap a half dozen shots from as close as I can get. "Hey, Jake!"

"What?"

"We got a ruler or tape measure in the car?" I like to keep one for just this sort of thing—measuring the width of tire tracks. Out here in the boonies, lots of people drive pickups as well as cars and SUVs. Tire tracks won't have DNA evidence on them, of course, but they can easily lead you to a type of vehicle. Even, if you're lucky, to a specific vehicle.

"It's in the back, I think. Tire tracks?"

"Yep. Be awful careful where you step."

"Hey, look. You stay where you are, Chief Inspector. I'll go get the tape. Stay there and I'll be back in just a sec."

And he is, with a small tape measure we keep in the trunk. "Looks pretty clear, Denise," Jake says. "But look, it's dried out. Could be a week old or even more. Got pictures?"

"I do." I bend to measure the width of the track. It's perfectly clear and maybe three feet long—long enough for the tire to have come part way around. Gingerly, I pluck off a few fallen pine needles to get a more perfect picture. "This look familiar to you, Jake?"

Jake's the car guy, even more than I am, since he got that Challenger last time the department bought vehicles. "Well . . ." and he looks at it closely. "It's a car, not an SUV."

"You sure?"

"Pretty sure. Here, look: No off-road tread. Wide enough to be a big truck tire, but not the right kind of tread. This is more of a racing-type tire, something that would go on a fancy-ass car."

"Like your Challenger?"

"Yep, he laughs. Except we never drove the Hellcat in here, not to this spot. *Could* be a pickup track, but I really doubt it. It's very clear. Tires look pretty new."

"I'm measuring close to twelve inches wide. That says a big tire to me."

"Maybe. But look. See these horizontal lines?"

"Yeah?"

"Those go on the outside of the tire, to channel water away from the tire on a slick road."

"And an unbroken longitudinal line. A groove that goes all the way round the tire, one on either side," I point out to Jake.

"My guess, a racing tire, a tire that would go on a really nice car." I'm a bit depressed at this, because that seems to say a teenage boy's new toy—some spoiled high school boy whose indulgent parents would buy him the car of his dreams when he's only seventeen. Not in the neighborhood where I grew up, tell you that.

"You been out here in the Challenger with that boyfriend of yours, Jake Leon? Fess up now!"

I'm just joshing with him, but he smiles at me. "Nope," he smiles, "but it's a very similar kind of tire."

"We find who this tire goes to, we might find who was out here."

"Yes, indeedy," he says.

"See if we find any more. We'll take pictures of those, print them at the office and see if we can match them to anybody's car."

"Got it. Let's look around some more. I'm just betting there's more out here than we had any idea.

And, sure enough, there is. Off in the bushes, three beer cans. Jake and I both notice at once that they're the same kind of beer Stanford Bass guzzles like he was trying to make Niagara Falls with his next pee.

"Well," says Jake, "This seems to say Stanford Bass was out here. Of course, a lot of people drink the same brand of beer, but I'll betcha his prints are on some of these cans." We pick up all three gingerly, trying to keep from putting our fingers where prints would be, and in the evidence bag they go.

"Yeah, but there's no way those tire tracks go to his old pickup."

"True enough. More likely to see bicycle tire patches in the dirt than a nice, new racing tire if it was Stanford Bass's truck."

And then, a gold mine. Or, rather, a silver mine. A little flash of silver glints through the weeds and palmetto fronds. I bend over to pick it up. "Jesus, Jake!"

"What? What?" He comes closer to look. It's a little foil packet with two white pills still visible in the plastic bubble. "Some kind of medication?"

"Ain't just some kind, Jake Leon. Ain't just some kind. Bet you any amount of money you want, this is Rohypnol."

"Roofies? Date rape drug? You sure?"

"Yep. Used for that," I say. "It's a legitimate sedative, ten times more powerful than Valium. Ain't prescribed in the U.S. where it's illegal, but that don't mean it can't be obtained. Unfortunately, it's used illegally and criminally almost more than it's used legitimately for real medical purposes. Double the dose on these things, you'll knock somebody out cold."

"Damn! You sure this ain't something else?"

"Ninety percent sure. Yes, I am."

"Well, now. Ain't this just something. You thinking what I'm thinking?"

"Well, as I said, great minds think alike. What you're thinking and what I'm thinking, is that Lavida was drugged out here, maybe on his way to the mound where he was going to show up for a surprise. But whoever brought him out here gave him a beer with about three or four of these dissolved in it. Then, boom, down went Lavida. Then, our culprit or culprits dragged him out of the car, murdered him by pounding wooden stakes through his eyes and into his brain, then carried him through the woods to the Indian Mound."

"Would'a' taken at least two people."

"Would'a', I agree. But what two?"

"My money's still on Stanford Bass as one of the culprits."

"You know what we need to do?"

"What?"

"Go talk to this Profesor Bacardi. No one seems to be able to account for the whereabouts of Lavida on the day before or the night of the murder. Rodriguez swears he wasn't down in Central Florida, so where was he? If he was around here somewhere, why is there no car? No car means somebody brought him out here, then murdered him, then drove away."

"Or helped move the body, *then* drove away."

"I'm beginning to see Bacardi written into a lot of this."

"Me too."

A further close analysis of the campsite yields nothing substantial. There's a mostly burned small cardboard box in the fire pit that I put in an evidence bag. The size of the box was just what you'd expect for a pill box. Only a small part of one end with no printing visible was salvageable, but I figured it might be possible to match it to the dimensions of a Rohypnol box, and it's possible there could even be a recoverable fingerprint on it—not likely, but worth a chance.

After about thirty minutes scanning the area, Jake and I decide to leave. It's getting late and we have a drive into Tallahassee tomorrow.

CHAPTER SEVENTEEN
FRIDAY, MORNING THROUGH
LATE AFTERNOON

RUM PUNCH

THE NEXT MORNING, I GET IN A LITTLE EARLIER THAN USUAL—
7:15 instead of 7:25, but Jake is still in ahead of me, as usual. By the way,
not that I'm playing my little sympathy violin, but getting in at 7:30 doesn't
mean I leave at 4:30 or after an eight hour day where I had an hour for
lunch. No such thing. In the Wassahatchka County Sheriff's department, a
ten or eleven hour day is pretty usual. I almost never get home until after
six o'clock, and when I'm on a major crime investigation, I may not get
home until ten or eleven o'clock. If I didn't love doing investigation, I'd give
it up. Ain't no overtime, ain't no Christmas bonus, and some years ain't
even no raise.

We're a big county with a lot of territory to cover, and just the six of
us to do it—Pee-Wee and us five deputies. And when Jake and I are on a
major crime investigation, that's just three deputies to do everything else:
look into burglaries, man the speed trap, provide security at the courthouse
(only job in the department I absolutely hate), break up domestic disputes,
find runaway kids, break up fights at school, attend high school games for
security. Well, you get the idea. I love the investigation; I don't even mind
the speed trap, long as I get to chase a Porsche or a Corvette speeding
through our little borough. But there's no way everything that needs to
be done can get done if everybody whines about going over an eight hour
day. Other, richer counties, maybe, but not Wassahatchka. Only perk I can

think of is that we get to keep our cruisers as our personal vehicle, as long as we're employed by the department.

All of that would just be useless information for you, except that it gives you an idea why Pee-Wee is a little reluctant to let me and Jake drive up to Tallahassee to see this Professor Bacardi. We'd be at least seventy or eighty miles outside the county, and if he needed us for some major emergency, like a gunman taking hostages at the courthouse, then we wouldn't be around to help. He can always call on the FHP to buzz in and help, but our county is lightly patrolled by the Highway Patrol, seeing as how there are no major state or interstate thoroughfares going through Wassahatchka. So, here's how it went down.

"Hey, mornin', Pee-Wee. Nice cologne you got on this mornin'."

"Don't wear cologne, Midge Sumpter. What do you want?" Pee-Wee is about the best sheriff in the whole wide world, my honest to God opinion, but don't make no mistake: when he wants to be gruff and no-nonsense, he'll out-gruff a grizzly bear woke up by a firecracker in his winter den.

"Well, Jake and I were just thinkin' . . ." I can see Jake grimace and hide his face behind his hand, like he was saying, "Midge Sumpter, what did you have to say that for?"

"Leave Jake Leon out of this. What d'you want? You want permission to do something or other out of the ordinary. Out with it."

"I'd like to drive up to Tallahassee to talk to Professor Bacardi." I can see Pee-Wee looking up at me like I just asked him if he could get me a new red Ferrari for my patrol car. "Look, Pee-Wee, I really need to. I mean, we really need to. No fooling."

"You can't talk to him over the phone from here?"

"I can, but there's a hundred things I can't see, Pee-Wee. I can't see how he reacts when I ask him a question. Plus, over the phone, I can't look around. I mean, we found a packet of Rohypnol at the campsite on Indian Mound Road yesterday. Date rape drug. Likely what put Lavida out so's he could be murdered. Suppose Bacardi opens his desk drawer at school and I catch a glimpse of a box? Wouldn't be admissible as evidence in court, but I'd know who we had to target for a search. Also, I need to see his car. We found good tire prints at the campground, wide tire with rain grooves on the side. I want to see if Bacardi is driving a car with those sort of tires. There's just so much I can't do over the phone, Pee-Wee. Please?"

"Jake stays here. Can't spare the both of you to go galavanting off to Tallahassee, which is sixty miles outside our jurisdiction. Ain't got enough of you scalawags to cover this county as it is. I'm letting you go by yourself because it's a murder investigation."

"I need Jake, Pee-Wee."

Shouldn't've said that. A stack of papers comes slamming down on the desk. I can tell Pee-Wee isn't *really* mad, but he's getting aggravated. "Look, Midge. I'm glad you and Jake are getting along so well together. It's a credit to you both. And you're doing a good job. But there's too much happening. Jonas Brothers Bagels had somebody throwing rocks at their plate glass front earlier this morning, possibly an anti-Semitic thing. That little group of skinheads at the high school are at it again. And one of them, I think it was the McCain boy, brought a Bowie knife to school in his backpack yesterday, if you can believe that shit. Somebody tried to sneak a loaded pistol into the courthouse past Junior Madison yesterday. I just can't *do* with just three deputies, Midge. You'll go yourself, you'll take the Crown Vic, and you'll be back by early this afternoon. Now . . . git. You ask for anything else, *anything,* the answer is no."

Don't know why I get the devil in me sometimes, but I do. "Well, I *was* gonna ask you for a kiss, but I see I'm gonna be out of luck *this* morning." I fish the Crown Vic keys out of my pocket, and head out the screen door. "Be a lot quicker in Jake's Hellcat," I yell back through the door as I'm going down the steps to the gravel parking lot. "But I ain't askin'. Just sayin'. And if Jake was drivin', we'd probably be back before we left, the way that man drives. You have a good day, Pee-Wee. Bye, Jake. Don't get shot while I'm gone."

I hear a belated "Bye!" From Jake. He wanted to go, but when Pee-Wee says "No," he means "No." From Pee-Wee, all I hear is, "Hurry up and git. I need you back here this afternoon. And no three-cocktail lunches on county expense!" Like I ever had a three cocktail lunch in my life. The number of two beer lunches I've had I can count on one finger.

I call the college from the car to make sure Bacardi will be in. He'll be in all day, doing whatever department chairs in Anthropology do at state universities. I let the department secretary know I'll be in, and she pencils me in for 10:30, which should be fine if I don't dawdle or have any hangups along the way.

The drive up to Tallahassee is nondescript: up County Road Two to CR Four, then to I-10, then west on I-10. In a little over an hour, I'm in the Tallahassee environs looking for a parking spot at the university. The campus is very big and a little confusing, but a question or two to the man at the entrance kiosk sends me in the right direction. The Anthropology department is in a very large, very nondescript modernist-style brick building, not one of the older brick buildings that look like they belong on a college campus. I manage to squeeze into one of only four "visitor" parking spaces in the little parking lot at the back of the building, snuggling in between a big SUV that's parked a foot over the line, and a sorry-looking hedge that borders the lot. The department shares the building with the Archaeology and Classics departments, I discover.

There really isn't a "waiting room" as there would be for a doctor's or lawyer's office, just a front desk where the department's administrative assistant sits, and an area out in the hallway populated by a few high tables with stools—comfortable for most younger students, maybe, but not for any normal person past nineteen or twenty. I'd expected an audience sooner than I got one, but after an hour's wait, I'm ushered into Professor Bacardi's office.

He stands and greets me: "Deputy Sumpter! Glad to meet you, finally, face to face. We've talked over the phone, now, What? Once or twice at least? So, what can I do for you?"

He ushers me into a seat, while he sits behind his paper-clogged desk. I see no order to his system, just a clutter of papers, a tissue box, a half-buried laptop, and a jar with some sort of candies that look like they're left over from some Christmas ages ago and are all gummed together. He's a spare man, short and thin, with thinning hair combed straight back. He looks at me through black-framed glasses with thick lenses. Obviously, his eyesight is poor. Skinny arms poke out of sleeves way too big for them. He has no tie. His face is leathery and brown, obviously tanned from many seasons of digging at sites around the world. I understand from a little background reading that he's world-famous. Despite what I assume is a school-wide no-smoking policy, he puffs gently on a pipe.

"Just want to ask you a few more questions, sir."

"Ask away, deputy."

"So, I'll be direct."

"Oh, my God, please! The more direct the better."

"Okay. So, you know most of what there is to know about the details of the murder. Professor Lavida was found in a trench at the Indian Mound in Wassahatchka County, face up, dead, with wooden tent or utility stakes pounded through his eyes and his mouth."

I can see Professor Bacardi wince when I say this. He fidgets a little in his seat. Obviously the description makes him very uncomfortable. "Horrible business," he says quietly, "just horrible. Can't imagine anybody doing that to Toulouse. To anybody!"

"Do you have any idea whatsoever why Professor Lavida would have been there at the Indian mound in Wassahatchka County when everyone at the dig site thought he was further south at another dig site altogether?"

"None at all. I can only say that if Estella Rodriguez says he wasn't with her or at her site, then he wasn't. I suspect he intended to drop in on the Wassahatchka group early and surprise them. My best guess. He was pretty interested in that particular site."

"Could you confirm for me the type of vehicle Professor Lavida drove?"

"An old Chevy pickup truck. It was a real working vehicle. Couldn't tell you what year it was. Maybe, I don't know, somewhere mid eighties, maybe a little newer. It was a rugged old beast. He drove it everywhere. I'd guess it had close to 200,000 miles on it."

"Thank you."

"I take it you haven't been able to locate his truck?"

Already I've learned something. "No, sir, we haven't. Didn't know until just now that it was even missing. I have an idea where it might be. Just an idea. But if it's in the woods somewhere near the Indian Mound, that's a lot of wild woods to search through to find an abandoned vehicle."

"Search by helicopter?"

"Wassahatchka County doesn't have one, and the county commission probably wouldn't spring for the cash needed to hire one. It ain't all like you see on TV."

"I'm sure."

"So, would Lavida have stayed in a hotel or in a tent, if he was going to surprise them early?"

"Well, I don't know. Toulouse was pretty rugged and pretty handy with camping equipment. I imagine he'd probably have gone right there and set up camp near the mound. Are there many accommodations in Seminole Pines?"

"A few, yessir. Well, one, actually."

"I see. Still, my guess is Toulouse would have camped out. He's famous for his campfires and his campfire-roasted potatoes."

I'm thinking, I know no more about *why* TouTouse Lavida was on Indian Mound Road than I did before, but learning that he would have been in his truck is important. Even as I'm talking with Professor Bacardi, I'm forming a couple of different scenarios for where Lavida's truck could be. I even think maybe I know. I decide to turn to the other main direction of my questioning. "Okay. So, I said I'd be direct. So, that body just shows up the morning that the digging crew is set to start excavations. That's Dr. Morgana, Regina Gentiles, Tuco Fairweather, Stanley Assice, and Rebecca Rubin. All five swear they had nothing to do with it, which doesn't mean they didn't, but it means I'm hitting a brick wall getting enough information to figure out who's guilty."

"Tough job," Bacardi says. "I wish you luck. Anything I can do, let me know."

"That's why I'm here, sir. So, also, all five people swear they heard no vehicles approach the camp the night previous. Now, assuming the five of them didn't bring the body in with them, which seems terribly unlikely . . ."

"Probably impossible," Bacardi butts in. "I mean, if one or two people are guilty of this murder, then there's no way three or four other people could have missed a dead body being hauled in in the van or the trailer. Once they're on site, they unpack everything. They would have found the body."

"Yes, sir. Exactly. That means *either* all five of them were in on the murder, which makes no sense because I can't see how any motive fits all five of them, *or* there's somebody else *outside* the group who was doing everything on their own, or maybe in concert with somebody *else* outside the group. Or, again, maybe somebody outside the group was working with somebody *inside* the group."

"And there would have had to be somebody outside the group because . . . ?"

"Well, think about it, sir. Professor Lavida must have been killed off-site and then his body brought in through the woods. Professor Lavida wasn't very large, but, still, that's 170 or 180 pounds of dead man that had to be carted on foot through the woods and deposited in that trench. Regina Gentiles swears she heard heavy breathing that night. I think that was the murderer or murderers carrying the body, probably already with the stakes pounded into his face, up to the mound. Then, they disappeared."

"Hard to do in the dark of night. Those woods get pitch black at night. Don't see how anybody could see their way through all the trees and palmettos and undergrowth." He shivers. "Can't even imagine it."

"Well, there are two young men working on that site who are ex-Army Rangers, and a young woman, Becky Rubin, who is or who was a Captain in the Army Rangers. Pretty tough soldiers, all of them."

"Okay," he says, "But what brings you to see me?"

"I said I think we have an outside operator, somebody either doing the deed or assisting one of the five at the campsite."

"Ahh, of course. How blind I am. So you'd like to know where I was and whether I have an alibi for the night before Toulouse Lavida was discovered in that trench?"

"Precisely."

"Well, I was at home all night with my wife. I know family members are not the most reliable witnesses, but, well, there you are. Early in the evening, say, about seven through maybe 8:30, we had two department members over for post-dinner drinks. But they both left right around eight-thirty."

"Who were those two people?"

"Two of our younger department members, Joe Stegerson and Amy Alderton. They were talking about teaming this summer on a site up in Nova Scotia that might produce the remains of an old ninth or tenth century Viking settlement, something like L'anse aux Meadows in Newfoundland, but about two hundred miles south. It would be very important if it turned out to be legitimate. Aerial photography seems to show the outlines of what could be longhouses under the sod, but we won't know until we dig what it really is. I'm really very excited about the prospect."

"So they were there with you just to get permission?"

He laughs. "Well, not exactly. They don't need 'permission' in the sense you mean. We were discussing strategy. Basically, funding. It all comes down to funding. What can the university do? Are there private sources? What might the Canadians be able to do? These things take money. They wanted to show me the aerial photograhs. My job is to allocate resources and personnel as best I can. I can't ask the university to help fund something that's totally off the wall. The photographs look promising, though. Maybe it will come through. We'll have to see."

"So, after they left?"

"Went into my study and pulled out some maps and files. Found a couple colleagues at McGill University in Montreal and the University of Ottawa that we might be able to team up with. Oh! Yes, that reminds me, I called Steve Fischer at The University of Ottawa probably about nine, nine thirty. I know him personally and I didn't figure he'd be too grumpy at being interrupted at nine thirty at night. Anyway, there will be a record of that call, I assume. And I can give you a number to call him. It's an international call. But he'll be happy to corroborate my story."

"How long did you talk?"

"Don't know. Maybe an hour. Pleasantries, first of all, you know, 'How are the wife and kids?' That sort of thing. But we talked over the project at pretty great length. He actually knew of the photographs, but they're just as cash-strapped there as we are here. Governors and politicos want money to go to STEM education and nothing but, or practical, business-type courses. Damn bullshit if you ask me. Real education? Pushing back the frontiers of knowledge? They don't give a crap. Anyway, his name is Stephen Fischer, department of history at the University of Ottawa. I'll give you the number before you leave."

"And I'd appreciate it. And the names of the two department members here so I can corroborate your whereabouts with them."

"Most certainly. You know, deputy Sumpter, Toulouse and I were life-long friends. Just to say. Of all the people in this world, I'd be the one least likely to be his murderer."

"So, I've asked you this before, but who would benefit from Professor Lavida being murdered?"

"Absolutely nobody. That's the honest truth."

"Well, both Professor Morgana and Dr. Rubin seem to think that with Lavida out of the way, they stand a chance of getting the inside track on being his replacement."

"Well, that's something I haven't decided on yet." Then he pauses: "Well, not for *absolutely* sure. Anyway, it really isn't my decision alone. The Dean of the College of Arts and Sciences would chair the hiring committee, and the committee would include several people in the department, not just me."

"Between those two people, Rubin and Morgana, where would your own preferences lie?"

"Between those two? Rebecca Rubin, obviously. She's a bit young and raw, and her Army service, though of great benefit to her country, doesn't help her in this particular situation. Still, between those two, she's the obvious choice."

"Obvious because?"

"Because Felicia Morgana isn't really up to the publication schedule required in a modern research university. She's a good enough site manager, but I've seen some of her actual work. She can't write, and she misses really important connections. There are too many things she doesn't know."

"Like?"

"Oh, my God, lots of things. For example, in one of her sample papers she submitted to me for possible recommendation to a certain journal, she completely missed the importance of isotopic analysis of tooth enamel."

"Analysis of what?"

He smiles. "I know it sound pretty arcane and strange, deputy, but it's something that's pretty well-known in paleontology. You can figure out a lot about the diet of a specimen by analyzing the stable isotopes of oxygen in tooth enamel. It's formed during one's lifetime, you see, and then stays stable after death. I can get more technical if you'd like, but that's the layman's gist of it."

"I see. And Becky Rubin?"

"Probably knows more about it than I do. The woman is a genius. Why she was in the Army is beyond me, but she'll be a star wherever she ends up. I'll confess, she'll have my vote in the hiring committee."

I decide to switch tacks. "Why would Regina Gentiles think Lavida was having an affair with Felicia Morgana?"

He's really taken aback by this. His eyes go wide and he breathes out hard. "Wow!" he says. "Didn't see that one coming. I don't know why she would think that. God Almighty! An affair with Felicia Morgana? Toulouse? Oh, my God!" Then he laughs. "Wow! Well, first, he's at least thirty years her senior. Second, I think Toulouse had . . . ahhh . . . other entanglements, so to speak."

"Like Estelle Rodriguez?" I ask.

He just throws up his hands. "I think Toulouse was something of a ladies' man. Or, that's how he saw himself. How the ladies saw him, too." He laughs. "Third, I'm aware, if only peripherally, that Dr. Morgana has a reputation for, ahhh, sleeping around, I guess you could say. Trying to use her good looks to get herself ahead in the world."

"That brings up another question I have for you. What's your first name?"

"Eh? Jeffrey. Why do you ask?"

"Because Becky Rubin seems to think a certain Jeffrey wrote part of Felicia Morgana's doctoral dissertation, a few years ago."

He throws up his hand and smiles. "Guilty," he says simply, "though it's not quite what you think, and not so illegitimate as you might suspect."

"Fill me in."

"Well," he hesitates, "every doctoral candidate has a committee who oversees their research. I was doctor Morgana's supervisor. It's pretty common for a supervisor or other members of the committee to suggest edits and offer suggestions. In Felicia's case, I probably looked through her manuscript far more than is ordinarily the case with most doctoral candidates. I didn't rewrite it, exactly, but I helped turn a mess into something the committe could at least live with. We even had a grad student from the English department proofread her manuscript because she makes far too many plain English errors, not to mention the anthropological ones. The long and short of it is, she's not a very good writer. In fact, she's awful! But she had finished her coursework, and her dissertation proposal, though nothing spectacular, was reasonable. It's really tough to see someone come that far only to be turned down because they can't write worth a lick and their actual research technique is sloppy."

"You've said yourself she has a reputation for sleeping around, Professor. Does that include you? Don't mean to pry, but I need to pursue every angle I have."

He's quiet for a minute. "I spoke with her at a faculty-student party once and I got the feeling she was trying to, well, not seduce me, exactly, but interest me, maybe. But I wasn't interested. I'm *not* interested. Actually, I couldn't *be* interested."

"I'm sorry, I didn't get that. Couldn't be? What do you mean?"

He's silent for a moment. "Do you know the character Jake Barnes from Hemingway's novel *The Sun Also Rises?*"

"Never read it."

"Oh, boy. Well, deputy, this is pretty private, but I'll share this with you because you're in a murder investigation. Jake Barnes is a character who was injured in the First World War. I hold this distinction in common with him, except in my case, it was in Vietnam when I was only eighteen years old."

"Injured?"

"Yes. I was made impotent, Deputy Sumpter. I lost both of my testicles to a Viet Cong mine. It ripped up the inside of my right leg, which has since been more or less surgically repaired, but it also destroyed my groin area. Yes, it was very, very painful and embarrassing. I almost died. But I didn't die. I lived. I was lucky to find a woman, my wife, who would marry me with no possibility of begetting children, and we've been married ever since. Thirty-eight years now. I can refer you to my doctor for medical reports. To this day, I have certain surgical implants and prostheses to be able to, umm, perform basic bodily functions. But sex? Not for a little over fifty years. July twenty-first, 1968. I was on patrol through the rice paddies about fifty miles south of Saigon—Ho Chi Minh City, now. Stepped on a mine even though five men ahead of me in line walking across the dike had missed it. I ended up in the adjoining rice paddy, bleeding like crazy, fully conscious, and in unimaginable pain. I was evacuated by helicopter about thirty minutes later. My very first patrol. And that happens. War is shit."

"Well," I say, "I'm so sorry for your loss." And even as I say that, I realize how dumb a thing that was to say. "Oh, my God, I'm sorry. I didn't mean . . ."

He laughs. "It's okay, Deputy. Please. Check with my doctor. I'll give you his name and phone number. So, an affair with Felicia Morgana? Not even physically possible. And not anything I'd desire. And as to having any part in the death of Toulouse Lavida, absolutely not. Phone records to Ottawa will confirm that I really was on the phone to Stephen Fischer until, I don't know, maybe ten thirty or so. Anyway, the loss of Toulouse was, personally, to me, the loss of a great friend, and professionally, the loss of the best, most trusted researcher in our department."

"So who the heck would want him dead?"

"Damned if I know. If it's one of the two women, murdering Toulouse to open up a spot in the department for herself, then I can't help you there. My opinion? I don't think Felicia Morgana has the, ummm, wherewithal to be able to plan and carry out such a deed. Rebecca Rubin could both plan it and carry it out, but we were more or less planning on hiring her anyway, so I don't quite see how she'd think she'd benefit from knocking off Toulouse. I mean, Toulouse was her mentor, her ticket. Toulouse thought very highly of her."

I sit for a moment thinking. But I can't think of another question to ask. I'm just thinking what a complete bust this trip has been. "So, one last question: What kind of car do you drive?"

He looks very surprised. "What kind of car?"

"Yes, sir."

"Why in the heck . . ."

"I can't explain that to you, sir. It figures into our investigation. So, what kind of car do you drive?"

"A Kia Soul. It's parked out to the side of the building in the faculty lot, if you want to take a look. Why do you want to know about my car?"

"Like I said, Professor, I can't explain that to you. What color?"

"White. It's the only one in the lot. I can tell you for certain it wouldn't have been seen in Wassahatchka County the night of Toulouse's murder. I'll one-hundred percent guarantee you of that."

Okay, thank you, professor."

"You're welcome."

I stand to leave, and he extends his hand to me to shake hands goodbye. As I open the door and leave, I hear him call to his secretary: "Julius! Could you bring me that file of Nova Scotia aerials in here?" And, listening to that, I walk out the office and down the hall.

Outside the building in the late fall heat, I walk around to the faculty lot and check out his car. It's the only Kia Soul in the lot, a very modest, practical professor's car. Clearly, Jeffrey Bacardi isn't the flashy type. One look at the car and a quick peek underneath the rear end to check out the tires tells me this is no match at all for the treads Jake and I saw at the campsite in the woods off of Indian Mound road. I notice, though, he has a specialty license plate: PALEO 001. It's not likely this car would have gone completely unnoticed had it been in Wassahatchka during daylight hours, but, then, at night it may not have been seen at all. Still, the tire treads just don't match up, and Bacardi's story about talking with that professor up in Canada sounds pretty legitimate, though I'll check it out. It just doesn't sound at all like he's the culprit.

What a bust, I think. But, then—not a bust entirely. If Bacardi is out of consideration for the outside person in this murder, then that circles us back around to Stanford Bass. Stanford Bass and his old truck— unless I'm missing something entirely.

I drive back to Seminole Pines in perfect silence, trying to think this all out. When I get in, I spend the rest of the afternoon catching up on paperwork. Pee-Wee is out doing something, so I'll have to report to him about the trip tomorrow.

CHAPTER EIGHTEEN
SATURDAY MORNING

STAN THE MAN AND FATA MORGANA

"HOW'D THE TRIP TO THE GREAT METROPOLIS GO?" PEE-WEE asks as soon as I get into the office next morning. Jake is over at his desk, filling out reports on our last three days' interviews. Paperwork: Hate it!

"More or less a bust, but not entirely."

"Fill me in."

"Well, Me and Jake figured that there *had* to be somebody outside the five at the dig site involved in the murder. The body didn't come in with them in the SUV or their trailer, so it had to have been brought in that night. There's a little campground about two miles up the road, almost exactly two miles from the Indian mound and another mile or so from County Road Three. We've identified it pretty certainly as the actual site of the murder. Lavida was drugged there and taken through the woods by somebody to the mound, where he was dumped into the trench and left there to be discovered the following morning. We had kind of gotten focused on Professor Bacardi, who seems central to everybody in the circle of people at the dig, but I'm ninety-nine percent certain he wasn't there. He has an alibi from about seven-thirty to eight thirty or so, then another alibi up until about ten thirty. I haven't checked them out yet, but we'll get that done. It seems unlikely he would have driven in the middle of the night to Indian Mound Road, and up the road with a drugged colleague in his car. Just doesn't seem likely. So I think he's out as the outside man. Besides, his car doesn't fit the tire tracks."

Jake looks up at me from his desk. "We're back to Stanford Bass, then, as the most likely culprit."

"Yep. Old Mr. Bass and his shiny red truck."

"Truck?" Jake asks. Pee-Wee looks up at me, listening.

"Have a feeling about Stanford Bass's old pickup truck, but if you all don't mind, I'm gonna keep it to myself for just a bit until I have a chance to check it out. But I think I know how LaVida got to the campsite, and I think I know why we can't find his old truck."

"We going to go see the old codger again? I, umm, I think *maybe* I know what you're thinking."

"Maybe. Maybe. Still, I'd like to have a chat with young Mr. Assice first. We've more or less skipped over him to this point."

"Sure enough. Of course, you'll need my expert advice and devoted backup during this interview. Darn! Have to get out from behind this comfy desk and out into the field, doing police work." I appreciate his sarcasm; Jake hates paperwork as much as I do. Pee-Wee just looks over at him with that serious look of his that says "Give me a break."

Then, he says it: "Oh, crimony! Give me a break. Finish your reports when you're done with this Assice guy," Pee-Wee says. Then he looks up at us both as we're heading out the door. "Tonight, before either one of you goes home for the night. Hear me?"

"We hear you Pee-Wee."

"You'd both better be sure I'm serious."

"I know you are, Pee-Wee. We'll get 'er done. Promise."

Probably when you think of a crime investigation or watch one on TV, all you read about or see is the actual investigation; interviews, statements, shoot-outs and chases. Nobody wants to read a book or watch a show where all the investigators are doing is sitting behind a computer at a desk filling out reports. But the truth of it is, every damn thing you do gets typed into a computer. Whole interviews, quotations from witnesses, witness statements, some accounting for where you're going and what you're doing. Everything becomes part of the record of an investigation.

You never know what will be important in court. It took me at least an hour to type up my report on the interview with Bacardi yesterday. Maybe you didn't realize how much paperwork is involved, but there's a lot. And it piles up quicker than you can imagine.

Meanwhile, though, Jake and I are outside on our way to the Hellcat. We're going to pay a visit to Mr. Assice at Seminole Lake Park.

As we pull into the campsite, no sign of Stan Assice or Tuco Fairweather, either one, though the tent is still there. The big Toyota Land Cruiser, however, is not. We get out and decide to poke around a bit. Wherever they are, they can't be too far. Maybe one or both are in town, probably grocery shopping. I see a figure in the distance down at the lake. Assice? There aren't showers at this county park, so a dip in the lake to freshen up would be mighty welcome, as long as the gators and moccasins stay out of range.

And, yes, in case you're wondering, that's not a joke. Seminole Lake has gators; every body of fresh water in Florida bigger than a swimming pool has gators. And moccasins, water snakes, even rattlers hang around bodies of water. You might not think of rattlesnakes as water snakes, but they swim really well and if you're swimming, you need to be careful that you don't bump into one.

We snoop around a little bit. Nothing extraordinary. The camp stove is still on the table. There are two reclining, low-slung folding lawn chairs under the spreading pine tree. The table is spread with a few random artifacts, pieces of bone, shells recovered from the mound. There must have been a fishing camp near the mound long ago, though the site is a long way from the ocean. Must have been fresh water mussels or something of the sort in the lake that used to exist there.

I'm about ready to walk down to the lake to see if it was indeed Assice that I saw, when he walks into the campsite in soggy shorts, a somewhat grungy towel wrapped around himself.

"Well, if it ain't deputies midget and faggot. How are you two, today? Solved this crime yet?"

I'm always sizing people up just in case there's some kind of con-frontation. I always want room to draw my weapon if I absolutely have to, or to avoid a witness throwing a punch. That "deputy faggot" was aimed at Jake Leon. I don't know how he knows Jake's gay, but the comment was mean-spirited and vile.

"That's deputy Leon, sir, and I'm deputy Denise Sumpter. I'd appreci-ate it if you could use our names."

Assice just smiles, throws his towel across the back of one of the lawn chairs. I can see he's still in Army shape. He doesn't have body-builder muscles, but he's lean and clearly very strong. I doubt either one of us, Jake or me, could take him by ourselves. Probably not both of us together. Pee-Wee's taught us a thing or two about self defense, but this guy is ex-Black Ops. I'm sure he'd put us both down really fast if he wanted to. I can see Jake isn't really bothered too much by the "faggot" remark, shitty as it was. But I can see him moving subtly over to the side, putting one of us on either side of Stan Assice. Jake is a smart one and knows how to handle himself in these situations.

"Is Tuco Fairweather down at the lake?" I ask.

"Nah," says Stan, "he's in town with Reggie Hen-tillies." He pro-nounces it that way, exaggerating the actual pronunciation, which is simi-lar. Is he making fun of Ms. Gentiles's hispanic background? This guy is a bit of a jerk. "What can I do for you folks?"

"Answer a few questions," I say.

"Already answered a few of your questions. Don't know what else I can add."

I'm going by instinct here. I don't really know what I need to know. I just want to start getting a picture of what happened, and so far, a blurry picture is all that's really shaping up. I'm fishing in my mind for a way to start that will get us somewhere: Tire tracks? Rohypnol? Sighting Toulouse Lavida's pickup truck? But once in a while sheer luck intervenes. Felicia Morgana crawls out of the tent, buttoning up her blouse as she emerges. She's in short shorts and she's barefoot. With her dressed in so little, I have to admit I can see why men find her attractive. She's flawlessly proportioned and very pretty.

"Ah! Dr. Morgana. How nice to see you here! Taking a nap in Stanley's tent, I see."

"Don't be stupid, deputy Sumpter. I was waiting for Stan to get back from the lake. I don't want to make love to somebody that stinks as bad as he stinks after a few days without a shower. You've interrupted our late morning plans."

"Well, so sorry about your plans. Do you mind telling me how long this has been going on, this affair, I mean?"

"None of your damn business, deputy. That's our private business."

I can see Stan standing over to the side of the table smirking. "It's all right, Felicia," he says. "Why don't we just tell her?"

"Because it's none of her damn business!" Morgana snorts.

"But it is my business if it has anything to do with the murder of Professor Toulouse Lavida."

"How does our little affair have anything to do with that?" Morgana snaps.

"I don't know that it does or doesn't, Dr. Morgana," I say very politely. "But there shouldn't be any shame in having an affair. You're both adults. When did this start, and why didn't you tell me you two were involved?"

She's silent. At last, she simply says, "A guy with a body like that? What woman would say 'no'?"

"Okay, So, how long has this been going on?"

Assice doesn't let up on the smirk as he answers: "Since last year, deputy Some-where. I was her student at the time, fresh out of the Army, taking classes at the JC. Saw this hottie, found out she was a professor, and signed up for her class. We started seeing each other about halfway through the semester. As you can see, she's a pretty hot potato. Was dying to get on her good side, you might say, from the minute I walked into her class."

"I see. So, why didn't you tell us you two were having an affair earlier?"

"Wasn't nobody else's business."

"But, what do you mean? Why not? You're two consenting adults. What never-mind would it have been to any other member of the excavation team?"

Stan stays silent, shoots a covert look at Morgana. She speaks up. "First of all, deputy snoopy, because it's highly frowned upon for teachers to have sexual relations with their students. I don't know whether I would have been fired, but Stan would at the least have been taken out of my class at JC, and I didn't want that. I wanted to further his career."

I can't help laughing at that: "Further his career?" Yeah, right. "And what of *your* career, Dr. Morgana?"

"Stan has nothing to do with my career. He's my lover. He satisfies my carnal instinct. He's quite animated in bed—animalistic, even, you might say." I can see Stan smiling along with this. "I like them that way—fundamental, crude, even. I want a man who wants me, who can't keep away from me." Stanley shrugs, as much as if to say, "She's right." But he doesn't say anything.

"Speaking of your career, Dr. Morgana," and as soon as I say this, I can see her stiffen up.

"Yes?" She says, very icily.

"Do you know I talked at length to Professor Bacardi at the college yesterday?"

"And what did that old geezer have to tell you?"

"That you wouldn't have been his first choice as a hire in his department."

She sits stiffly. I can see her jaw tighten. She looks down at the ground, as if trying to contain herself.

"Yes, deputy. I'm aware of that."

"He says you're not a very good writer and that you miss important things."

"Does he? Did he mention something about examining isotopes of oxygen in tooth enamel?"

I'm surprised by this. "He did."

"Yes, well, he seems to think it would have been germane to a paper I wrote and asked him to review for me, for a fee, by the way."

"Did he earn that fee, in your view?"

"What he told me, deputy, for your information, is that no peer reviewed journal would accept my paper, at least, not that one."

"That must have been devastating."

"I'd call it disappointing. I didn't include anything about analysis of the tooth enamel of paleo finds in western Alaska because I didn't see it as that important. They were big game hunters. Everybody knows that."

"Maybe they weren't, or maybe they supplemented their diet with fish, like salmon. They're abundant in Alaska, I think, aren't they? Couldn't that have been important?"

She looks at me. "I see you've been talking at length with Bacardi. Fucking rumhead." She says this with a definitely venomous hiss. I don't say anything to her, but I thought of that angle on my own. I can see myself why it might have been important to do the tooth enamel analysis. Maybe the people being dug up were fisher-folk. Maybe they were transitioning to a settled lifestyle along the Alaskan coast way back then. Who knows, maybe they even traded for maize with some tribe further south. That would be a big deal to miss, if you're trying to reconstruct how people lived.

"So, were you a bit resentful that your work was dismissed as inferior?"

"It needed brushing up, that's all," she says, but I get a distinct feeling it's about a lot more than just "brushing up." She's very defensive. I can see more clearly now that she really, really wanted to move up to the big time at the university. She was working at it, but she was just a bit short on knowledge and technique. I begin to see anger and jealousy—anger at Bacardi, jealousy of Becky Rubin—seething beneath the pretty dark eyes and the glossy black hair. Was this a motive for murder? So far, though, nothing substantive to go on. There might be a motive, but too many loose ends. What physical evidence?

"Deputy Leon, do you have any questions?"

"I do. Mr. Assice, everyone seems to think you drank yourself into a stupor the night before Professor Lavida's body was found."

"I drank a bit, maybe a bit too much."

"Becky Rubin says she saw you dump a beer out onto the ground. What was that all about?"

"I'd had enough. That's all."

"Not faking drinking more than you really were?"

"Why the hell would I do that?"

"I don't know. Maybe you could tell me."

"I don't do that."

"Did you fall asleep in a stupor? Or did you go over to Dr. Morgana's tent?"

He smiles, then answers. "Might have. Hard woman to resist, you know. Not that you'd know anything about how hard it is to resist some women."

"No, you're wrong. I understand it perfectly well. I find it pretty hard sometimes to resist my partner. Just to let you know, though, I'd have no problems whatsoever resisting *you*."

Stan Assice grins a bit nastily at that comment. "You'd never get the chance, buddy. I don't go that way."

"I'd never look for the chance, and you can go whatever way you want to."

This is getting us nowhere, though I understand why Jake wants to spar with this butthead. So I interrupt. "Do you know what kind of truck Professor Lavida drove?"

I'm watching his face carefully, and I can see that, just a tiny bit, he winces when I ask this. There's a bit of an evasion there. It's a question he wasn't expecting. Sometimes when you catch people unawares with a question sort of out of left field, they're unprepared and they reveal themselves just a little. I can see his face well enough to know that he knows about Lavida's truck. Will he lie to me, or make up a story? I can see he's quickly calculating his moves. I can also see that Morgana glances over at him quickly with her eyes, sort of quietly saying, "Don't screw up!"

"Hmmm," he pretends to muse, "I think I do. I've seen it before in the faculty parking lot at the university. An old Chevy pickup, right? Maybe it was a Dodge. Umm, no, it was definitely a Chevy. Yeah. Old, beat-up thing. Dusty beige color. A real archaeologist's truck."

"Umm-hmm, I say. And when was the last time you saw it?"

"Well, like I say, in the faculty parking lot at the U. Maybe a day or two before we left to go do the dig. Why? Who'd want that stinking old bucket of bolts? Wouldn't mind a spin in your little chariot, though. Dodge Challenger Hellcat! Biggest engine in any production sedan in the world. Performs like a sports car. Been a while since I got behind the wheel of something like that. How does a deputy in a rinky-dink outfit like the sheriff's department in Whatchacallit County rate a car like that? Do you guys even know how to drive a car that fine?"

"We manage," I say. I can see that Stan has recovered completely from the initial surprise of hearing the mention of the truck. Still, I know for a near certainty that he knows more about that truck than he's saying.

"Do you know where that truck would be now?"

"How the hell would I know that? Probably back in his spot behind Building A at the university."

"Only," I say, "It's not. It disappeared evidently at exactly the same time Professor Bacardi was murdered."

"You're suggesting somebody killed the man for his truck?" asks Dr. Morgana.

"Not necessarily," I say. "It's more likely whoever killed him found a way to get rid of the truck so it couldn't be found."

"Wait a minute," Morgana says, "How do you even know Lavida's truck was around here?"

"Unless he rode in with you guys, which you all deny, he has to have gotten to Seminole Pines some way. We assume he drove in under his own power."

"And then what? Just lay down on the ground while somebody pounded stakes into his eyes?"

"Nope. He was drugged. The toxicologist's report isn't in yet, but we know they're going to find drugs in his system."

"Drugs?" Morgana sneers. "What drugs?"

I can see right off I didn't set that up right. I should have said Rohypnol directly, caught her off guard, studied her reaction to that discovery. But I said just "drugs," generically, which could be anything, and I gave her time to recover before I mentioned Rohypnol.

"Rohypnol."

"Christ Almighty! A date rape drug?"

"Who the hell would want to rape that old bag of bones" Stan scoffs.

"Wasn't a case of date rape. He was rendered unconscious, then murdered."

"And how the heck would you know that?" Morgana asks.

I know she's fishing for how much we know, or at least I think she is. I decide to play cool, though. I don't know what harm it would do to our case if I told them we found a packet of Rohypnol tablets at the campsite off of Indian Mound Road. But I decide against it. Better to let them stew.

"Oh, let's just say an educated guess, Dr. Morgana. Just an educated guess."

"Going on guesses now, are we?"

"Oh, well," I say. "Sometimes a guess is the best we've got."

"Well," Stan sneers, "If that's the best you've got, you've really got *nothin'*."

"I wouldn't say that, Mr. Assice," I say calmly. "We may have more than you think we do. But that's all right. We'll call it a day here and head on back to the office. But you two need to stay in the area for a bit, just in case we might have another question or two."

"Aye, aye, little deputy lady," Stanley sneers. "A little black cop and her gay partner! What's the world come to?"

"Maybe the world's coming around to reality, at last," Jake says, very mildly. "We'll see you two around."

With that, we head back to the car and get in. They both stand where they were during the interview, Stan by the side of the camp table where he threw his towel, and Morgana in front of the tent, one button at the bottom of her blouse still undone. By the time we pull completely out onto the park road, I can still see them where we left them.

"So what do you think?" Jake asks.

"Same thing you think, Jake Leon."

"And what's that, Chief Inspector?"

"Those two are our murderers."

"My guess too. But we can't arrest them. On what? We'd need something like fingerprints on the foil cover of those tablets, and I can tell you that isn't all that likely. Or we need to find that truck, and see if their prints are on it. I tell you, one thing we do have is motive."

"Yep. For Morgana, anger at Lavida for being passed over in favor of Becky Rubin. But if it's anger and jealousy, why not go after Rubin?" I ask.

"My guess, Denise? Rubin's too tough a target. She'd be hard to sneak up on. Hard to sneak drugs into her beer. Lavida obviously made it clear he was recommending Rubin for that open position, so she directed her anger at him. But, what would be Stan Assice's motive?"

"Sleeping with her. Bet you what you want she's got him wrapped around her little finger."

"Yep. I could see that. So . . . how do we nail 'em?"

"Don't know that yet, Detective Sergeant." I decide to play the "Chief Inspector" game and make him my second in command. That might rile him a little since he's actually senior to me in the department by several years—years that he spent mainly manning the speed trap on County Two where it leaves town. But Jake is a hard one to rile. He just looks at me and smiles.

"I'm sure if they had Rohypnol on them, they've long since gotten rid of it in some dumpster around town."

"Yep," I say.

"We've still got to figure out those tire tracks at the campsite, and we need to find Lavida's truck."

"Yep. You got any ideas about them tire tracks?"

"Nope. You got any ideas about that truck?"

"Yep, I do. Bet you anything."

"Woo-hoo! What you thinking?"

"Thinking I want to pay another visit to Stanford Bass."

Suddenly, Jake sits up square in his seat. "Oh, my God! I know what you're thinking!"

I smile a big smile at him. "And what am I thinking?"

"That truck isn't hidden at all! Stanford Bass is driving it! And he's hidden his old truck, which is probably near the same year . . ."

"Where? Where's he hidden it?"

Jake waits for a few seconds. "In the old sawmill!"

"We'd better be right on this," I say. "Let's head over there now to check it out."

And we do.

AN OLD TRUCK WITH NEW PAINT; AN OLD MAN WITH A NEW STORY

STANFORD BASS IS ASLEEP IN THE SAME OLD LAWN CHAIR HE was asleep in last time we saw him. We leave him asleep. He blinks a few times and tries to wake up, but he's too groggy and nods back asleep.

"Leave him sleep. Come with me, Jake. Let's take a look at that truck of his first."

What had been merely an old red truck last time we visited, on closer inspection reveals itself to be a newly painted truck—painted by an amateur, but painted carefully. There are only a few splatters on the windshield where he didn't cover it up sufficiently, and a few spray splatters on the tires, but you'd have to look really closely to see them. I take a key out of my pocket and gently scrape away a tiny bit of red paint on the left rear fender near the bumper. Sure enough, underneath it's a dusty beige.

"Well, well, well." I hear Jake say. "Looks like we nailed that one, Chief Inspector."

"Let's go take a look in that old sawmill."

We have to wade through some tall weeds. There's an old, deeply rutted gravel road that leads from Bass's shack to the sawmill, but it's a roundabout walk. Going through the weeds might scare up a snake or two, but it'll get us there faster.

It doesn't take but ten seconds to find the truck, Stanford Bass's old beat-up red pickup. It's not the same year, I don't think, as Toulouse

Lavida's truck, but it's close enough that the body style is still the same—an old mid eighties pickup truck, stacked square headlights, a single bench seat in the cab.

"We got it, Detective Sergeant."

"Looks like it, Chief Inspector. We gonna go arrest Mr. Bass for murder, for grand theft, or for aiding and abetting?"

Suddenly, a deep, gravelly voice: "You ain't gonna arrest me for nothin'. I ain't *done* nothin'."

And, sure enough, there's Stanford Bass himself standing in the broad, open barn-doorway of the sawmill, conspicuously shotgun in hand, glaring at us like we were aliens.

"Got another man's truck in your driveway, and your own hidden away in this old sawmill, brother," I say, trying to sound as calm as I can. His shotgun is pointed down. "You ain't gonna do anything with that old shotgun, are you?"

"What 'chu mean? Always bring this gun with me when I raid the old mill. Place is crawling with snakes. Seen a six foot diamondback in here several times. Left it alone to keep the rats down, but I'll blast it if it gets near me or won't get outta my way."

"That right? You wouldn't be pointing that thing at sheriff's deputies, now would you?"

The barrel of the gun drops completely so it's aimed right at the floor beneath Bass's feet. "Hell, sister, I ain't never done nobody no harm in my life, not shootin' nor otherwise. I'm telling you the truth; I ain't done nothin'. Don't got no idea about that murder."

"Well, now, Mr. Bass," I say. I'm picking my was across stacks of old, over-dried cut lumber, watching carefully for that six foot rattler he said inhabited this maze of hiding places. "You know how this looks: we got a dead man, drove himself to Seminole Pines, left his truck somewhere but we don't know where, and now we see you've got it. You've got the dead man's truck. A few years newer than yours."

"Better shape, too," Bass sings out. "Man took care of his truck. I ain't never had the means, you know what I'm sayin'? Had to do all the maintenance myself. My old Betsy is worn down. Parked her here to git her outta the way."

"Parked her here to hide her, more like," I say. Out of the corner of my eye, I can see Jake has moved around behind Mr. Bass. His weapon isn't out, but he looks ready. "Come on, Mr. Bass, you know how this looks to us in the sheriff's department. You got a dead man's truck, for God's sake. What you think we're thinkin'?"

"You're thinkin' I killed him and stole his truck, but that's ridiculous."

"How'd you come by his truck?"

"I was told I could take it if I'd tow it out of there and not say anything. Honest to God truth."

"Told you could take it? Stanford Bass, that sounds hard to swallow. Are you bein' straight with me?

"Absolutely straight."

"Who told you. that?"

He's quiet for a minute, shakes his head. "Don't know for sure. Got a phone call. Told me to come pick it up from the camping spot on Indian Mound Road. I was suspicious, but I couldn't pass up a new truck, so I went out there late Sunday night, and there she was. I was skeptical there was something going on, but I didn't see nobody there."

"Yeah? So, you found the truck. So, go on."

Then, he shakes his head and is silent. He looks very worried. "Same evening that man was killed. It was parked there. Parked in the clearing. I knew who it belonged to, that old professor. The one I showed to the mound a few months back. One who I found out later was killed. But he was gone, wasn't there. I walked a bit into the woods, but there wasn't nobody there. I was thinkin' maybe he left me that truck on purpose, as thanks for the way I showed him where the mound was. I know that sounds like so much bullshit, but that's what I told myself. Thought maybe it was him called me. Don't rightly know how he got my number. But, damn! A new truck that runs good? How'm I supposed to pass that up? Then I find out from that boy at the store he'd been killed, and you all showed up the very same afternoon. Scared the damn *shit* out of me. I take the man's truck and he's been killed. Makes it look like I done it. But I didn't. Swear that to God Almighty."

"Why'n't you tell us all this before?"

"Scared. How's it look? I got his truck and he's dead. But I'm swearing to God in heaven I didn't do it."

I don't know whether to believe him or not, but he seems serious. There's something curious, though, in all this. He *has to* have gotten a 'phone call from somebody, or he'd never have known that truck was there in the first place. So his story has got to be at least partly, or mostly, true. And I just don't see him killing for a truck. My head is spinning. I glance at Jake and I can see his own mental gears spinning round. "Okay, Mr. Bass," I say. "When you went out there to pick up that truck, about what time was it, and did you see anybody else out there?"

"Went there, maybe, nine o'clock? Not sure. It was late, and dark, but not midnight yet. And nope, I didn't see nobody else there. Just a car or two on the road before I pulled into the woods, a couple coming the other direction and one that passed me up later. But nobody at the campsite itself. There'd been somebody else there, though, because there was beer cans I could see in the headlights. I don't leave cans at the campsite, so somebody else must'a' left 'em."

"So . . . you just took the truck. Weren't you worried there was anything strange going on?"

"Was I worried? Sure. But . . . a new truck! I ain't lucked into nothin' so good in longer'n' I can remember. They's lots of thieves around, and I didn't want nobody to come along and swipe my new truck, so I decided to hitch 'er up to old Betsy and tow her out. Except the keys was still in it, so instead, I roped old Betsy to his truck instead, and towed the old girl home, real slow. Did some damage to the bumpers, but nothin' too serious. You can believe me or not, whatever you like. But I was goin' to let them folks

know I had his truck. Was fixin' to drive down there and *let 'em know*. I
didn't know what was going on. Honest to God, I didn't. When I heard the
next day from that boy at the hardware store that that man been killed, I
got pretty worried. But the new girl, she's better'n mine. So, sure 'nough, I
repainted 'er myself. Hid Betsy away, like you said. You didn't even notice it
first two times you was here."

"True enough, we didn't. But, Mr. Bass, let's be honest. You repainted
Professor Lavida's truck so it would look like yours. Then, you didn't tell us
when we dropped by the first two times we were here. Basically, you didn't
want us to know you had the dead man's truck."

"Yeah, well . . . I guess I'm goin' to jail for that. But I never had much
luck in my lifetime. Never had much luck. Never did. Live in a old shack
I had to build myself, mostly out of leftover lumber that none of it fits
together proper. Feed myself out of my own garden, mostly, and by fishin'
in the lake with a low-down cane pole. Don't got no fancy equipment.
Couldn't possibly afford to buy another vehicle. What'd I get for Betsy for
a trade-in? A hundred dollars, maybe? If'n I did, it'd be the only hundred
dollars I had to my name. Been living on Social Security so long I don't
know no other way. Then, sudden, this gift just drops into my lap. Find out
the man is dead, so he don't own the truck no more. I figured I couldn't
hurt nobody if'n I kept it. Can't say I stole it from him. He ain't even alive
to claim it."

"Well, Mr. Bass, technically, the truck belongs to the estate of
Professor Lavida. I don't know anything about his next of kin, but it's their
truck now. Not yours. You'll have to give it back."

He looks terribly mournful. "Ain't that just the way? A man has the
first little bit of luck in a long time, and he gets hisself in trouble. Warn't
figuring on no trouble. But I guess as you're right. Truck's got a nice new
paint job. Guess I can't even charge 'em for that. What I'm supposed to do
now? I got to drive this truck all the way into Tallahassee? That's where that
man lived, I guess—taught at the university there."

"No, sir. We'll impound the truck and tow it to our secure lot at the sheriff's office. We'll notify the next of kin. You should'a told us, Mr. Bass. You should'a told us. You cooperate from here on out, and I'll ask Sheriff Marion if we're gonna charge you. It *would* be grand theft auto. That's a major crime."

"Yeah. I guess. So now, on top of it all, I'm a criminal."

"Look, you cooperate, give the truck back, tell 'em you were keeping it safe and you even repainted it for 'em, and maybe Sheriff Marion won't charge you. I can't promise anything. You might not 'a' *known* you stole it, but as of now, it ain't really yours."

"'Preciate anything you could tell the sheriff. Don't want to spend my last few years in Raiford. Ain't got long left now. I'm upwards of eighty years old, you know. Prison wouldn't be no place for me to live. Swear to God I was gonna tell the man about his truck. Swear to God I was."

"Okay, I believe you. But now I have some other questions for you. Can we please go back to your place and sit in the shade? And you can put that shotgun away, okay?"

"Sure enough deputy, whatever you say."

Within minutes, we're back in Stanford Bass's "yard," such as it is. Bare dirt, gravel, weeds and junk strewn all over. Bass is back in his chair, the shotgun is propped against the wall of his shack, I'm seated on an overturned plastic five gallon paint bucket, and Jake is leaning against the hood of the Hellcat.

Bass takes his face out of his hands, looks up at me: "So, what can I tell you?"

"Let's go over this again. What time were you there at the campsite?"

"Pretty late. It was, I don't know, at least nine, maybe ten. I wasn't watchin' the time too close. Thought for a minute as long as I was there, I might drive in further to the Indian Mound. I was gonna drop by and visit, tell them archaeologists about the spirits. Tell 'em digging there wasn't a good idea. They wouldn't have listened to me, but it is what it is. Should never have showed 'em where that mound was, anyhow. Needed the money. Damn! Needed the *money*; it's all money nowadays. Ain't nobody doin' right because right is what it is. *Never* should'a' showed 'em. So, I had their money from before, and I had a new truck. I felt lucky, and I just left."

"So, nine or ten o'clock. And the professor's truck was there waiting?"

"Yessum. Already there."

"And no professor?"

"No professor, no, ma'am."

To this day, I have to tell you it feels weird to me to be addressed as "ma'am," especially when a man is over eighty and I'm all of twenty-seven. "Did you see anybody else?"

"No, ma'am, I sure didn't."

"Everything you're telling me is the truth?"

"Everything."

"Didn't see anything. Didn't hear anything?"

"Said I didn't see nothin'. Didn't never say I didn't *hear* nothin'."

"Okay, what did you hear?"

"Heard that big SUV of theirs. Down the road a ways."

I'm confused by this. "Heard the SUV? Down the road? Down the road which way?"

"Down toward the Indian mound. Of course. I thought it was comin' up the road toward me, but it wasn't. It was going away from me. After a bit, I didn't hear it no more."

Jake and I look at each other. The SUV, according to everybody at the dig site, was there all night. Yet there was a vehicle on Indian Mound Road. Could it be the vehicle that left the wide-tread tire tracks? I can see by Jake's face he's wondering the same thing. But if it is, who's car?

"So, Mr. Bass, about what time did you hear that vehicle?"

"Oh, it was late. Not but a little bit after I got there. I was trying to fig-ure out how to tow that truck back to my place. I was working by flashlight, so it was going pretty slow."

"How did you finally manage it?"

"Well, you can see the professor's truck got a tow hitch on it. I ain't got none. All I had in my truck was some heavy rope. So I wrapped the rope around the tow hitch on his truck, tied it in two places to my front bumper, wrapped some blankets around my bumper that I keep for camping out, put 'er in neutral, and towed her all the way home. She smashed into the tow hitch a dozen times and smashed up my bumper, but I wasn't goin' but ten miles an hour, tops, and it didn't do the tow-hitch no harm. Put a couple scratches on it. Got 'er all the way home without nobody seeing me, except maybe once."

"Oh? You were maybe seen by somebody?"

"Yeah. Just one car drove by me like a bat outta hell once I got out on County Three. Yelled at me out of the window, then sped on. Son-'va-bitch nearly run into me."

"So they passed you?"

"Yep, on the way into town. I don't go all the way into town, of course. I come down Sawmill Road to my house. They was miles ahead of me by the time I got back."

"So, this car that sped by you—did you get a look at it?"

"Oh, God, no, ma'am. It was one o'clock by that time, even later. Pitch black. Just saw his headlights, saw the road ahead of me with my own headlights."

"Any guess at all what kind of car it was?"

"Not no clue, deputy Sumpter. Fast car, though. Could tell that by the sound."

"What do you mean? Explain, please."

"Sounded like a souped-up job, know what I mean? Them pipes was low and really loud. He slowed down when he caught up with me, then swerved around, yelled out the window, and gunned his engine like he was dying to get someplace."

"Could you tell by the sound of the voice who it might be?"

He looks startled at this. "No way I could tell you that, deputy."

"Deputy Leon," I turn to Jake. "Thank you for your patience. Do you have any questions for Mr. Bass?"

"Yes, thank you. Mr. Bass," and Mr. Bass turns to look at Jake. "Mr. Bass, did you catch maybe a glimpse of his license plate?"

"No, sir. Didn't see no license plate."

"The person who yelled out the window at you—man or woman?"

"Definite a man. Didn't see 'em, but it was a man's voice."

"How well did you hear it?"

"Couldn't miss it. They was yellin' at the top of their lungs."

"So, a man, definitely?"

"Yep. And I think it was a brother, too."

"I'm sorry. A brother? You mean the person sounded black, African-American?"

"Exactly what I mean. Didn't yell like no white man. 'Git outta the way! What 'chu doin, motherfucker.' That's what he said. And sounded black." Jake looks quizzical, as I must look.

"And coming from the direction of Indian Mound Road?"

"Well, comin' from that direction, yes. Don't mean nothin'. That road goes past Indian Mound Road all the way out to County Two."

"And the only other vehicle out there at the campsite when you were there was the professor's truck, the pickup?"

"Yep."

"How did you know he wasn't going to be back to pick it up?"

"Didn't. It was just so late. Like I said, I was told to come get it. It was easy ten o'clock, maybe ten thirty before I started hitchin' old Betsy up to the professor's truck."

"You said the keys were in the truck?"

"Yep."

"Why'd you figure the old professor wasn't there?"

"Must'a walked on to the mound, I guess."

"It's a good two miles, maybe three, through the woods, middle of the night, from that campsite to the Indian Mound."

"Likely."

"And you think he must've walked?"

"Look, deputy Leon, I don't know for right sure. All's I know is, I showed up, truck was there with the keys in it, and I figured it was a blessing."

Jake stops, seeming perplexed. Something occurs to me. "Mr. Bass, did any of them people, them at the Indian mound doing the digging, did any of them know you were there at the campsite?"

He's silent for a minute. Then, "Maybe."

"Okay, so . . . Who?"

"Well . . ." Then, he falls silent.

"Mr. Bass, this is really important."

"I didn't *see* none of 'em. Not that night."

"Not what I asked you. Did any of them know you would be there?"

He's silent for a moment. "They told me over the phone not to say nothin'; I could just pick up the truck and nobody wouldn't say a thing. Then, later, that one man come and reminded me to hide the professor's truck, and told me if I said anything about it, it would go pretty bad for me. But I decided since it looked so much like mine, I'd repaint it and hide mine instead. There wasn't nobody supposed to find out about it."

"They called you. Do you remember anybody you gave your number to?"

He thinks a minute. "That professor who I took out to the Indian mound. Him and them that was working with him."

"Including a nice-looking white woman?"

"As I recall, yes."

"So, Mr. Bass, that man who came to you, came to see you *after* the murder, and threatened you?"

"Yessum."

At this point, I'm frustrated by how people just won't see the sheriff's office as a support. It gets to me. "But, when you found out about the dead man, didn't you figure you needed to come tell us about the man who threatened you, and about the truck?"

Again, he's silent for a moment. "That one man, he said shut up about the truck. Get it out of there, and I'd get a hundred dollars—the one called me about picking up the truck. That was Sunday night. Told me they didn't need it no more, and I could take it. So I done it. I couldn't figure what was goin' on, but I decided not to look a gift horse the mouth, as the old sayin' has it. Didn't know there would be no *murder*. That man, he was one *scary* as shit dude. Come to see me Monday afternoon, before you-all came, which was Tuesday. He pulled an assault rifle out of that SUV they got. Put a full clip into that tree across the road, that tall one. Go look for yourself. That's well more'n a hundred yards off. He said every one of them shots hit the tree just below the first branch. I went and looked myself after they left, and it was true. Didn't want to get killed."

"Don't you figure that's what we're here for, Mr. Bass, your Sheriff's Department? To take care of miscreants like that? Protect you?"

He's quiet for a moment again. "You don't go tanglin' with somebody like that. Tellin' you. You think I'm fuckin' with you. Ain't fuckin' none with *nobody*. Not no more. He's gonna kill both of you if you go tryin' to arrest him. *Telling* you. You listen me. Take the truck, I don't give a shit no more about the truck."

"Hmmm . . . so you decided to repaint it instead of hiding it?"

He's quiet for a moment. "Thought I'd put one over on 'em. Two trucks look most identical. But his runs lots better'n mine. I repainted it and switched 'em, hid my own truck instead of the professor's, like they said to do. I just wanted a newer truck. Get me into town more reliable. Get me to the lake so's I can go fishin'. Swear to God, when I took 'er, I didn't know there'd be no murder. Then, I was scared half shitless when that man come afterwards. But he didn't know the truck was repainted, same as you didn't know at first. I done a good job of it. I was feeling pretty smart. Ain't feeling so smart right now." He lapses into silence. Then, "Almost pulled 'er off. But now I'm in deep shit. But you listen to me, deputy. You folks treated me right, even if you end up arresting me. So I'm telling you this for your own good. That man, he's a crazy fucker. *Crazy*. He's the kind don't matter to him what he does. He'll kill you and make a run for it. He was in the Army, the special Army, forget what it's called."

"White man or that Indian-looking one?"

"White man. Short brown hair. Big smile."

"Okay, Mr. Bass," I say. "You just sit tight, you hear me? In a day or two we'll send a tow-truck to impound the pickup. In the meantime, just leave 'er be where she is. That man shouldn't be back. And if he is, we were never here and you're just the same as you were before. I'm going to tell Sheriff Marion all about this. We won't let nothin' happen to you. You hear me? You sit tight, stay put. Leave the truck where it is."

"Okay" is all he says.

When Jake and I are pulling out, Jake says, "Stan Assice, for sure."

"Yep."

"We going to arrest him? We'll need backup."

"Oh, we'll get backup all right. Get Pee-Wee and Junior Madison out there at the park."

"You're about to say 'But,' aren't you."

"Got one loose end to tie up."

"The vehicle that Mr. Bass heard in the woods?"

"Exactly."

"Is it the same vehicle that passed him up on the road?"

"Yep."

"And that left the tracks at the campsite?"

"Yep."

"And how the hell are we going to find out who those tracks belong to, I mean, whose car they belong to?"

"I know whose car they belong to," I say.

Jake's eyes go wide because he hasn't figured it out yet. But I have. On our way to talk to him, I radio Pee-Wee. We've got someone to see, and it's gotta be fast.

HOW TO SAVE UP TO BUY A BUSINESS

As we're leaving Bass's Pro Shop, I call Pee-Wee. "I've figured out the murder, Pee-Wee."

"What the hell?"

"Ain't kidding."

"Who?"

"Stan Assice and Felicia Morgana."

"Explain."

"Sure." I'm driving and talking at the same time, but I spew it out pretty quick, because I've got it all figured out. "Early the evening before the murder, they'd met Professor Lavida when they went on their beer run. The beer run was just a convenient excuse. They'd arranged by phone to have him meet them where Indian Mound Road comes out onto County Road Three, probably promising to lead him to the mound site. Instead, they led him to this campsite halfway between County Three and the Indian Mound, maybe about seven o'clock. There, they gave him a beer spiked with Rohypnol, and he was out like a light for the next several hours. They drove back to the Indian mound camp with their beer, as if everything was normal, had their party. Lavida's out cold back at the campsite. After the party, Morgana and Assice hike out in the dark to where they left Lavida; Assice has night vision goggles, betcha anything. On the way, she calls Silvio. This is probably, what, nine or nine-thirty or so. Poor Silvio must'a' thought he was going to luck out with Morgana, but instead, he finds a 'drunk' man passed out in his truck, and Morgana and Assice waiting there to 'convince' him to help them move him part way down the road. I've puzzled all this out. I'm telling you, I know what went down. When Silvio got there, expecting something else was going down, they loaded up Lavida into Silvio's car, then called Stanford Bass to come haul Lavida's truck away. Told him it had to be that night. Make it look to everybody like they had no idea at all how Lavida ended up in that trench. Then they threatened Silvio and Mr. Bass both not to mention anything to anybody. And neither one directly knew then or knows now anything specific about the murder. Neither one actually witnessed it."

Jake is sitting next to me, wide-eyed.

"How the hell you figure that one out?" Pee-Wee asks.

"Tell you that later. Right now, I'm going to talk to Silvio at the store, make sure of my theory. But when we go to arrest Stan and Morgana, we're going to need backup. Stan's ex-Special Ops, a real super-soldier. He's gone off the deep end, but he's an expert marksman, and I don't doubt he has some heavy artillery, so to speak. I don't know if we'll have to take him down, but I'd consider him very well armed and extremely dangerous."

"Okay, listen, Midget," Pee-Wee says, with some urgency in his voice, "I know from experience you and Jake like to think you're immortal. You're not. *Don't move on that man* until I'm there ready to back you up. I mean it."

"Ain't that dumb, Pee-Wee. I'll tell you when we're ready to go after him."

"You do that. Have both of your phones open to my number, and don't stray too far from the car radio if you can help it."

"Will do, Pee-Wee." And I put the car's ancient radio speaker back in its cradle on the dashboard.

Jake is looking at me like he just can't figure out what's going on. "Okay, Chief Inspector. I take it it's Silvio Treadwell's car that Mr. Bass heard?"

"Yep. Morgana and Assice timed it all pretty well. They'd have time to meet Lavida, drug him, then get back to the mound campsite in plenty of time to make it look like nothing was going on. Just a beer run. Later on, after the party, and not as drunk as they wanted everybody to think, when everybody was asleep, they just hiked on down the road and met Silvio at the campsite. Lavida was still out cold. Once they had Lavida loaded up, they called Mr. Bass. Simple. Whole operation was maybe two and a half hours."

"Wow. Goes to show you, the more people in on a secret, the less secret it really is. But why'd Lavida get there so late? What—around seven o'clock or so?"

I look at him. "He was *going* to drive down to Sarasota to see Estella Rodriguez, but the way I figure it, they had an argument. She sounded awfully jealous of Morgana. I guess he couldn't convince her there was nothing to it. He'd hired Morgana to be assistant site manager, so Rodriguez immediately got jealous and suspicious—with good reason, as it turns out."

"Okay so far. But why hire Morgana in the first place? Seems like everybody knows she's an academic lightweight."

"Don't know for sure. Maybe just her looks. Maybe Lavida really was smitten, who knows? Whatever the case, he hired her. I'm betting Rodriguez didn't tell us the whole truth. Probably told Lavida she didn't want to see him that night. Not sure about that one, but that's what I'm guessing."

"Seduced by Morgana's good looks, then," Jake says. "You know, seems every case we look at, there's always either sex, money or drugs—or some combination of the three."

"Seems to fuel most of what's wrong with the world, Jake."

"I guess if Morgana offered to meet him where Indian Mound Road comes out onto County Three, he would have shown up."

'Exactly. Love and hormones, Jake. Love and hormones. Tellin' you, they make us crazy."

"God! My head is spinning. Morgana must've talked to Silvio, too, eh— when she bought those stakes at the hardware store? Turned his head a little."

"I figure it that way. Then, that night, called him up to see if he knew where the campsite was. Told him she was waiting for him. She and Assice met him at the campsite. Lavida was out cold, and they got Silvio to help them move him. We'll talk to Silvio, see if I'm right."

"So much plotting, so much evil. For what?"

"Love, hate, jealousy, bitterness. They eat people up, take over."

"Morgana was that jealous of Becky Rubin?"

"Riddled through with jealousy and hatred."

"Then why not target Rubin? Why Lavida?"

"Lavida passed her over, Jake. As for Rubin, she's a tough target. But after Rubin betrayed her, I'm certain she's been plotting revenge."

"They could still be thinking of taking her out."

I look at Jake. "Yep. What was that story you told me about? Fata Morgana? The woman might be bad news, but she's got a certain magic about her. Main reason we got to move on this quickly. Betcha they're gonna try to lure her out to the mound, murder her there, and then get outta there. Say they don't know squat about it."

"Why not drive over the the park right now?"

"Right now, it's all theory, Jake. Got to talk to Silvio, see if I'm right."

"Better get on it, then. Now you got me worried. How about we call Pee-. . . I mean, sheriff Marion, and ask if he can go check on Ms. Rubin at Seminole Lake Park?"

"Good idea." So, I radio Pee-Wee.

"Yep?" He says, in his best gruff bass voice.

"Say, Pee-wee, me and Jake are worried that Assice and Morgana might have Becky Rubin in their sights."

"To murder her, you mean?"

"Exactly. Hey, please, I know I ain't giving no orders, Pee-Wee, but could we get you to drive down to the park to check and see if she's okay?"

"All right. Hope you're wrong. But if this is a double murder in the planning stage, got to head it off. I'll head down there myself. Hope you're wrong about this, Midget."

"Hope I am, too, Pee-Wee. But we sure appreciate it. Look, we just got to the hardware store. If you get there before we get back in the car, call us on the phone."

"Will do," he says. And I can hear over the radio him going out the creaky screen door, heading to his Suburban.

We park, get out. But before we walk in, I take Jake around to the back parking lot where the staff parks. There it is, a shiny red Chevy Camaro with mag wheels on the back, chrome hubcaps, even fuzzy dice I can see inside hanging from the rear-view mirror. All decked out. A boy's dream car.

"Check out them wheels, Jake," I say. He bends over to look from the back.

"Shit," he says. "I'll be damned. If this isn't the car, I'll eat my hat. This *is* the car that left those tracks at the campsite."

I laugh. "You don't wear no hat, Jake Leon. You're too proud of your sexy little curl. You'd never hide it under no cap."

He smiles. "How'd you know?"

"Silvio mentioned that he'd gotten new wheels last time we talked. And I know Silvio Treadwell from school. He used to drool over all the hot cars in the senior parking lot, more than he drooled over the girls that was hanging around him."

"That include you?" Jake laughs at his little tease.

"Maybe so, Jake Leon. I wouldn't go teasing on little ol' me, though. If you'd gone to school with Silvio Treadwell, you might've had the hots for him yourself. And don't fool yourself, I had a few beaus were eager to go out with me. Wasn't no wallflower, Jake Leon. You be nice to me."

He just smiles. I think he sees I'm just a bit sensitive on the subject. Truth is, Silvio Treadwell never did, never would, ask me out, as many hints as I dropped about my interest and availability. He was always after Roxy Cornwell, tall and beautiful—a basketball star like him. And Doria Lake, of course. My best friend, but . . . yeah, I'm jealous. Enough of that. Don't want to talk about it. "Let's go in and talk to Mr. Teadwell, shall we?"

Silvio Treadwell is there behind the counter checking out some customer who has a stack of boxes that look like screws or nails. There are no other customers in line, so we head to the counter.

"If it ain't Supercop and her trusty sidekick!"

"Knock it off, Silvio," I say. I hate for people to call Jake my "sidekick." He's actually senior deputy between us two. He respects my investigating ability, and he's super polite about letting me take the lead, but he's my partner, and a really good one. "Jake Leon ain't my sidekick, Silvio. He's senior to me by five years in this department. We're partners. Respect that."

I can see he looks nervous. "Whatever you say, Denise. Say, heard your boss calls you Midget. Kinda fits, don't you think?"

"Don't change the subject on me, Silvio Treadwell. You look nervous. What you so nervous about?"

"I ain't nervous," he quavers. But I see he is.

"Yeah, you are. How come? You got something to hide?"

"Ain't got nothin' to hide, Denise Sumpter."

"Yeah, Silvio, you do. Saw your car out back. Nice car. Got nice, wide mag wheels on the back."

"Yeah? So? You like my car? Want to take a ride in 'er?"

"No, Silvio, I don't want to take no ride in your car. What I want is for you to be straight with me."

"'Bout what?"

"'Bout where you been with them shiny new wheels of yours."

"Been to work. Been home. Been out a few times."

"Ain't interested in whether you go home or whatever. 'Course you go home."

"You ain't still jealous of Roxy Cornwell?"

"Damn it, Silvio. You knock this shit off." I whisper it, but loudly and with force. I don't want the rest of the store to hear, but I want Silvio to know I'm serious. "You listen to me, Silvio Treadwell. You're gonna be straight with me, or I'm going to have that car impounded. A good, close inspection will reveal whether you've been up and down them forest service roads. You know that? Particles get left in the tire treads. Tires kick up sand and mud and pine needles that get stuck in the wheel wells or in the back bumper. You want me to go check on that right now?" He's probably had the car washed since he drove down that road, and I don't really know whether there'd be any such evidence as I'm hinting at. But I actually will impound his car so we can look, if he doesn't cooperate.

"What forest service road would this be, Detective Sumpter?"

"You know which one. So why don't you tell me all about it? Why don't you tell me who you had in there as a passenger?"

He's silent for a few minutes. Then, "Can we go in the back office? It's a bit slow."

He motions me to the back of the store, and Jake and I follow him back. When we're in the office, a small room set up strictly for business with a desk, computer, filing cabinets and stacks of invoices on the corner of the desk, he closes the door behind us.

"So, super-cop, what do you want to know?"

"Where you've been with that car, and who you've had in it as a passenger."

He's silent for a minute. He doesn't know how much we know or don't know, but he's thinking about my threat to have his car impounded. Taking away his car has got him stewing.

"Okay, look. Here's what happened. That lady, the good-looking one, did come in the store to buy those wooden stakes. That's the truth. Didn't see no harm in telling you that until I found out those stakes were used as murder weapons. She didn't come in with that guy, the grim-looking white dude. But I could see him in their van, their SUV, outside."

"This was the afternoon before the murder?"

"Late afternoon. Not that far from closing time. So, she sees my car out there, and starts teasing me about it—got 'er decked out pretty sharp, if you ask me. So I say, 'What you want, lady. You want a ride in 'er?' I didn't expect her to say nothing, but she did. 'Maybe I do,' she says. Well, I don't really get what's going on. But, you know, if you see a little chance at some sharp-looking pussy, 'scuse me, you do the suave, you know what I mean? And you see how far it gets you. So I give her my phone number, tell her to call me any time she's interested. I don't figure she's really going to call, good-looking white lady like that, but sometimes they go for a black stud, know what I'm saying? So she takes my number, puts it in her purse. Calls me later that night, pretty late, and tells me to meet her out on the forest service road that goes out to the mound. It's late, and I'm past ready for bed, but I change my plans. Asks me if I know where the Indian Mound is, and could I find it in the dark. I say of course I do. I'm surprised and curious, but I can't see no harm in it. So I drive out there, drive down the road, and about two miles in, I see a flashlight. It's her. She gets in the car and says 'drive to the campsite.' I don't know where it is, but she's in the car and she shows me the way. I've actually been out there when we was in school, but it's really dark."

He pauses for a moment. "Okay," I say, "Go on. Finish your story."

"Well, needless to say, I'm thinking we're going to get some tent action, you see what I mean? But we pull into the campsite, and there's no tent. What there is, is an old, beat-up chevy pickup, and somebody's in it asleep. She tells me to get out, so I do, but I'm pretty confused. Then, out of the darkness, this guy comes up behind me. It's that grim dude, I can tell, but I can't see him. At first, I figure they're automobile robbers, but that wasn't what's going on. The guy says, 'We want you to transport our friend in the truck there part way down the road to the Indian Mound. You don't got to ask no questions. There's five hundred bucks for you if you do what we ask and don't ask no questions.' And he waves a wad of bills in front of my face from behind. Looks like a lot of money, and I need it. Also, I'm a little scared, to be honest, because what's going down seems weird to me. It don't make no sense. But I take the money and say 'Okay.' But I ask 'em, 'What the fuck's going on here?' 'Just a little joke,' the lady says. 'Just a little joke. Our friend in the truck there has had too much to drink, and he's passed out. We want to get him to the Indian Mound worksite where we've set up a camp.'"

He falls silent again. This time I say nothing. Silvio continues. "'Why not drive his truck?' I ask 'em. 'Conked out,' they both say. 'We've got somebody to tow it out of here. Take it to the shop. But we can't carry him all the way.' So, weird as it is, I agree. 'Okay,' I say. Let's get him in the back seat.' So all four of us cram into my Camaro, and I start down the road to the Indian Mound. They tell me it's a sort of joke. They're going to take him into the camp they got set up there at the mound, but they tell me to stop only about half way there. 'Help us get him out,' they say. I can see the dude is bad off. Had way too much to drink. 'Why not just let me drive you in to your camp?' I say. But they say, 'No, we'll take it from here.' I'm figuring something bad is happening, but I don't know what. Then, the dude kind of loses his cool. Man, that dude is wound up tighter than a spool of twine. 'Just follow our instructions,' he says. 'Ain't nothing bad's going to happen. We just want to surprise the folks in the camp.' He's saying all this like he's trying to be rational and cool, but I can tell he don't want me asking questions. It wasn't 'til the day after the murder when you guys showed up that I found out the man was murdered. But I swear to God, he was alive when I picked them all up and drove down toward the Indian Mound. Swear to *God*."

"You see anything on the way back into town?"

"Yeah. I did. Seen that pickup truck towing another truck looks most like it. Looks to me like Mr. Bass's truck. Dark at night and the truck he's towing don't have no lights, so I near plowed right into them. *Think* it was Mr. Bass's truck pulling the sleeping guy's truck, but it's dark at night and and I can't see 'em that good. Look," he pauses, clenches his hands: "When I found out that dude been killed, I got scared. That wound-up dude comes by the store early next day, about an hour before you-all showed up, acting all cheerful, and says 'Thank you.' But then, he looks at me like he's ready to kill me, and just says, 'You're not going to mention a word of this to anybody. Our little secret. May have another couple hundred bucks for you if you can keep this to yourself.' I say 'sure' because I don't know what's going on, and I need the money. But the guy heads out to his big van, and

I can see he's got a big military-type rifle perched on the dashboard. Then, I found out from Mr. Pruitt that the professor's been *killed*. Then, you two showed up and I found out, indeed, that man's been killed. I near told you all about what I done, but I was scared. Scared of that dude, first of all. I don't know how I knew this, but I could tell that guy was crazy, and I was scared of getting shot. Also scared that you'd link me to the murder. Hey, you know . . . white man's been killed. He's been in a young black man's car. How's that going to look? Might as well just book my stay in Raiford for the rest of my life. Don't want nothing to do with that. So I decided to stay shut up about it. But here's the most important thing: I swear, I *swear*, Denise Sumpter, I swear to you and Mr. Jake here, that man was alive when they got out of the car together, all three of 'em. I couldn't figure out what the hell was going on, why they wanted me to drop them right there in the middle of the woods, but I figured there was some shit going down that I didn't want no part in. Started out thinking I was gonna have a good night with that hot white lady, ended up carting a man through the woods that I found out later is dead. *Nobody'd* fess up to that, knew what he was saying."

"Well, I'm glad you finally come clean, Silvio. I'll ask Sheriff if we're gonna charge you with obstruction, and we'll have to impound your car to look . . ." But he cuts me off.

"Guarantee ain't no blood in that car, Deputy Sumpter. If them two killed that man, they done it on the side of the road out in them woods, and I didn't see it and don't know nothing about it."

"Did that lady call someone while you were in the car?"

"Sounded like she was calling a towing company, but now I think about it, she was calling Mr. Bass. How'd he get that truck outta there, no tow-truck?"

"Towed it with a rope. But I think we're about done here."

As soon as I said that, my phone rings. It's Pee-Wee.

"Hey, Midge. Our Army gal ain't in her tent. She and Gentiles both are gone. I checked the boys' campsite and they're gone, too. The van is gone. Think they headed up to the Indian Mound."

"Damn! Meet you out there as soon as we can get there, Pee-Wee. Make that Suburban fly. I have a feeling we're gonna need you. Got your Remington?"

"Got it, Midge. Don't move in on them 'til I'm there. I'm calling Junior for backup."

Then the phone clicks dead, and Jake's looking at me like we'd better hurry our butts up. He didn't hear everything, but he overheard enough to know what I know. Stan Assice and Felicia Morgana have kidnapped Becky Rubin and Regina Gentiles, and they've taken them out to the mound.

"Better step on it!" Jake says. And in just a minute, we're flying down the highway to County Road Three, blue lights flashing, traffic moving out of the way.

BACK WHERE THE PARTY STARTED

IN NO TIME, JAKE AND I ARE BOUNCING DOWN THE FOREST service road to the Indian Mound. As we get closer, I start to think that somewhere between the turn to the campsite and the emergence out of the woods of the Indian Mound itself, we have passed the spot where Silvio dropped off Assice, Morgana and Professor Lavida, insensate and barely alive. What must that poor young man have thought, poor Silvio, who couldn't have known what was going to happen when they got out of the car? Somewhere along this narrow, sandy, rut-filled road, Toulouse Lavida was dragged out of a car entirely unconscious, slammed to the ground, and had wooden stakes pounded through his eyes into his brain. Was he aware at all of what was happening? Did he feel pain? Was he awake even for an instant?

We're making the best time we can in Jake's Hellcat, but the advantages it has on good roads are lost in what are basically off-road conditions. Pee-Wee's Suburban will make better time on this road than we will. He's on his way, somewhere behind us. He had to drive all the way from Seminole Lake Park, about four or five miles further than we had to go from the hardware store.

We had to stop by the office after we left Pruitt's Hardware for just a few seconds—literally, less than a minute—to get one of the department's two assault rifles out of the arms locker. Wassahatchka doesn't have an actual trained SWAT team. The Sheriff's department is basically Seminole

Pines Police, County Sheriff and a substitute for the Highway Patrol. We do it all. Problem is, though I've fired my pistol more than a few times at our range and done respectably well, and though I've fired the rifle in practice, I'm not really comfortable with it. It's a bit heavy for me, and I don't like it. I've fired my pistol at perpetrators before (read my last book, The *Motel Murder),* but never the rifle. Jake may have to do the honors if Assice won't come peaceably.

Within about a mile of the Indian Mound, we pass a small clearing with grass growing on either side, about enough for a car like Silvio's to do a four or five point turn. Sure enough, the grass is matted and, even though we speed past, now that I'm looking for it, I can see the pattern of tire marks. How did I miss something that now seems so obvious? All I can say is, when you're out in these woods on these narrow forest roads, you're looking to avoid slamming into pine trees and thickets of palmetto. But I missed the place, sure enough.

We pull up to the big SUV with the Indian Mound clear in the distance, maybe fifty yards away, and things get really dicey really quickly.

We've been pretty noticeable in pulling up. We didn't surprise anybody. Jake's Hellcat makes a lot of exhaust noise. Beautiful sound, if you ask me, but all the same, wish this time it had been quieter.

Wouldn't have mattered, probably. The second we get out, I hear Assice:

"Get the fuck out of here, you little black tar baby, you and your faggot boyfriend. Get out! I've got little miss Ph.D Captain Rubin and little squeaky Reggie Gentiles, and they're two dead pieces of bitch if you get in my way. I want this road *cleared.* I happen to know how to get out of these woods to safety, and not you nor nobody else is going to stop me!"

I don't see him, but the voice is coming from somewhere in the woods on the passenger side of the car. That's where I am. I scoot out as fast as I can, getting as low to the ground as possible. I do a real Army crawl around the back of the car. Bam! Bam! Bam! Quick and automatic. I'm so low and the bullets so close that I hear them ping into the lower part of the door frame and the hubcaps not even inches above my back. A bullet nicks my butt, but I can tell it doesn't hit anything vital. A bit embarrassing to get hit there, but better than if a bullet had grazed my skull.

As soon as I'm on the driver side of the car, first thing Jake says is, "You okay? You're bleeding." The bullet must've hit more solidly than I thought. Sure enough, I've got blood dribbling down my pants.

"Like having a bullet in your ass? I'll let you two fuckers go if you get in the car and turn around *now*."

Then I hear Rubin: "Don't do it, deputy Sumpter, Deputy Leon. Don't do it!" The voice is hers, for sure, but it's garbled and hard to understand, as if she were talking through a mouthful of blood. "The second you show yourselves, he'll shoot you. He's a miserable fucker, and he'll kill people to get out of here. If you let him go, I swear to you, he's off his rocker, and he'll kill again. I'm not shitting you! He'll kill me and he'll rape and kill Reggie. She's tied up and unconscious." As she's screaming I hear Assice trying to yell over her, "Shut up, bitch."

The voice draws me to a pine tree about twenty yards off in the palmettos. Rubin is partially obscured, but I can see her clearly enough to see she's been badly used. She's tied to the tree, and I can see her face is a bit bloodied. She's got her tan shorts on and her work shirt, both a bit mussed but, to my quick glance, not torn. Her arms and legs are all over cuts and huge bruises, like she'd fought in the rough palmettos and been scratched up. Her face is swollen and it looks like her hair has been chopped off with a machete.

"You go ahead and listen to her, and she'll die and then you'll both die. In fact, I've changed my mind. Don't get out of here! Stay! Because I've decided I'm going to kill you! But first, little Rubinski."

A blast of bullets hits the tree where Rubin is tied and branches fly off. By some sheer luck, Rubin is tied facing us; Assice is somewhere back in the woods on the other side. Maybe because he's decided to prolong this, he's tormenting Rubin and messing with us. The bullets shred the tree, but I don't think any go directly into her. But Assice has a high-powered assault rifle, and another burst or two like that and the tree will simply disintegrate and Rubin will have a dozen bullets in her back.

"Hey, Jake." I say, "Let me talk to him from the back of the car. It may draw his line of sight toward me. Poke your head up quick between the front windshield pillar and the fender, and see if you can spot him."

"Hey, Stanley Assice. You're a pretty good shot, but you barely nicked me with one bullet and hit the car with about ten. You ain't such a hot shot as you think you are. You drop that rifle, come outta the woods, and we'll arrest you peaceably. You'll get a fair trial, and I'll even testify that you gave yourself up willingly. How about that?"

A burst from his rifle shatters the back windshield, and I hear bullets thunking into the door panels on the passenger side. Three or four hit the trunk. I'm wondering where Felicia Morgana is.

"Hey, Stanley. Where you got your girlfriend? Where's Morgana?" I yell out. "By the way, you missed. Don't know that you could hit a barn door with that rifle. Come on! I gave you a good deal. You ain't getting out of here, so why not give up?"

Bam! Bam! Bam! In quick succession from the front of the car. Jake is up and firing into the trees and palmettos maybe thirty, forty yards off into the woods. Then I see Assice! All painted camouflage green. His face, his clothes are all camouflaged. No wonder we didn't see him at first. I'm still wondering why I haven't heard from Morgana. Where is she?

I glance in Rubin's direction. Her head is hanging down. I have a feeling that if we don't get her out of here soon, she could collapse from blood loss. She may even have severe internal injuries.

"Missed me, fuckers!" That's Assice. I've lost him in the undergrowth. But I can see, barely, palmetto fronds moving. He's moving from his spot in my direction, to his left, my right, toward the back of the car. While he's moving, he's not aiming or shooting. I fire off seven quick shots. The clip holds seventeen, so I'm good for two more bursts. Damn! The assault rifle is in the back of the car still! I just thought of that.

I pull open the driver-side passenger door, reach in and pull the rifle out by the barrel, slam the door shut, as three or four more shots from Assice's rifle clunk into the passenger side door, through the door into the back seat. When I slam the door shut, I hear a bullet hit the inside of the door just opposite where I'm crouched down. That shot went through the passenger side rear door and hit the inside of the driver side rear door. There's one thin stretch of steel between me and Assice's shots.

Jake is up on the front end of the car. He's been following Assice's movements through the trees and palmettos. Bam! Bam! Bam! His shots are more aimed and deliberate than mine. I'm looking from around the back of the car, but I don't see Assice's movements any more. Has he been hit?

"You've been hit, Stanley Assice!" I call out. This is a gamble, I know, but when things are desperate, they're desperate. I have to go on instinct.

"Dumb fucks!" I hear him call out. "Damn little tarbaby got one lucky shot. I ain't hurt, though. Little nick. Ain't going to bleed to death. I been shot before. I've killed a dozen Taliban were better shots than you are. I hear his voice. So does Jake. He's standing full up, fires a half dozen shots into the bushes where the voice is coming from. I can see palmetto fronds swaying and I think I see a bullet or two splash a handful of bark off a tree.

Then I see something terrible. As if from nowhere, Assice appears right behind the pine tree where Becky Rubin is tied. I can see the rope around her right wrist, and where it disappears behind the tree. I don't see her left hand, but I know it's tied and the rope around both wrists binds her tightly to the tree.

Assice's gun is up, the barrel pointed at Becky Rubin's head.

But Assice was lying. He wasn't nicked. I can see blood soaking his camouflage shirt. He's been hit somewhere in the chest or abdomen. The blood soaks the lower part of his torso. "Get the fuck out of here! Or she gets it! Drop your fucking weapons, you two! Drop 'em, or I'll put a bullet right into Captain Rubin's brain! *Drop 'em!*"

Then, I hear a voice echo: "Drop 'em!" And it's Felcia Morgana, standing in the roadway on our side of the car, not ten feet away, holding a rifle of her own, pointed right at Jake. Jake and I both turn quickly, a shot goes off and I can see Jake squeeze his left arm over his left side and scrunch over. He's still holding on to his gun. She's got the rifle aimed right at Jake. I can see her shaking a little, but she won't miss at this close range.

How it happened so quickly, I don't know, but I swing around fast and fire three shots quickly, less than a second, right at her midsection; I can't see all three bullets go in, but I know at least one does. No sooner has my third shot hit, but her whole head explodes in a bloody mangle. A quick glance to my left shows me Pee-Wee Marion standing beside his parked Suburban about fifty feet away. One shot, and he blows her head apart. But he doesn't lower his rifle. He quickly swerves around and aims at the tree where Assice is standing.

I glance quick at Jake and he's staring at me. He's dropped his gun and is holding his left side with his hand. Blood is oozing through his fingers. I think he's hurt pretty bad. "Hang on, Jake, Hang ON!" I whisper. "We'll be outta here soon." There's a first-aid kit in the car and one in Pee-Wee's Suburban. I need to put some sulfa powder on the wound and gauze it and bandage it around his waist.

I look up toward the tree where Rubin is tied. Assice is standing behind it, his rifle barrel pointed at her head. But then, suddenly it's not pointed at her head; it's pointed at Pee-Wee's Suburban, and a flurry of shots, several seconds worth, whistles through the trees, and I can hear them clunking into the Suburban. Pee-Wee doesn't bend over very well at his size, but he's on his knees behind the front of the truck and the bullets riddle the truck without touching him.

I swivel fast around to Assice again, and the most amazing thing happens. Rubin has somehow worked loose. Bloody as she is, she's grabbed Assice's gun by the barrel, even though it's probably blazing hot, and she's kicking his right side with her left foot again and again. Kicks slam hard into his ribs where I can see he's been shot by either me or Jake. But Becky Rubin is weak, I can tell even from this distance, and Assice manages to fling her to the ground, holding his rifle which she's grabbed onto. His gun barrel is lowering toward her when a half a dozen shots from me and just one from Pee-Wee whack into Stanley Assice, and he crumples onto the ground. The gun falls from his hands, and I know he's dead.

Pee-Wee is running toward Rubin. He yells at me, "Get the kit! Bandage up Jake and get him into the Suburban. As fast as he can move his considerable bulk, he thrashes through the palmettos, gathers Becky Rubin up in his arms, and carries her back to the truck.

"Hey, Midget," I hear Pee-Wee yell, "Captain Rubin here just whispered to me that Gentiles is in the back of the university van. Help Jake get into the suburban, then you untie Gentiles and drive into the clinic behind me. See you sat on something sharp. You okay?"

Lordy! Really? Even when we got dead people at the site of a shootout, and live people we got to get into the clinic, Pee-Wee's still joking around with me. "Yeah, accidentally sat on an Army issue .25 caliber bullet, and somehow it went off."

"Serious," he cries out as he's trying to sit Becky Rubin up in the back seat, "You okay?"

"I'll live, Pee-Wee," I yell back, "But you ain't getting me on no desk job for a while. Won't be sittin' long in my present state."

I turn around, my butt starting to really ache, and I open the back door of the university van, and, sure enough, there's Regina Gentiles, duct tape over her mouth, her wrists bound and attached to her ankles. I can see by the look of her hands that the bindings are way too tight. Hopefully I can cut them off in time to restore some circulation. Fortunately, I'm Ms. Preparedness, and I whip out a little pocket knife I carry with me—everybody in the department has one—and within seconds I've cut the cords binding her up, and I've ripped the duct tape off her mouth.

"God, thanks!" Is the first thing she says. "I heard all the shooting. What's happened? Is Becky still alive?"

"She's alive, but hurt pretty bad," I say. "You're lucky to be alive yourself." She doesn't ask about Jake, which kind of annoys me, so I add:

"Deputy Leon has been shot, too, and he's lost a lot of blood. Sheriff Marion is taking him and Captain Rubin to the clinic in town."

"Oh, my God!" She says. She looks really scared, like she's almost in shock. "Stan and Felicia? You know, they're the one's who did the murder. You got them under control?"

"They're both dead," I say simply.

All I hear from her then is a quiet "Jesus!" Then, I decide not to follow Pee-Wee's instructions exactly. I put Gentiles in the back of Jake's patrol car, shot up as it is, and try to turn the engine on. Crap. The keys are still in Jake's pants!

I drag Gentiles out, as she's starting to cry, and we both get in the front seat of the university SUV. Fortunately, those keys are still in the truck, in a little cup holder between the two front seats. I'll be driving it out. Jake's beauty will have to wait. One good thing: there are no bullet holes in the university's big SUV.

Jake tells me later that on the way into the clinic, Rubin was drifting into and out of consciousness, wrapped in a blanket. I don't know what Assice did to her yet, but she's pretty beat up. Her clothes are on, so I don't think she got raped, but I can tell they fought. I find out later that she got quite a few licks in before Assice was able to take her down. Jake says later he was conscious most of the way into town, sitting quietly holding the bloody gauze against his left side. But he'd lost a lot of blood and passed out, in shock, just as the bullet-riddled Suburban, lights going crazy, pulled into Doctor Leon's clinic.

When I get there, about two seconds behind Pee-Wee in his Suburban with its splashing red and blue lights, I move to get up, but I'm stuck to the seat for a second. My bloody butt has glued itself to the driver's seat. Damn embarrassing.

All Pee-Wee has to yell is, "Your son's been shot, Doc!" And everything explodes into action. I help support Jake as we hobble inside. I'm about to sit in a plastic chair outside the emergency room when Nurse Polk turns to me: "Don't you dare sit there. You get your butt into room

Two, right there, and lay down on your stomach. You been shot in the butt, honey, and you ain't ruining perfectly good chairs. I'll be in with you in a minute; right now we got to take care of this lady and Jake first. You'll keep for a minute." I lie down as she told me to, and I feel but don't see the needle she jabs into my arm.

And I do keep for a while in that room. Somehow, I've drifted off to sleep before they get to me, despite the fact that my rear-end hurts like crap. I know I'm going to wake up to see Pee-Wee's huge face staring down at me from a hospital bedside, and I'm comforted by that. I don't know what I dream. Maybe I don't dream at all. All I remember is waking up in the hospital and nothing else.

CHAPTER TWENTY-TWO
SUNDAY MORNING

AIN'T NO SITTING DOWN AT THE DESK FOR ME, NOT FOR A WHILE

SO, I WAKE UP IN A HOSPITAL, NOT IN SEMINOLE PINES, BUT IN Tallahassee. Don't know what Nurse Polk stabbed into me yesterday afternoon, but it put me out for a good while. So, I can see outside and it's still dark. I'm in what obviously is a hospital bed. Thought I'd be lying on my front with a gunshot wound in my butt, but I'm not. I'm on my back, and I check and see, and I have a heavy gauze pad on my backside taped around my front with a wide white hospital tape. My butt feels numb, so I assume they've shot me or it up with some kind of pain medication. I actually feel pretty comfortable, though the room is colder than a polar vortex. I decide to hit the "Nurse Call" button to see if I can get the temperature increased in here.

I want to know what's up with Jake, Captain Rubin and Reggie Gentiles. And where's Pee-Wee?

A tall, middle aged black woman comes in. Her name tag says Henderson. "Mornin' there, young lady. See you're up. How you feelin'?" she asks. She's looking at my chart as she's speaking.

"I'm all right, ma'am. Feelin' okay. You said 'good morning'. So, what time is it?"

"About six a.m. Sun will be up in less than half an hour. You been sleepin' like a baby. That nurse at the clinic in Seminole Pines gave you a

233

sedative that knocked you out good. Doctor sewed up your backside yesterday evening, and you never even knew you was in here."

"Sewed up my backside? So I didn't have no bullet in there, then?"

"Nope, but it was a serious wound. Bullet tore a hole in your rear end about three inches long and a half an inch across. It wasn't that hard to close up, but you're gonna have a pretty prominent scar once it heals up proper. You'd lost a bit of blood. Probably one reason you were out so long. That nurse in Seminole Pines gave you a dose of Propofol that would'a' knocked out a grown man. Took you a good while to recover from it. Blood loss didn't help. That uniform you had on—total loss. Got a tear in the rear end, and there's so much blood down the right leg, you may as well toss it out because you ain't never goin' to wash it all out."

"Probably I'll do just that," I say. "Say, ma'am, do you know where my sheriff is? He's that great big white man stands about six-seven, has a buzz cut, has a face like a bulldog about to bite the mailman. Maybe you've seen him?"

"Sure I've seen 'im. Can't miss 'im. Takes up most of the hallway. You want to see 'im? He's down in the waiting area."

"I sure would. Say, could we make it a little warmer in here?"

"I can get you another blanket, honey. But I don't control the AC. These rooms don't have individual thermostats."

So she gets another blanket out of a cupboard across from my bed. It's wrapped in filmy plastic, which she rips off and throws away. She spreads it over me chin to toe.

"Thank you," I say. "Feels better. Say, when could I get some breakfast?" I'm a big breakfast eater. Like my bacon and eggs in the morning. Eat a good breakfast every day, though I can't get an extra pound on me to save my life.

"Breakfast service starts at seven. You got about an hour to go. I'll be back in about a half hour, or an orderly will, to give you a menu. We got a pretty good food service here. Now, you relax. I'll call downstairs to have them send your big boss-man up." She adds, "You like him? That's one big white man. Police officer that size, and he's white, would'a' scared me most half into the grave I'd 'a' seen him back when I was a teenager. Ain't really my business, but he treat you right out there in Seminole Pines? You're a little off the beaten track out there, you know what I mean? Lots of white folks with guns. Know what I'm sayin'? He treat you right?"

Actually, she's right, it's not any of her business, but she's being protective of the little black deputy. But Pee-Wee looks so much like the quintessential badass white Southern sheriff, I know where she's coming from. Here I am, a—ahh, normal sized—young black woman, and there's Pee-Wee—big, white, buzz-cut and old school-lookin'. Looks like the kind of sheriff would'a' been there just to harass black folks back when. Maybe even today, some places. But I ain't got a bad word to say about Beaumont Marion. He's as honest as the day is long, fair, and treats all his deputies the same. Only knock I ever had on Pee-Wee is, he don't know how to deal with the County Commission, get us the funding we need to build this department and get us some equipment wasn't made back before General Custer's time. Everything about law enforcement he's an expert, but Pee-Wee ain't no politician, that's for sure.

"Yeah," I say, "He treats me right. He's a good sheriff, no kiddin'. Don't matter a lick to him you're black or white or zebra-striped. He'll treat you fair, and follow the law to the letter, no matter who you are."

"Well, good to hear," she says. "Wished as more were like him, then."

"So do I," I say. And I mean every word of it.

In about ten minutes, Pee-Wee walks in just as the nurse is leaving. "Well, well," he says in his best gruff voice, "If she ain't finally woke up. Lord 'a' mercy, thought you was going to sleep through your whole shift. When they gonna let you out of this place?"

"Can't wait to get out of here, Pee-Wee. They ain't said yet when I can go. When they bring me my breakfast, I'll ask about when I'm gonna get discharged."

"You know I'm just gonna have to send you back out in the field when you get outta here. You and Jake got a lot of paper-work to do when you get out. Got a rash of smash-and-grabs going on at Seminole Lake Estates; got a robbery at Mel's gas station; crook stole a case of beer. You remember Titus Chancey and Emaine Handlan? Well, she konked him with a cast-iron frying pan and knocked him cold. Can't for the life of me see why them two stay together. I don't think he's ever goin' to hit her again."

Good news about Titus and Emaine. I mean, people smackin' people with frying pans ain't good. I don't mean that. But if them two are ever goin' to be more than a curiosity item, they're going to have to stop the violence against each other—and mostly it was him against her. She's always been loyal to him, God knows why. But she has. She's always believed she could reform him. Maybe she can, after all.

"Can't wait to get back at it, Pee-Wee," I say, and I really *can't*. This hospital thing is for the birds.

"So, I got a bone to pick with you, Midget Sumpter." He looks really gruff when he says this, and for a second, I think I'm in trouble. Then, he looks straight at me, and says: "You know this is the third patrol car you've got all shot up since you started working for me? Next contract I have you sign, gonna say you pay for any damage to the car. Can't hardly get the County Commission to give us what we need as it is. Keep destroyin' cars like you're doin', can't find no money for raises for next year. I calculated it all out, and I figure I'm gonna have to cut your income by fifty percent for the next three years to pay for all the repairs gonna be necessary for that car. You realize that maniac put one bullet hole in the front right fender, four in the front passenger door, five in the rear passenger door, three or four in the trunk lid, and smashed out the entire rear window? And, damn it, he put a few bullets in my Suburban! Now *that* really makes me mad!" He says "mad" but he's smilin', laughin' at his own joke.

"Pee-Wee Marion, you reduce my income by fifty percent, I'll be livin' on the streets and eatin' outta garbage cans. Gonna have to start rollin' all the drunks that hang out at Bam-Bam's Liquors, just to get pocket change for food. Hell, reason I can't put on no weight as it is, is because after I pay for rent and clothes, only money I got left for food is just enough for one

PB and J for breakfast and another one for dinner. And it ain't my fault if some cuckoo ex Special Forces dude likes shootin' up patrol cars." I act all serious, but I know he's messin' with me just like he knows I'm messin' with him back. We been playin' this game for four years, ever since I got hired.

I decide to rub it in a little, long as I'm messin' with him. "Besides, Pee-Wee, you're gonna have to pay for them bullet holes yourself, seein' as how late you showed up at the scene. What was you doin'? You stop off at Burger Butt to have their Swamp Ape special before you decided to mosey on out and help us with a dangerous armed perp?"

I can see I zinged him with that one. But after a minute, I see him crack a smile. "Shoot, are you kidding? First thing I did when I got there was I got out to watch the fireworks. Just like a cops and robbers movie. Shootout out in the piney woods. Damn good stuff. Wasn't 'til I saw he was gettin' the best of you that I decided I had to butt in to your little private duel and save the day." Then he spreads his hands all shy and humble-like, and says, "Like I always do."

Now I laugh full out. Pee-Wee's a funny man. He makes me laugh near every day. But I make him laugh too, so we're even. "Come save the day? Pee-Wee Marion. I got three shots in that woman before I saw you got just the one." That's actually true, though it's not like what you might imagine. The three shots I fired at Felicia Morgana when she was holding that rifle on Jake didn't take but, maybe, a half a second. Wasn't even a second. Amazing how fast you can fire 'em off when you have a semi-automatic pistol. Pee-Wee probably pulled the trigger exact same time as my first shot. But his old Remington is a bolt-action. Old as he is, but a damn fine firearm.

"Hate to tell you this, Sugar-lump," he says, "but your three shots. One went into the bushes behind Morgana, and one grazed her right side, just about where she shot Jake, but on the other side."

"Uh-huh. That leaves the third shot."

He pauses for a minute. "Right through her solar plexus, smack into her right ventricle. Probably would'a' killed her on the spot. Bullet probably

THE INDIAN MOUND MURDER

got there a hair of a second after her head blew up from a 30.06. Couldn't just let her shoot Jake, you know?"

Now, for a minute, our game is over. Jake is a serious concern. "How is Jake, Pee-Wee."

"He's still asleep. You lost some blood, but he lost twice as much as you did. You didn't need any blood or plasma. Jake needed about three pints. He was white as a sheet when he came in. In a state of shock. That sucker just wouldn't stop bleeding out. Thought for a minute while we were waiting for the helicopter, that we could lose him. But he's sleeping comfortably for right now. They got him all stitched up. Bullet went in through his left side, just below his rib cage. Missed his kidney by about a millimeter. In and out. Exit wound was ragged and looked like a whole chunk of his skin had been hacked off. Really nasty wound. But as I say, doctors got him patched up, he's got some new blood coursing through his veins, and he'll be up and around in a couple of weeks. You, on the other hand, will probably be outta here today or tomorrow. Soon as you're on your feet, I need you back in the office. Got Junior keeping an eye on the town and Dennis touring the woods looking for meth labs and pot farms. Can't keep a lid on things with just me and three deputies."

"I'll be back before you know it, Pee-Wee. Do you some good in the meantime to get outta the office and walking around. Don't mind my sayin' so, them donuts from Carly's Donut Shop ain't just disappearing into thin air when you eat 'em. I can see 'em popping out again on your waistline."

I don't seriously rag on Pee-Wee for his weight, but the truth is, he really is getting too big, even for his huge size. He's probably about 330 pounds right now, and he really doesn't get enough exercise. So I'm kidding him, but sort of not kidding. He takes it okay, though.

"Yeah," he says, patting his ample stomach where it hangs over his belt. "Carly's maple bars, and the lemon-filled. Umm, hmmm. Need to cut back to one each a week. Ain't doin' me a lot of good at my age."

"So," I change the subject, "How's Becky Rubin, and how's Regina Gentiles?"

"Well," he says, "Gentiles got some topical treatment for rope-burns on her wrists and ankles, but we took her back to her tent at Seminole Lake Park last night. Dennis is driving her to the sheriff's office this morning, or he's going to soon, to pick up her, or the university's, SUV. She's okay. Pretty shook up, but she was tied up in the back of their SUV for the whole gun battle. Nothing she could do. Once you untied her, she was safe and sound."

"Rubin?"

"Another story. Good news is, all of her wounds are superficial, if by 'superficial' you mean no more than skin deep. Bad news is, doesn't seem like there's a square inch of her body that isn't bruised from a punch or kick, cut from twigs or branches out in the woods, or scraped raw from colliding with some pine trunk. Not sure yet how Assice and Morgana got her into the van and out to the woods, but it looks like once they were there, she woke up from whatever they gave her, and gave Assice a hell of a run for his money. He ended up getting the better of her, but he outweighs her by sixty or seventy pounds. He's got bullet holes in him, but he also has bruises and cuts all over the place. Looks like she gave a pretty good account of herself." Pee-Wee pauses a minute while I frame the picture in my head. "She'll take a while to heal, but so far as we can tell, no deep internal injuries. Some of the punches and kicks Assice gave her could have ruptured a kidney, but she went through a CT scan and the doctor tells us everything inside looks to be okay, or at least there's no internal bleeding that he can detect. Poor woman's face is a mess. Broken nose. Swollen lips. Looks like a few of his punches connected with her face, and it looks like just out of meanness he took a machete and chopped off her hair. Got just a tiny bit of her scalp, but we haven't found the weapon, yet. As I say, she'll recover, but she may not have lasted too much longer if you guys hadn't shown up."

So, I think, they had her tied up when we got there. Probably fixing to torture the poor woman. Not surprising from a pair who would drive wooden stakes through the eyes and mouth of a man so drugged up he was completely unaware of his surroundings. "They were going to torture her then kill her, Pee-Wee," is all I say.

"Yep, that's how it looked," says Pee-Wee. But he doesn't say any more.

"Where was Tuco Fairweather all this time?"

"He'd walked into town from the campground at the park for supplies. Five miles. Walked all the way in, all the way back. We found him by himself at the two men's campsite when we took Regina Gentiles back. Right now, he's in the room down the hall with Becky Rubin. He asked if we could give him a lift up here, so I brought him up with me early this morning. Oh, I should let you know that you and Jake and Rubin were all flown in by helicopter. You were out like a light. So I just drove up about five o'clock this morning. Been here for maybe half an hour. That young man don't say a lot, but it's clear he was thinking about Becky Rubin. Last I saw, he was at her bedside. Holding her hand. I poked my head in, asked if she was doin' all right, and she looked over at me and said 'uh-huh.' She can't talk because they've got about twenty cuts on her face all stitched up. . . . Well, maybe not twenty, but several, at least. Once she answered, I just left 'em be. She'll recover. Hopefully, won't be any need for reconstructive surgery, my guess."

You wonder how people can do to each other some of the things they do.

"How're you holding up, Pee-Wee?"

He's silent for a minute. "Getting tired, Midge. Getting tired. Not ready to quit just yet, but next year, maybe the year after next at the latest, you and me—we're gonna have to sit down and plan out an election strategy. I want you running for sheriff when I retire. Jake's a great deputy, might be able to do the job, too, but I don't think he wants it. There's a reason I put you in charge of the investigation, and that last one in the motel. You've got a lot more brains than most people. Probably more'n' I got. Whatever. I don't mean Jake isn't smart. Like I say, I think he's more comfortable with you in the lead. He's dependable as heck, and he's a good one to bounce ideas off of. But there's that spark of drive, you know, energy, that he just doesn't have. No knock on him. He's a great guy. Then, Dennis is an old hand, but he's a textbook guy. He's the guy passed every course he took with a C. He passes as a deputy, too, but same grade. Junior Madison is four, what, three? years younger than you are. Another Dennis Martin in the making. You can depend on him to follow orders and get things done. But ain't got the imagination for any leadership role."

"Appreciate the support, Pee-Wee. Ain't looking to get rid of you, you know. If I'd 'a' missed that vicious woman, Jake might be dead right now. I think it was your shot dropped Stan Assice. You hadn't been there, Becky Rubin might be dead."

He just shrugs. "Don't know, Midget. That might be or might not be. Who knows? But, yes, it was one shot from the Remington, smack into the middle of his chest cavity. He was dead in a microsecond. He may have died anyway, you know. You guys were spraying bullets into the woods like crazy, and between the two of you, you put two bullets in him. One, it looked like, went through a tree first because it stopped at his fifth rib and didn't break it. No way a nine millimeter's gonna stop that way unless it's been slowed down some way. Haven't got no more than that from Doc Leon, yet. The other one hit the soft tissue between his hip bone and his femur. How come you guys didn't get the assault rifle out as soon as you got out of the car?"

"Pee-Wee, as soon as I got out of the car, Stanley Assice was shooting at me. I didn't have time to open up the door and pull it out. Didn't get it out until I was on the driver's side of Jake's car."

"Ummm," is all he says. Then he says. "Oh, yeah. I've added up the cost of all the bullets you two clowns wasted on the trees out there, and I'm gonna have to dock you both 25% of your salaries to pay for the loss."

"Pee-Wee," I say, pretending to be exasperated, "You dock us 25% of our paychecks, that'll only be a down payment on a box of cartridges for our old, used Glocks. I got to go out on the street and trade all my old clothes for food as it is. Why I'm so damn skinny. Why'n't you get with the County Commission and see if you can't get us what we need to run this department?"

That last thing I said was a bit of a dig, honestly, but it's true. To his credit, Pee-Wee doesn't take too much offense; he does his best, and the County Commision is cheaper than used socks at the Goodwill store. He smiles and turns to leave. "I'm gonna ask the nurse when you're gonna to get out of here. Looks like your breakfast is coming in. Need to go downstairs and find me a donut shop. Hear a maple frosted donut calling my name. Then a cream-filled chocolate frosted one. Coffee had better be good, too."

I smile. Then, before he's out the door, Pee-Wee turns to me to add one last thing. "Say, odd thing. You know, I picked up a piece of bone fragment looks something like that piece of skull cap you brought in? Had it in an evidence bag along with the cigarette butts. Didn't really think anything of it at first. But I got out the evidence tray with everything we collected at the mound, and I remembered I'd half-consciously picked it up. Almost didn't register with me that it might be important. Reggie Gentiles only planted *one* such bone. The other one might have actually been in the mound for thousands of years—many thousands. That old man, what's 'is name, Bass? Might be right. I'll call Bacardi some time today after I get back to the office. Guess we'll see."

I just smile. Can't wait to pay another visit to Professor Bacardi and to Mr. Bass. Nicer visits this time.